PRISON BREAK
THE CLASSIFIED FBI FILES

Paul Ruditis

Based on the series created by
Paul T. Scheuring

With Contributions by Christian Trokey,
Kalinda Vazquez, and Tim Morgan

Pocket Books

New York   London   Toronto   Sydney

Acknowledgments

Thanks to Paul T. Scheuring, Margaret Clark, Tommy Day, Anne Diaz, Jeff Drushal, Zack Estrin, Sylvia Franklin, Michael Glenn, Jennifer Heddle, Seth Hoffman, Bethany Jones, Monica Macer, Tim Morgan, Amanda Norris, Matt Olmstead, Debbie Olshan, Nick Santora, Dave Sliozis, Evan Snider, Jim Sodini, Nicole Spiegel, Christian Trokey, Karyn Usher, Kalinda Vazquez, Jason Zakarian.

POCKET BOOKS, a division of Simon & Schuster, Ltd
Africa House, 64-78 Kingsway, London WC2B 6AH

Designed by Timothy Shaner, nightanddaydesign.biz

ISBN-13: 978-1-84739-008-0
ISBN-10: 1-84739-008-0

This Pocket Books trade paperback edition May 2007

1 3 5 7 9 10 8 6 4 2

CONTENTS

FBI Files

on the Fugitives and
Other Persons of Interest

CLASSIFIED

C H I C A G O

To: FBI Headquarters
From: FBI Chicago Field Office
Subject: Complete Files on Manhunt for Fox River Eight

The following pages represent the complete files on the FBI manhunt for the escapees from Fox River Penitentiary. The information is complete up to and including the events of June 17. These files contain all the pertinent information on the prisoners and persons related to the case, as well as an in-depth analysis of the escape plan and reports on known sightings of the fugitives.

　　The ongoing investigation has brought to light key elements of the intricately plotted scheme to break out of Fox River Penitentiary, but our primary focus remains the ongoing manhunt that has already covered most of the country. Four fugitives remain at large, but the Bureau has been close to apprehending each one on several occasions. We have no doubt that we will achieve total success on our current timeline.

MICHAEL SCOFIELD

All evidence gathered to this point indicates that Michael Scofield was the mastermind behind the escape from Fox River Penitentiary. It is believed that his very incarceration was nothing more than a setup to help his brother, Lincoln Burrows, escape from the penitentiary prior to his execution for the murder of Terrence Steadman. The entire plan hinged on the fortunate coincidence that Burrows was incarcerated in the same prison that Scofield helped design.

Michael Scofield graduated at the top of his class from Loyola University with a B.S. and an M.S. in Civil Engineering. Prior to graduation, he had already accepted a prominent position as structural engineer at Middleton, Maxwell, and Schaum, one of the better design houses in Chicago. He quickly worked his way through the ranks at the design firm, handling high-profile projects as well as becoming the "go-to guy" for special assignments, such as the Fox River redesign. Though Scofield believed his mother's life insurance paid for his education, records show that no such policy ever existed. It is believed that the finances came via a loan his brother, Lincoln Burrows, took out from Crab Simmons, a reputed loan shark.

Scofield achieved his success in spite of a difficult childhood. His father, rumored to be an abusive alcoholic, abandoned the family before Michael was born. As a result, Scofield took his mother's maiden name for his own, which explains the different surnames for the two brothers.

FOX RIVER INMATE FILE

Inmate Name: Michael Scofield

Prison Handle: Fish / Snowflake

Age: 30

Back Number: 94941

Location: General Population, A-Wing, Cell 40

Crime: Armed robbery

Sentence: Five years

Time Left on Sentence: ~~Five Years~~ TBD—AT LARGE

Eligible for Parole in: ~~Two years, six months~~ TBD

Former Employment: ~~Unemployed~~ Structural Engineer

Next of Kin: Nika Volek   **Relationship:** Wife

Michael Scofield

440 West Ardmore Avenue, Apartment 11
Chicago, Illinois 60660

Education **Loyola University, Chicago,** Chicago, IL
M.S. in Civil Engineering
▪ Earned *magna cum laude* distinction for graduating with a grade point average in
the top five percent of his class (3.89).
▪ Studied under professional engineers Eduardo Rivera, Megan Costa and Ravi
Rajendra.

Loyola University, Chicago, Chicago, IL
B.S. in Civil Engineering
▪ Earned *magna cum laude* distinction for graduating with a grade point average in
the top five percent of his class (3.98).

Experience **Calloway/Drushal**, Chicago, IL
Intern
Assisted partners Peter Calloway and Jeff Drushal with various aspects of managing
their architecture firm for four consecutive summers. Duties included:
▪ Applied creative and analytical problem solving skills to multiple advanced building
systems.
▪ Developed schematics for sustainable designs in developing urban communities.
▪ Spearheaded low-income renewal project through corporate outreach initiatives.

Honors and **Phi Beta Kappa**
Awards Elected to nation's oldest academic fraternity in first year of eligibility.

Dean's List
Achieved Dean's List honors (by earning a grade point average of 3.5 or better)
in every semester, both undergraduate and graduate.

Percival Stern Award
Received award from the Engineering Department honoring "most promising young
structural engineer" upon undergraduate graduation.

Activities **Chicago Youth Outreach Mentor**, Chicago, IL
Mentored over 50 inner-city children during five year involvement with the program.

Food For Kids, Chicago, IL
Helped found this service that provides free breakfasts to all schoolchildren in the
Morgan Park area of Chicago

Scofield's mother died from liver cancer when he was a child. From that point
his older brother, Lincoln Burrows, effectively became his primary caregiver.
Following the death of their mother, the boys moved in with the family of
Lincoln's friend, Veronica Donovan. That situation was short-lived. Afterward, the boys traveled in and out of different foster home situations. Though
they were usually kept together, there were periods of time when circumstances required them to be placed separately.

Once such instance occurred when Lincoln did a six-month stretch in juvenile hall on an assault charge when he was seventeen and Michael was eleven. Michael was placed with a foster father in the Pershing section of Chicago. Though several reports had been filed suggesting the man was abusive and routinely locked his charges in a small storage shed, no formal inquiry had been made prior to Michael's placement. Six months into Michael's stay, his foster father was found dead in his home, a victim of a violent attack. For better or for worse, young Michael Scofield repressed all memory of what had occurred and was not able to help police in their investigation. To this day, the murder investigation remains unsolved.

In high school, Michael took an elective survey class in Arts and Crafts, which had a large section devoted to the Japanese art of origami. He was immediately drawn to the precision and patience that the practice required. He was particularly fond of constructing cranes and began to do so out of any material he could find.

Michael's practice of making paper cranes carried over into his adulthood. Stashes of origami paper were found in Michael's cell after the escape, and several constructed pieces, including a few birds and one flower, were discovered in the Fox River drainage pipes and in the desk drawer of one of the infirmary physicians, Dr. Sara Tancredi. It has been concluded that the cranes were yet another piece of Scofield's methodology of escape. The cranes were used as markers to tag certain key locations inside the prison.

Scofield continued to use the cranes once outside Fox River's walls. He created an elaborate code, which he used to communicate with Dr. Sara Tancredi. Scofield wrote phone numbers on paper cranes, which he then mailed to her. However, these phone numbers were not actually phone numbers. As discovered by Agent Alexander Mahone with the help of Agents Wheeler and Lang, Mahone realized the numbers were indicative of the alpha-numeric keypad on a telephone. Though Mahone did not have all the pieces of the puzzle (it was deduced that Scofield had sent Tancredi a total of four birds), it was enough for him to get a jump on the fugitive's location. That is how Mahone was able to trace Scofield and Tancredi to Gila, New Mexico.

In any case, despite being bounced around the system with a brother who was constantly in and out of trouble, Michael Scofield grew into a successful

adult who, by all accounts, lived a comfortable life in the Streeterville section of Chicago. Though his relationship with his brother had become strained in recent years, Scofield was the one person who stood by Burrows's side throughout the Steadman murder trial and appellate process. During this period, Scofield apparently grew determined to help his brother escape from Fox River Penitentiary. Though Scofield showed few outward signs, he was secretly making dramatic changes in his life.

What could be considered the first noticeable change in his demeanor was his sudden interest in getting a tattoo that covered his full torso and both arms. The otherwise clean-cut, proper businessman had never before considered so much as getting an ear pierced. Subsequent interviews with friends revealed that he had withdrawn from his closest associates in what is now assumed to be the time he spent planning the escape. And then there was his sudden marriage to Nika Volek, a woman from Kladno, Czech Republic, whom he reportedly met through a mail-order bride organization. But nothing was more surprising than the fact that the day after his wedding to Volek, Scofield was arrested in a failed bank robbery.

According to police reports, Michael Scofield entered Chicago Trust &

Savings Bank armed with a .38 and demanded cash from one of the tellers. After filling a duffle bag with a half-million dollars in cash, he fired three shots into the ceiling, demanding access to the vault. The teller was unable to meet this demand, as the branch manager is the only one with access to the vault, and he was out at lunch. Scofield fired another two rounds into the ceiling and repeated his demand. At that point, CPD and SWAT converged on the bank. Scofield pulled another gun from his belt and dropped both weapons, surrendering without further incident.

Against the wishes of his attorney and childhood friend, Veronica Donovan, Scofield pled no contest to the charge of armed robbery. In her ruling, Judge Tonya Willis cited the following:

Excerpt from Ruling in the Michael Scofield trial:

JUDGE WILLIS: Given your complete lack of prior criminal conduct, I am inclined toward probation. However, the fact that you discharged a deadly weapon during the commission of the crime suggested malice to me. For that reason, I feel it incumbent that you see the inside of a prison cell, Mr. Scofield. It says here that you've requested to be incarcerated somewhere near your home here in Chicago. I'm willing to honor that. The closest Level One facility—

VERONICA DONOVAN: Level One? That's maximum security, your honor.

JUDGE WILLIS: I would ask counsel to refrain from interrupting me. As I was saying, the closest Level One facility would be Fox River State Penitentiary. As for the term of your sentence, I'm setting it at five years. You'll be eligible for parole in half that time. Sentence to be carried out effective immediately.

Michael Scofield was placed in Cell 40 in the A-Wing of Fox River State Penitentiary, in a cell also occupied by Fernando Sucre. At first, it seemed like the cellmates hit it off, with Sucre introducing his new cellmate to prison life. But Sucre soon requested a cell transfer for unknown reasons. Scofield seemed to make enemies quickly at Fox River, engaging in confrontations with convicted mob boss John Abruzzi and murderer Theodore "T-Bag" Bagwell.

For a brief time, Charles "Haywire" Patoshik was assigned to Scofield's cell, but the psychiatric ward patient reportedly attacked Scofield and was sent back to the psych ward as a result of his actions. Sucre returned to the cell, seemingly having gotten past whatever it was that had occurred between him and "Fish," as Scofield came to be called. After a time, it seemed that Scofield had also moved beyond his problems with Abruzzi and Bagwell, as they all worked together on the same Prison Industries team. At the time, the prison staff was unaware that this was simply a cover for a crucial part of the escape plan.

Prison Industries was the inmate work program established by Warden Henry Pope when he first began his position years prior. Pope believed it would benefit both the prison and the prisoners, as it would help with upkeep of the facility but also give the inmates something productive to do, serving as a form of rehabilitation. But however fond Pope might have been of the program, he did not keep a particularly close watch on it and left the day-to-day affairs to correctional officer Captain Brad Bellick. Bellick succumbed to the corruption of prison dynamics and decided to auction Prison Industries, hoping to get an extra kickback from whoever owned it. Inmate and mob boss John Abruzzi was the highest bidder and took over Prison Industries years before Michael Scofield was incarcerated in Fox River. It is believed that Scofield knew details about P. I. before he even entered the prison, and that this knowledge aided in his escape.

Prisoners made a rate of nineteen cents an hour and their duties ranged from clean-up crew to construction.

When Scofield was admitted to Fox River, the prison staff did not know that he was the brother of death row inmate Lincoln Burrows. This information soon became public knowledge when Scofield was scheduled for a prison transfer. He initially asked Warden Pope if he could be allowed to stay at Fox River until his brother's execution. In an effort to force the situation, Scofield filed a Motion for Interlocutory Injunction, citing that the air by the river was beneficial to his chronic sinusitis. Though the initial motion was reportedly lost, Warden Pope did honor the request. Off the record, members of the prison staff have alleged that the brothers—particularly Michael—received special treatment from Warden Pope due to Scofield's assistance on a project. Warden Pope's assistant, Rebecca Gerber, described the project in her interview with the Department of Corrections investigating team.

Excerpt from DOC interview with Rebecca Gerber:

DOC: According to prison logs, Michael Scofield was in Warden Pope's office at 4:00 P.M. every Monday, Wednesday, and Friday. Can you tell us what he was doing there?

REBECCA GERBER: It was a . . . It was a special project for Warden Pope. A personal project.

DOC: What was the nature of this project?

GERBER: The warden's fortieth anniversary was coming up, and he wanted to make a special gift for his wife. A model replica of the Taj Mahal. She really loved the Taj and, well, as warden, he spends so much time working that—

DOC: Please, just stick to the facts. Does Warden Pope often assign personal projects to the prisoners?

GERBER: The warden really believes in rehabilitation. He's always saying that. . . . I'm sorry. . . . When he found out that Michael had a background in architecture, I think he saw it as a way to kill two birds with one stone . . . to get some help on his model and give Michael something to do that matched with his training. Michael seemed like a really great guy. Not like some of the other prisoners. Like he had just made a mistake and wound up somewhere he shouldn't have been.

DOC: In light of the escape, do you think the warden may have been too personally familiar with the prisoner? Given Scofield too much leeway? That he may have provided certain opportunities for Scofield to capitalize on?

GERBER: No! I mean, sure they became friendly. I know the warden is really hurt by what's happened. But I don't, for one minute, believe that the warden did anything wrong. Scofield used the warden. He betrayed that man.

Clearly, Scofield did use his proximity to the warden to his benefit in orchestrating the escape plan, and this level of access was directly responsible for gaining Burrows's freedom from solitary confinement on the night of the escape. Though Scofield was known to be close to the warden, he was conversely at odds with Captain Brad Bellick throughout his brief incarceration. But, as mentioned earlier, Scofield was not quick to make friends, and his time at Fox River was marred by several violent incidents, as indicated in his medical records.

As was the case with the warden's office, Scofield's proximity to the infirmary was integral to his plan. When admitted to Fox River, Scofield informed the medical staff that he suffered from type-1 diabetes. Dr. Sara Tancredi's initial observations suggested that this might have been a misdiagnosis. The insulin shot she had administered did not normalize Scofield, but rather overloaded his adrenal glands and brought on a hypoglycemic reaction. Subsequent blood tests did reveal, however, that he was, in fact, diabetic. After the escape, a search of Scofield's cell netted a small stash of PUGNAc, an insulin blocker. Scofield clearly knew that by feigning the need for insulin, he would have to be taken to the infirmary for daily shots. Scofield's repeated trips to the infirmary, which was the weakest link in prison security, laid the groundwork for the escape. It also led to what is believed to be an intimate relationship with Dr. Sara Tancredi, though it is currently unclear if that relationship was genuine or if he was just using her in his escape plan. Contact Scofield has had with Tancredi since the prison break seems to suggest that his feelings are genuine.

In addition to his regular trips to the infirmary, Scofield was also taken there for several emergency procedures. This is not unusual in prisons, as the inmates are prone to violence. However, Scofield did meet with an excessive number of "accidents" in his short time at Fox River.

Within the first week of his incarceration, Scofield was rushed to the infirmary. His file indicates, "Right foot trauma, transmetatarsal amputation." In layman's terms, two of the toes on his left foot had been cut off. There was a note in the file that the prisoner requested that no formal incident report be filed. Later, Scofield was badly burned. Like the first incident, Scofield refused to explain what had happened. When Dr. Tancredi found fragments of a guard's uniform in the burn, she was forced to report the incident to the warden. At first, Scofield refused to admit what had happened and was placed in solitary confinement until he admitted that Correctional Officer Roy Geary had been shaking down prisoners and was behind the burning. Though it would have been within his rights to lodge a complaint and sue the DOC, Scofield dropped the matter. Geary admitted to the shakedowns, but he denied any involvement in the burning incident. Evidence has since come to light that exonerates Geary in the matter.

While in Ad Seg (Administrative Segregation), Scofield appeared to experience a psychotic episode in which he became nonresponsive and nonfunctional. Dr. Tancredi diagnosed him as having trauma-induced delusions with self-destructive tendencies. He was placed in the psychiatric ward, where he was reunited with his former cellmate Charles Patoshik. As the eventual escape route took the Fox River Eight through the psych ward, it is now believed the entire episode was faked to provide Scofield access to the psych ward, and possibly to Patoshik as well.

Our current investigation has revealed that Scofield never anticipated his team becoming the so-called Fox River Eight. All evidence points to the fact that several members of the team were not expected to make it out of Fox River, especially not Theodore Bagwell. While Scofield clearly believes he was justified in helping his brother, it is likely that he is experiencing remorse over allowing convicted murderers to escape along with him. His subduing of Warden Pope at the start of the escape seems to have been unpremeditated as well. He was likely unprepared to commit this level of betrayal. Evidence points to Scofield experiencing a great deal of regret over his actions; that may prove beneficial in aiding in his capture.

For more on Scofield's medical history and mental state, please see the attached note found in Scofield's file.

The attached letter found in Dr. Tancredi's files has given investigators great insight into Michael Scofield's thought processes. This could be beneficial in our attempts to anticipate his actions. Further to our investigation, agents have interviewed Jennifer Mandel, the head of Chicago Youth Outreach, where Scofield volunteered for several years as a mentor to at-risk children.

The horrifying incident where Michael Scofield's toes were amputated led me to contact his personal insurance company. From them, I found out that before Michael was sent here, he was being treated by a clinical psychologist named Dr. George Brighton. I don't know why I needed to talk to Dr. Brighton, but he agreed to meet with me to talk about Michael.

Dr. Brighton said that Michael suffers from low latent inhibition, a condition where he apparently processes every single element of what he sees. Dr. Brighton used a desk lamp as an example. Michael would see the lamp like I would, but his mind would also fixate on every element, down to the bolts and washers inside. His brain is more open to incoming stimuli in the surrounding environment, which the typical brain would shut out through a process called "latent inhibition." We have to do this in order to keep our sanity.

Apparently, if someone with a low IQ has low latent inhibition, it almost always results in mental illness. If someone with a high IQ has it, it almost always results in creative genius. When Michael went to Dr. Brighton, he was feeling no sense of self-worth—no surprise since Michael lost both his parents when he was a child. Normally a child in that situation would become very withdrawn or self-centered. But, according to Dr. Brighton, the low latent inhibition made Michael extremely attuned to all the suffering around him, to all the people he perceived to be experiencing the same sort of pain he was. It was a constant bombardment that he couldn't shut out. And so, Michael became a rescuer, more concerned with others' welfare than his own. As a result, Michael started putting in a lot of community work in mentoring programs and such. This is a perfect description of the Michael Scofield that I've come to know. But it still doesn't explain what he's doing here.

Excerpt from Jennifer Mandel interview:

FBI INVESTIGATOR: Mr. Scofield was involved in your program for five years, is that correct?

JENNIFER MANDEL: Not quite. Mikey was with us as a full-time mentor for five years while he was in school. He usually worked with the kids after classes and on weekends. He went part-time when he got his job. I remember we had a party for him to celebrate him being employed. Many of our volunteers do it for school credit and then disappear once the commitment is over, but not Mikey.

FBI: So, he worked with you until his incarceration?

MANDEL: His attendance was spotty in the months before. . . . But he always let us know when he wasn't coming in. I know he hated letting these kids down, but sometimes life just gets in the way.

FBI: That's a funny way to refer to a federal crime. A bank robbery doesn't just "get in the way."

MANDEL: Someone on the news said that maybe that bank thing was just a way to get him into his brother's jail. Mikey wasn't a criminal. He hated the lowlifes that hung around our kids and did everything in his power to keep them away. If he really did what they said he did, I know there was a reason.

FBI: How can you be so sure?

MANDELL: There was this time. . . . One of our kids was having problems with the local gangbangers. Mikey tried everything to reach that boy. Got him a job running deliveries for a design firm a friend of his worked at. Mikey even took time off from work to make sure the boy was doing his job. . . . Getting to school . . . staying out of trouble. It looked like Mikey had reached him. That boy had a future all laid out in front of him. And that's something we can't say about many of the kids we help. Everything looked perfect. Till the cops arrested the boy for dealing. Turns out the kid was using his delivery route to cover for drug deliveries for

the local gang. Michael was devastated. Not only did
we lose the boy, but Mikey was betrayed by him. It hit
Mikey hard. Didn't even come back in here for three
weeks. He'd lost kids before. Not every child is a success story around here. We take what we can get. But
there was something about this one. I think it was the
betrayal. Mikey'd been alone for so much of his life. He
didn't place his trust in others easily.

With few friends, and no family to speak of, Michael Scofield has few
options for a safe haven upon his escape from Fox River. His wife, Nika Volek,
seems to be little more than a marriage of convenience so she could get a
green card. Initial interviews with Volek have netted no useful information.
Volek was placed under surveillance, though she managed to disappear for a
few days. Her whereabouts during that time are still unknown, and her car
is missing. Agents have also been dispatched in search of Veronica Donovan,
who has been missing since the escape.

Scofield has been sighted at various points across the Midwest and Southwest.

The following is a crime report filed on June 3, 2006, in Tahiti, New
Mexico.

TIME: 5:00 P.M.
LOCATION: Hal's Fishin' Shop
CRIME: Theft and Assault
REPORTED BY: Hal Beandep
STATEMENT RECORDED BY: Officer Carlos Vazquez

Mr. Beandep, owner of Hal's Fishin' Shop, reports that at approximately 3:30 P.M.
this afternoon a white male in his early thirties entered his establishment asking
for an entire case of fishing reel oil. Mr. Beandep states that he found it odd for
anyone to purchase that much oil in one go, as an ampoule can last a fisherman
months at a time. Mr. Beandep claims that he went in back to his stockroom to
retrieve the oil, and when he emerged, the male had picked up a GPS unit and
placed it on the counter. Mr. Beandep remarks that at this point in time, the suspect seemed amiable and non-threatening.

Mr. Beandep rung up the two items on the register, which came to a total of ninety-six dollars and twenty-three cents. The suspect proceeded to tally up his cash, but discovered that he did not have enough money to purchase both items and decided to take only the fishing reel oil. The transaction was completed, and after handing the suspect his change, Mr. Beandep states he began to converse with another customer who had just entered the store, an acquaintance of his, Gregory Furnace.

A few moments into his conversation with Mr. Furnace, Mr. Beandep states that he noticed, out of the corner of his eye, the suspect walking quickly toward the exit, with the GPS system in hand. Mr. Beandep yelled at the suspect to get his attention and told him that he needed to pay for the item he was holding. At this point, the male became aggressive and shoved Mr. Beandep into a product display. Mr. Beandep tumbled to the floor, sustaining injuries to his right shoulder and left knee in the fall.

Once on the ground, Mr. Beandep claims he acquiesced to the suspect, telling him to take it, and asking the suspect not to hurt him. The suspect turned and ran, taking the GPS unit with him, which is valued at $65.

The witness, Gregory Furnace, corroborates the story and believes he can make a positive ID on the suspect.

FURNACE: I walked into Hal's and saw this guy leavin'. He looked like a regular joe, only there was something familiar about him. Hal and I started talking about the currents in Hollow's Creek and then Hal sees him runnin' out with that GPS device and tries to stop him. He nearly plowed through Hal. As he stood over Hal I realized I knew where he was from. He's one of the escaped convicts from that prison over in Illinois. I hope they find those guys soon before they stir up any more trouble. Lucky for Hal I was there so nothing too bad happened to him.

On June 5, Michael Scofield and Lincoln Burrows released a video via the internet claiming Lincoln Burrows's innocence and asserting that they, and others they know, are merely victims in a larger "conspiracy."

Scofield and Burrows, accompanied by an unidentified male posing as a government agent, had just been ambushed by authorities at the Cutback

Motel in Montana. Authorities quickly realized that the unidentified male herding the convicts out of the motel was not a federal agent. The fugitives and their accomplice grabbed local news cameraman Greg Rydenour and used him as a human shield, taking him hostage as they commandeered a vehicle and fled from the scene.

Rydenour emerged hours later with a tape in hand. Though physically unharmed, his life had been threatened and he was forced to cooperate in capturing the brothers' plea of innocence on tape.

The following are excerpts from the tape:

LINCOLN BURROWS: My name is Lincoln Burrows and I'm innocent. I escaped from Fox River Penitentiary because I was sentenced to die for a murder I did not commit. I didn't murder Terrence Steadman. He committed suicide last night in the Cutback Motel thirty miles outside of his home in Blackfoot, Montana.

MICHAEL SCOFIELD: He killed himself out of fear. Fear of the people who have been hiding from him for the past three years—the same people who want my brother dead. They don't want you to know who they are. But know this: they are working with the highest level of government, including the president of the United States. . . . They operate with impunity, under the cover of the Secret Service. The very people meant to protect and serve. . . . Much blame has been placed on another innocent person, Dr. Sara Tancredi. She had nothing to do with our escape. Sara, if you're listening, I know I can't ask you for another chance. I only hope by now you have found your safe haven. I took advantage of you—your commitment to help others—and put you in a place that's every doctor's nightmare. I've considered many ways to apologize, but I must arrive at one. . . .

The FBI command center in Chicago, Illinois, brought together its finest analysts to deconstruct the meanings and intentions of the tape, in the hope that it would expedite the capture of Scofield and Burrows. Although many theories were circulated as to the motives of the tape, including a precursor to the assassination of President Caroline Reynolds, it was Agent Mahone who eventually realized the tape's true purpose. Meant to serve as a communication to Sara Tancredi, Scofield layered the dialogue with allusions to text from the Alcoholics Anonymous blue book. Mahone deciphered that they were going to rendezvous at St. Thomas Hospital in Akron, Ohio, but the fugitives had already fled the location by the time he arrived at the locale.

On June 7, a young boy by the name of Andy Lerhop ran home to his mother, Joan Lerhop, showing off the twenty dollars that a man on the street had given him. Concerned, Mrs. Lerhop asked her son where he had gotten the money, and he told her an outlandish story. Mrs. Lerhop was hesitant to believe him until a news flash appeared on television about the Fox River Eight, and her son recognized one of the escaped fugitives. Mrs. Lerhop immediately called the Chicago PD, who sent an officer to her home to question her son and file a report. The following is an excerpt of the interview between Officer Joshua Benson and Andy Lerhop:

> JOSHUA BENSON: Son, your mom tells me you had a run-in today with Michael Scofield. Is this true?
>
> ANDY LERHOP: Uh, yeah, I guess so. But I didn't know his name. And I didn't know he was running away from the police.
>
> BENSON: How did you meet Mr. Scofield?
>
> LERHOP: I was over at the mini mart buying some snacks, and after I paid for 'em, he walked over to me and said, "You wanna make some more snack money?" and I said, "Sure."
>
> BENSON: Were you scared? Did you get the feeling he was dangerous?
>
> LERHOP: No, he seemed okay. He was standing there with another guy, who kinda looked like he was his brother or something.
>
> BENSON: That would be Lincoln Burrows. Does he look like the guy in this picture?
>
> LERHOP: Yeah. Anyways, the other guy, Mike—
>
> BENSON: Did he tell you that was his name?
>
> LERHOP: Uh huh. Mike handed me one of those cells that you can throw away when you're done with it. He told me to wait by the train stop and give it to the first guy

I saw who was soakin' wet. Once I did that, he said I
should tell the wet guy to give me twenty dollars.

BENSON: Didn't you think this was strange, Andy?

LERHOP: Yeah, it was kinda weird, but it didn't seem like
I'd be doing anything wrong, so I figured, why not. So
I took the phone and waited by the train stop near
the park. For a while I was worried the wet guy would
never come, but he did.

BENSON: And then you gave him the phone?

LERHOP: Yup, and he gave me twenty dollars.

BENSON: And you never saw those other men again?

LERHOP: No sir.

The search for Scofield continues at the time this report was filed.

Last updated on 6/16 by Agent Wheeler.

FBI Files

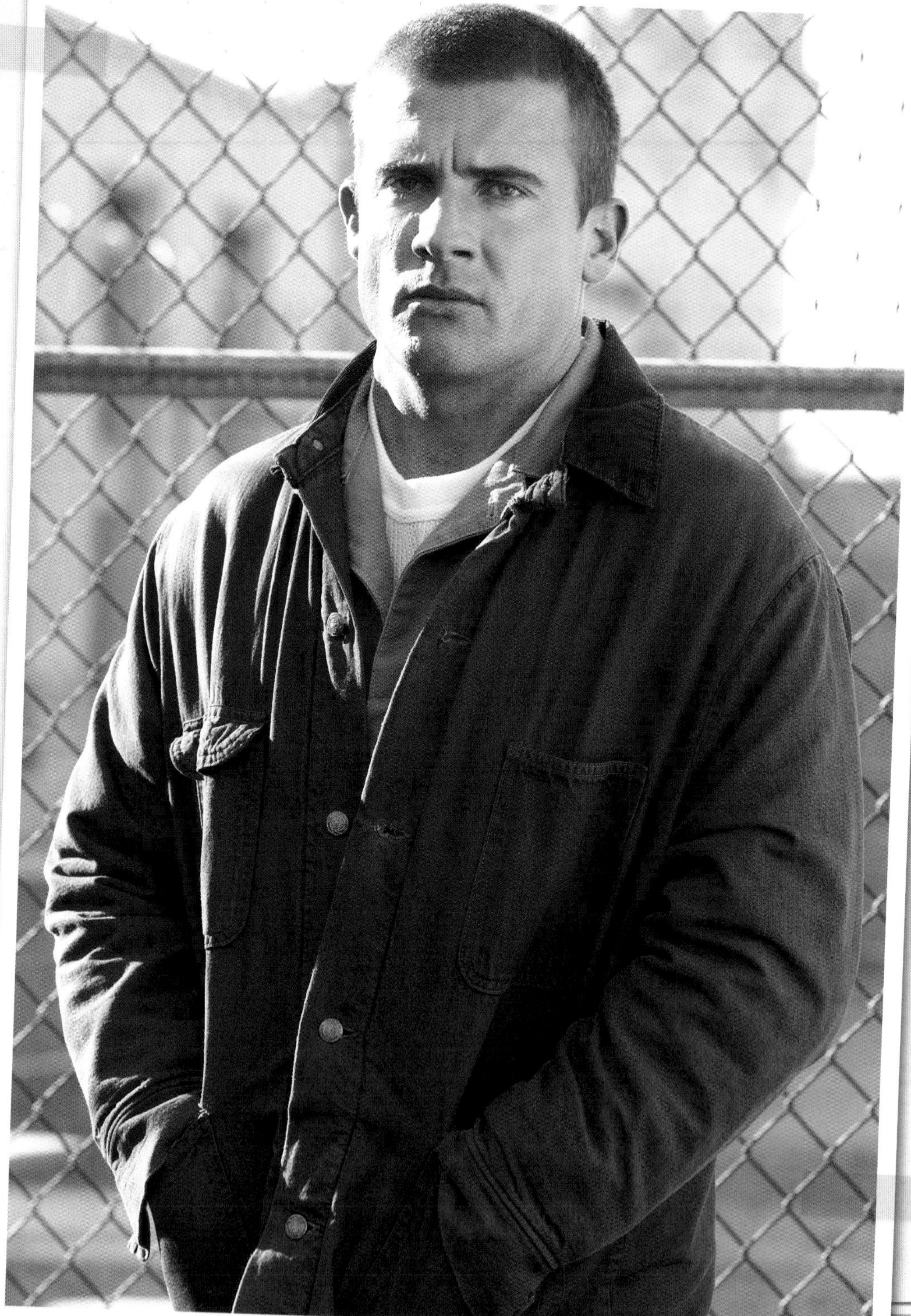

LINCOLN BURROWS

It is now evident that Lincoln Burrows's freedom was the motivation for his brother's incarceration and the goal of Michael Scofield's entire escape plan. This is surprising in that the brothers had been estranged for much of their adult lives, as Scofield's successes pulled him further and further away from a brother who seemed doomed to failure.

Problems began early in the Burrows family. Lincoln's father, Aldo Burrows, was reputed to be an abusive alcoholic who abandoned the family when his eldest son was six. Unfortunately, all formal inquiries into the Burrows family history have revealed very little about the father. In fact, there is very little record of the man and nothing on him following the disappearance from his family's life.

The tragic childhood of Lincoln Burrows continued when his mother died of liver cancer. Following the mother's death, the family of his childhood friend, Veronica Donovan, took in Lincoln and Michael. That setup was brief, which likely had something to do with the fact that Donovan was also reported to have grown up in an abusive family situation. It is unlikely that someone with Lincoln's temperament would not intervene when his friend was being hurt.

Left to care for his younger brother, Lincoln did the best he could, as

21

FOX RIVER INMATE FILE

Name: Lincoln Burrows

Prison Handle: Linc the Sink

Age: 34

Back Number: 79238

Location: Death Row, Cell 18

Crime: First degree murder, aggravated discharge of a firearm

Sentence: Death by electrocution

Time Left on Sentence: ~~One Week~~ TBD—AT LARGE

Eligible for Parole in: Inmate is not eligible for parole

Former Employment: Unemployed (Formerly employed by Ecofield)

Next of Kin: L.J. Burrows

Relationship: Son

they were shipped to various foster care situations. His juvenile file is filled with reports of violence, as Lincoln literally fought to keep his brother safe. One such violent incident resulted in charges, and Lincoln was sent to juvenile hall for a period of six months, while his brother was placed in what was reportedly an abusive foster home.

Through all of his relocations and run-ins with the law, Lincoln managed to maintain his friendship with Veronica Donovan, and it eventually grew into a romantic relationship during their teenage years. Although Lincoln continued to act out, it was widely known among his crowd that Veronica had a calming effect on him, but that abruptly came to an end when she left for college. The two initially tried to maintain contact, but Lincoln eventually took up with another woman. He and Donovan attempted to reconcile after college, but by then Burrows's attitude had changed severely, and Donovan pulled away seemingly for good. However, it is believed that Veronica Donovan's recent work on Burrows's behalf—combined with the loss of her fiancé—has led to a reunion of sorts between the two.

The woman Burrows became involved with after Veronica Donovan left for college was Lisa Rix. This relationship resulted in an unexpected pregnancy and the birth of their son, Lincoln Burrows, Junior. Though he and Rix never married, Burrows tried to be a part of his son's life, in spite of the fact that his own was rapidly falling apart. Burrows's constant legal problems prevented him from getting to know his son better. By the time Burrows was sentenced to Fox River, he had already spent time in various institutions, serving two months for theft, three months for possession, two months for disorderly conduct, six months for battery, six months for assault, and ten months for battery.

It is rumored that Burrows secretly bankrolled his brother's high-priced education at Loyola University, via a deal he made with loan shark Crab Simmons. To this day, Burrows maintains that the deal led to him being at the scene of Terrence Steadman's death, though most members of the law enforcement community believe that the convict is effectively grasping at straws. Taking Burrows's checkered past into consideration, it is more likely that he killed Terrence Steadman in a revenge scenario. However, there has been an increasing public outcry that Burrows may be innocent. This idea, initially spearheaded by the now-missing Veronica Donovan, is beginning to take hold, especially in the internet community. Regarding Burrows's conviction, these are the facts as they are known:

Lincoln Burrows worked in one of the Ecofield warehouses. This was the company owned by Terrence Steadman. Reportedly, the two had a public altercation that resulted in Burrows being fired, although Burrows claims to have never met the man. Two weeks following this incident, Terrence Steadman was found dead from a gunshot wound in a parking garage. An eyewitness saw Burrows fleeing the parking garage, and

Killer of VP's Brother Scheduled to Die May 11

The attorneys of Chicago Southsider and convicted murder Lincoln Burrows suffered another and final setback in their calls for a re-trial Tuesday. Acting Judge Laslow Manckiewicz ruled that the Illinois Department of Corrections has legal right to move forward with the execution, which will be by electric chair on May 11th.

Burrows, who rose from obscurity to regional prominence with the high-profile case, issued a letter through his attorney maintaining his innocence.

Local groups opposing the death penalty decried the ruling. Marcos Canton-Williamsburg, president of the anti-death penalty group An Eye For An Eye Makes the Whole World Blind, indicated that a retinue of more than a hundred protestors will stage a week-long sit-in outside the prison to protest the execution.

Lincoln Burrows, Killer of VP's Brother awaiting death sentence.

Lincoln Burrows' Final Appeal Denied
Execution Will Proceed as Scheduled

Lincoln Burrows, it seems, has
fi........ ..t ....ites. The

later he was discovered at home, washing the victim's blood off his clothes. The murder weapon—a 9mm gun—was found in his apartment. Parking garage surveillance cameras recorded the event, showing Burrows walking up to Steadman's car and firing into the driver's side window. He then crossed around to the passenger's side and rifled through the glove compartment, trying to make it look like a robbery before he fled the scene.

Burrows was charged with Murder One for Steadman's death and sentenced to become the thirteenth person executed in the state of Illinois since 1976. His lawyer, Tim Giles, went through the usual round of appeals; however, he managed to exhaust all avenues in three years. Once the final appeal was lost, Burrows's execution was set for May 11. The following are the transcripts of an interview a reporter from the Chicago FOX affiliate conducted with Burrows's lawyer. It occurred outside the courthouse on the afternoon that the ruling on the final appeal came down.

REPORTER: Mr. Giles, were you surprised that this—what many people are considering the final ruling—came so quickly? Doesn't it take about a decade for these things to run their course?

TIM GILES: I'm very surprised. If you look back over the case, every step along the way the proceedings have been expedited. While it's not entirely unusual in a high-profile case, such as this, it definitely took us by surprise.

REPORTER: Now that all of Lincoln Burrows's appeals have been exhausted, what is your client thinking?

GILES: As I'm sure you can understand, Mr. Burrows is upset and very frustrated with the way things have turned out for our case. Whoever killed Terrence Steadman is still at large, and meanwhile, my client is still sitting behind bars, convicted of a crime he didn't commit. But he's strong. Lincoln's maintaining his innocence, and reading his Bible for guidance and comfort. He's confident that new evidence will come to light that will ultimately exonerate him of this crime and in the eyes of the American public.

REPORTER: Why was there no talk of a plea bargain? Could a deal have been struck that would have kept your client away from the electric chair?

GILES: Lincoln Burrows has not wavered once from his claim of innocence in the entire time I have worked with him. He refused to even consider a deal. Accepting a deal means wrongly convicting an innocent man of this heinous crime and letting the guilty party go free. Is that how justice is supposed to be served?

REPORTER: Was there any indication that Vice President Reynolds may have used her influence to expedite this trial?

GILES: I cannot comment on what Vice President Reynolds may or may not have done. But there's no question that in our society, cases that revolve around the wealthy and privileged are measured against a different set of standards than those that are not.

Burrows was incarcerated at Fox River Penitentiary, where he earned the nickname, Linc the Sink, because when threatened, he was said to "come at you with everything but the kitchen sink." Aside from the typical prison scuffles, Burrows was initially a model prisoner, even being allowed out of his death row cell to participate in the Prison Industries (P.I.) work program. He and his brother, Michael, reunited in prison and seemed to work through their years of estrangement. Little did anyone suspect that they were also working on an escape plan.

While incarcerated, Burrows also grew closer to his son, L.J. When his son had his own legal troubles (he was arrested for possession of marijuana—see file on L.J. Burrows), L.J.'s parole officer assigned him to a "scared straight" program, scheduling regular visits with his father. However, L.J. was soon implicated in the murder of his mother and his stepfather and went on the run to escape prosecution. It is believed that he still managed to communicate with his father during this time and may have sought refuge with Burrows's old friend, Veronica Donovan.

Though at times he appeared the model prisoner, Burrows did have some run-ins with other inmates and guards. The day before his originally scheduled execution, Burrows punched a C.O. outside the break room where Burrows was working P.I. As a result, Burrows was sent to Administrative Segregation. That evening, he suffered a sudden and violent stomach malady. It was later determined that this was a ruse to get him to the infirmary for the initial escape attempt. When that attempt failed, Burrows returned to the Secure Housing Unit, where he awaited his execution.

Though his new lawyer, Veronica Donovan, continued to work their appellate options, Burrows prepared for the end. With his son missing, Burrows spent the evening of his execution with Michael and Veronica. His last meal consisted of blueberry pancakes. With all the necessary elements in place, Burrows was set to die on May 11. He was taken to the death chamber, where he said good-bye to his loved ones and was then strapped into the electric chair. With only seconds to go before his death, a last minute reprieve came from Judge Randall Kessler. New evidence had come to light, suggesting that

Terrence Steadman was not really dead. The execution was delayed, and Steadman's coffin was exhumed for examination. Dental records confirmed that the body inside was Steadman's and Burrows's execution was rescheduled for May 26.

At the same time, Burrows's brother, Michael Scofield, was presumably moving ahead with a backup escape plan. There was, however, another suspicious event that may or may not have been an escape attempt, which occurred shortly before the actual breakout. The following report was found in the internal prison files. It was never formally reported to the DOC.

FOX RIVER INCIDENT REPORT

INMATE: Lincoln Burrows
INCIDENT: Possible escape attempt
REPORT PREPARED BY: Rebecca Gerber

SUMMARY OF EVENTS: In what Warden Pope considered a highly unusual precedent, the DOC approved a petition to allow the prisoner, Lincoln Burrows, a one-hour visit with his son, L.J. Burrows, who was charged with two counts of attempted murder. All necessary precautions were taken to transmit the prisoner, Burrows, to the Cook County Courthouse. The prisoner was Y-cuffed and taken in a transport van with armed guards. En route to the courthouse, a truck crashed into the van, sending it rolling into an embankment. The truck continued on, leaving the wreckage behind. Correctional Officers Jeffrey Nathan and Adam Rabinowitz were killed in the crash, while Officer Michael Roker was left in critical condition.

The accident occurred in Kane County, which is under the jurisdiction of Sheriff Ballard. The sheriff immediately rendered assistance, agreeing with Fox River C.O. Brad Bellick that it would be best not to alert the media until the situation was under control.

A bystander named Roy Hawkings happened on the scene and attempted to render aid when another car drove up and the driver knocked out Hawkings. When Hawkings regained consciousness, the car and driver were gone, and so was Lincoln Burrows. The unknown driver was in a 2006 Mustang, either black or dark blue. Hawkings was unable to get the license number. Sheriff Ballard set up checkpoints at 171 by Lemont, at Sage Bridge, and at the river toward Romeoville.

Three hours into the search, the Sheriff received a call from Steve Schimek at Smitty's Salvage Yard, reporting that the missing car was on the premises. Local police and Fox River Correctional Officers converged on the junkyard and apprehended Burrows without incident. Burrows was returned to Fox River and placed under 24-hour surveillance. Burrows maintained that he had not been making an escape attempt, but rather that someone—presumably the unidentified driver—had tried to kill him. The fact that Burrows had been found at a junkyard eight miles away from the accident site made this claim difficult to believe.

Whether or not the incident was an actual escape attempt is still unclear. With the clock ticking down to Burrows's execution, Michael Scofield's backup plan for escape was put into action. On the night of the escape, Michael Scofield forced Warden Pope to have Burrows transferred to the infirmary where Burrows and Scofield escaped along with six other inmates.

Outside of Fox River, Lincoln Burrows has no friends beyond Veronica Donovan and her co-counsel, Nick Savrinn. All attempts to contact Veronica Donovan have failed and she is now officially listed as a missing person. When agents went Nick Savrinn's apartment the day after the escape in order to question Savrinn about Burrows, they found him and his father dead on the premises. To this day, the whereabouts of Burrows's own father remain unknown. Other than Scofield, Burrows's only known relative is his son.

Security was tightened at the Cook County Courthouse when, on the day after the escape, L.J. Burrows was scheduled for a hearing in his murder case. Posing as Nick Savrinn, Burrows placed a call to his son, and evidently passed along a secret message. As L.J. was waiting to be transported to a facility in another state, his father and uncle staged an attempt to free L.J., presumably to take him on the run with them. FBI Special Agent Alexander Mahone managed to thwart their efforts, and L.J. remained in custody, but Burrows and Scofield escaped. On Route 38, near mile marker 12 just outside of Chicago, the brothers attempted to fake their own deaths to avoid capture, driving a car rigged with explosives into a ravine. The subsequent investigation into the crash determined that the blood, bone fragments, and DNA evidence found in the wreckage did not belong to Burrows or Scofield but were, in fact, dismembered pig parts.

The brothers continued on the run together until they separated at a private residence in Tooele, Utah. At that point, Burrows left to find his son, who had been released from jail in Arizona. The charges against L.J. had been dropped on the grounds of insufficient evidence. Shortly after the father/son reunion, the pair was caught and taken into custody in Willcox, Arizona, but managed to escape soon thereafter. It is believed that Burrows placed his son in a safe location, before moving on as the pair was not seen together again for some time.

Ten days after the escape from Fox River Penitentiary, agents of the FBI and U.S. Border Patrol captured Burrows and his brother only a few miles

from the U.S./Mexico border. The prisoners were taken into custody and kept under tight security as arrangements were made for their return to Fox River. As they were being transported to Chicago, they managed yet another escape from custody. During the escape, Special Agent Mahone was shot and wounded. It is unclear where Burrows and Scofield retrieved the firearm they used against Special Agent Mahone, but conversations with D.O.C. officials who were involved in the transport have led us to believe that one of the guards transporting Burrows and Scofield may have been carrying an unauthorized firearm. Subsequently, the firearm used against Special Agent Mahone has not been recovered by investigators.

At a nearby roadblock on Route 46, two state troopers stopped a black Suburban shortly after the escape. The driver, who identified himself only as Agent Kellerman, argued with the officers before being allowed to proceed through. A check of various defense and intelligence-gathering databases at Quantico concluded there is no such person with that name working within any of the departments of the United States government. Hours later, the Suburban was found parked at a private air strip in New Mexico. A witness at the scene said three men matching the descriptions of Michael Scofield, Lincoln Burrows, and "Agent Kellerman" boarded a small plane.

At a private airport in Cutback, Montana, several hours later, a witness positively identified all three men who deboarded a small plane and left in a black SUV. Authorities were notified and roadblocks were put in place on every major road and highway in the surrounding area, but to no avail. Several hours later, a call from Michael Scofield was placed from a room at the Cutback Motel to the Channel 11 news station. On the call, Scofield stated that he wanted to turn himself in. As law enforcement officials and news organizations descended on the motel, the man identifying himself as Agent Kellerman took Channel 11 cameraman Greg Rydenour hostage and, along with Burrows and Scofield, fled the scene. Inside the motel room, authorities later discovered the body of Luc Tkachuk, a custodial employee for the motel. He had been shot in the face, though it is unclear at this time as to which of the three men shot Mr. Tkachuk.

Using Mr. Rydenour's camera equipment and technical know-how, the fugitives drove to an undisclosed location where they read prepared statements while Mr. Rydenour filmed them. After they were finished, the trio dropped Mr. Rydenour at the side of the road and instructed him to take the tape back to Channel 11. The station later broadcast the tape nationally. (A partial transcript of the tape can be found in Michael Scofield's file.) Agent

Arthur Montana from the Billings office spoke with Mr. Rydenour afterward. Below is a partial transcript of that discussion:

Interview with Greg Rydenour, Cameraman, News Channel 11:

AGENT MONTANA: Let's talk a little about the gentleman in the suit. You never heard Burrows or Scofield say his name?

RYDENOUR: No. Not at all. But the tape—it wasn't his idea. It was Scofield's. The suit just went along with it.

MONTANA: I'd like to bring a sketch artist in a few minutes, so we can try and create a composite of what he looked like.

RYDENOUR: Sure. I'll try my best.

MONTANA: Now, take me back to the moments right after they asked you to tape them. What followed?

RYDENOUR: They hung a sheet behind their heads, on the wall. One of them, the guy in the suit, found it on the floor while Burrows and Scofield were talking about how far they had to go. Burrows said something about "four hundred and fifty miles in six hours."

MONTANA: Four hundred and fifty miles to where?

RYDENOUR: I don't know.

The next sighting of Burrows and Scofield occurred in Akron, Ohio, at St. Thomas Hospital, although it is unclear what the two men were doing at that location. They fled before authorities arrived. They were next seen in Evansville, Indiana, at a train station. The man identifying himself as "Agent Paul Kellerman with the Secret Service" told a ticket taker he was transporting a fugitive to Chicago and requested an empty train car. The alleged "fugitive" he was transporting was later identified as Michael Scofield. Burrows and a woman believed to be Sara Tancredi were also seen by passengers in the same car. (See the fugitive sightings file.)

Last updated on 6/8 by Agent Wheeler.

FOX RIVER INMATE FILE

Name: John Abruzzi

Prison Handle: None

~~DECEASED~~

Age: 44

Back Number: 81004

Location: General Population, A-Wing, Cell 96

Crime: Murder (two counts), conspiracy to commit murder (two counts)

Sentence: 120 years

Time Left on Sentence: 119 years, six months *TBD - AT LARGE*

Eligible for Parole in: Inmate is not eligible for parole

Former Employment: Vice President, Falzone Enterprises

Next of Kin:

	Relationship:
Sylvia Abruzzi	Wife
John Abruzzi, Jr.	Son
Nicole Abruzzi	Daughter

JOHN ABRUZZI

Chicago crime boss John Abruzzi has a colorful history of violence and suspected underworld activities. He first became a member of the Falzone crime family as a young man. It is suspected that he started as a wheelman for the organization, but quickly worked his way through the ranks. As his power base grew, he began dabbling in a variety of criminal activities ranging from extortion to murder.

Local police and the FBI organized crime unit suspected Abruzzi of numerous criminal endeavors operated out of several shell companies. Neither organization was able to come up with any proof of Abruzzi's activities. That all changed when Otto Fibonacci stepped forward.

Fibonacci was a supervisor at one of the warehouses under Abruzzi's control. For the first several years of his employment, Fibonacci was unaware of his employer's underworld connections.

One night, Fibonacci was working late and accidentally stumbled across Abruzzi ordering the execution-style murder of two men. At first Fibonacci was reluctant to come forward, fearing for the safety of his wife and children. Eventually, his conscience won out, and he was the key witness that sent Abruzzi to prison for two counts of murder and two counts of conspiracy to commit murder. But Otto Fibonacci's value to the government did not end there.

**Excerpt from the testimony of Otto Fibonacci
in the Abruzzi murder case:**

PROSECUTOR JAMES RILEY: Mr. Fibonacci, can you
    describe exactly what you saw the night in question?
OTTO FIBONACCI: I was working late. I handle all of the
    books for the warehouse.
RILEY: You're speaking, of course, about the C&O ware-
    house that Mr. Abruzzi owns, correct? Off Castlio Road
    downtown.
FIBONACCI: Right.
RILEY: How long have you worked there, Mr. Fibonacci?
FIBONACCI: Almost fifteen years.
RILEY: That's a long time. I take it you like your job, then?

FIBONACCI: Very much.

RILEY: And the people you work with?

FIBONACCI: I like them, yes.

RILEY: I understand you're known as "Lucky" around the warehouse. How come?

FIBONACCI: I run a football pool every year. Ya know, just with some of the guys who work with me. A few years ago I had a pretty good run.

RILEY: Picking winners?

FIBONACCI: Right. Picking winners. In the pool. It seemed like I couldn't be stopped. So a few of the guys started calling me Lucky. And it just stuck.

RILEY: So you've got a good job. And you're friendly with your coworkers. So up until the night in question, you held no ill will against your employer?

FIBONACCI: None at all.

RILEY: Please continue.

FIBONACCI: Due to the schedule of trucks coming in and out of our place, I'm not able to leave until after the last shipment has come in. That usually isn't until after 10 P.M. As I was proceeding to the vault, where I lock away our statements, I heard a noise. Thinking it was George, our custodian, I walked over to the warehouse to say good night. But as I got closer, I heard voices.

RILEY: And did you recognize these voices?

FIBONACCCI: Not at first. But as I turned the corner I saw two men on the ground, and three other guys standing over them with guns. One of the guys who was kneeling was crying.

RILEY: Did you know any of these men? Either the three with the guns or the two who were kneeling?

FIBONACCI: Yes.

Young, 93, retired in the mid-1980s   Security retirement bene

Life Sente
Mob Boss

Mob Boss John Abruzzi was sentenced yesterday to a life term with no parole

Tuesday, Judge Ricard sentenced John Abruzzi to a life term without parole.

RILEY: Are they in the courtroom today?

FIBONACCI: One of them is. John Abruzzi.

RILEY: Mr. Abruzzi was there. And what was he doing?

FIBONACCI: He was just pacing, listening to the man's pleas. Then he touched one of them, silencing him. He nodded to one of the other guys who had a gun. Then that guy executed them. Just like that. Real quick. And both men slumped over. Dead.

RILEY: And what did you do, Mr. Fibonacci, after you realized what happened?

FIBONACCI: I just stood there. Frozen. Like I couldn't move. Like it was all a dream. I've never seen nothing like that before. And I hope I never do again.

Due to his management position in Abruzzi's company, Fibonacci had access to financial records and reports on many of his employer's holdings, as well as those linked to Philly Falzone. Once he realized the true nature of the illegal dealings, all it took was a little digging on Fibonacci's part to find what the FBI believes is enough information to take down the entire Falzone organization. Fibonacci agreed to further testimony under the condition that he and his family were placed in the witness protection program and moved to a safe location.

During Abruzzi's rise to power, he married Sylvia De Luca, daughter of a high-ranking member of the Falzone family. Though she clearly knew of his mob ties before they were wed, their lifestyle has become increasing stressful on her and their two young children. Those concerns only deepened once Abruzzi was imprisoned. It has been widely reported that while Abruzzi was incarcerated, Philly Falzone used Abruzzi's family as some form of bargaining chip against him.

Once he arrived at Fox River, Abruzzi quickly asserted himself as a key player in Prison Industries, a work program for inmates. He struck a deal with crooked C.O. Brad Bellick. In exchange for money, which was deposited directly into Bellick's bank account via a contact on the outside, John attained full control of P.I. He assumed control of the prison work program and asserted his influence over who could and could not work inside prison walls. Not only did this increase Abruzzi's power base in the prison, it also gave the eight fugitives the opportunity to dig underneath the prison's guard shack every day.

It is unclear whether or not Scofield knew of Abruzzi's hold on Prison Industries prior to his arrival at Fox River. What is clear is that Abruzzi did play a part in Scofield's plan from the start. Information found on Scofield's

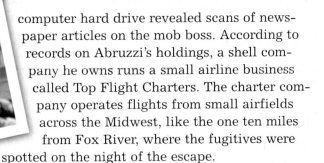

computer hard drive revealed scans of newspaper articles on the mob boss. According to records on Abruzzi's holdings, a shell company he owns runs a small airline business called Top Flight Charters. The charter company operates flights from small airfields across the Midwest, like the one ten miles from Fox River, where the fugitives were spotted on the night of the escape.

Abruzzi nearly missed his chance to escape when, on the day of the failed escape attempt, an unknown assailant attacked Abruzzi and slashed his throat, leaving him for dead. Abruzzi's crew found him lying near death in the landscaping shed. Though none of the men would talk, it was rumored that Theodore "T-Bag" Bagwell had done the deed. Abruzzi was airlifted to the University of Chicago medical hospital, where he underwent emergency surgery. Miraculously, Abruzzi lived. He was placed under guard while he recuperated for several days and was then readmitted to Fox River. As a result of this event, the prison chaplain believes that Abruzzi went through a spiritual reawakening. It is unclear whether or not this was a ruse. Certainly his behavior following the escape would lead one to believe that it was all an act.

While it is clear what a man of Abruzzi's connections brought to the escape plan, it is more difficult to understand what Scofield could have brought to the table in order to get Abruzzi on board. Though the possibility of escape would have been enough motivation for most inmates, Scofield would have needed a compelling incentive for Abruzzi to even agree to an audience with Scofield in the first place. It is likely that Scofield had information on the whereabouts of Otto Fibonacci.

It is suspected that Scofield discovered a glaring weakness in the Federal Witness Protection Program, one which has been a source of concern for this agency for many years. Before a witness is transferred to the U.S. Marshals Service to be placed in witness protection, a local sheriff from the county where the trial will take place is required to guard that person at a distant location. If an interested party determines which sheriff from the county is inexplicably missing from the office while guarding the witness, all it takes is the ability to track down that sheriff to find the witness's location.

FOX RIVER PENITENTIARY VISITORS LOG

Date: May 1st

Officer on Duty: S

Name	Visiting	Time in	Time Out	Secured	Unsecu
Todd Marcus	Jackson	2:38	3:08	X	
Phillip Falzone	Scofield/Abruzzi	2:45	3:01		X
Maria Jimenez	Jimenez	3:00	3:23		X

Most likely Scofield used this knowledge and was able to ascertain that Fibonacci and his family were initially placed at an undisclosed location in Topcka, Kansas.

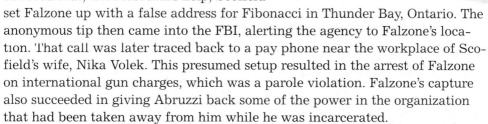

Prior to the prison break, an anonymous tip came in to the FBI regarding Philly Falzone and a planned execution. This incident occurred only one day after Philly Falzone visited Michael Scofield at Fox River. It is believed that, with Abruzzi's help, Scofield set Falzone up with a false address for Fibonacci in Thunder Bay, Ontario. The anonymous tip then came into the FBI, alerting the agency to Falzone's location. That call was later traced back to a pay phone near the workplace of Scofield's wife, Nika Volek. This presumed setup resulted in the arrest of Falzone on international gun charges, which was a parole violation. Falzone's capture also succeeded in giving Abruzzi back some of the power in the organization that had been taken away from him while he was incarcerated.

Following the escape from Fox River, Abruzzi was seen with the main group of fugitives for a short time before they all went their separate ways. Reports indicate that he reunited with his family in New York and was set to leave the country. One of his associates later admitted that Abruzzi had booked passage on a container ship that had a stateroom listed as a cargo hold on the manifest. The ship was docked at the Navy Yard and scheduled to leave for Sardinia a day after Abruzzi had reunited with his family. Abruzzi never had the chance to make the trip.

Special Agent Alexander Mahone found Scofield's preliminary escape plans on a hard drive dredged up from the Chicago River. Mahone made the connection to Otto Fibonacci based on the assumption that the location of the witness was what Scofield had offered Abruzzi to get his assistance with the escape plan. Suspecting that Abruzzi would still want vengeance on the man that had sent him to prison, Agent Mahone leaked false information regarding Fibonacci's location, hoping that Abruzzi would take the bait. Within hours, Abruzzi arrived at a motel armed and ready to take out Fibonacci.

On Agent Mahone's orders, Abruzzi was allowed to enter the motel room, while his associate waited in the car outside. At that moment, FBI vehicles swarmed the motel parking lot, trapping Abruzzi in the room. The fugitive was ordered out of the room and told to drop his weapon. Abruzzi refused. When the fugitive raised his weapon at officers, Mahone gave the order to fire. Abruzzi was shot dead.

Last updated on 6/1 by Agent Wheeler.

FERNANDO SUCRE

Fernando Sucre was born and raised in Chicago in a large family that, to all outward appearances, seemed perfectly normal. He has no prior criminal record, though people in the neighborhood where he grew up recall several instances where he "borrowed" cars for joyrides around the neighborhood. He always returned the vehicles, and no one ever pressed charges.

Sucre was convicted on one count of aggravated robbery of a liquor store, although it apparently was not his first offense at that store. According to the store owner, Sucre had robbed the store on one prior occasion, but only took $100 from the cash register. Interviews with his friends indicate that his first theft was to pay for a date with his girlfriend, Maricruz Delgado. Because Maricruz was from Chicago's Pill Hill neighborhood, some felt that she was out of Sucre's league. This seemed to be substantiated when he felt the need to make a return trip to the liquor store to supplement his income enough so he could buy her an engagement ring. That theft was thwarted when police received an anonymous phone call alerting them to the robbery.

Sucre had been dating Maricruz for two years prior to his arrest. The couple remained together during his incarceration, in spite of the fact that Maricruz moved to New York after accepting a job as a buyer for a major Manhattan fashion retailer. The pair became engaged while Sucre was incarcerated. As Sucre was largely a

FOX RIVER INMATE FILE

Name: Fernando Sucre

Prison Handle: None

Age: 30

Back Number: 89775

Location: General Population, A-Wing, Cell 40

Crime: One count of aggravated robbery

Sentence: Five years

Time Left on Sentence: ~~Four years, one month~~ *TBD—AT LARGE*

Eligible for Parole in: ~~One year, six months~~ *TBD*

Former Employment: Landscaper

Next of Kin: Francisca Sucre

Relationship: Mother

model prisoner, he was allowed conjugal visits with his fiancée, which is usually only reserved for spouses.

Though Sucre generally exhibited exemplary behavior, he was not a perfect prisoner. He lost his conjugal visit privileges when he refused to admit to having a cell phone, after another prisoner indicated that he did. Sucre was also sent to solitary confine-

ment on two occasions. The first occurred when a weapon was found in his cell during a routine shakedown. The second incident occurred when he was found outside in the yard after count. At the time, he claimed he was retrieving a pair of panties his girlfriend had thrown over the wall for him. However, subsequent interviews with Maricruz indicate that she was in New York at the time. It is possible that his being in the yard at night was related to the intricate escape plan.

Sucre would have been the first unknown element in Michael Scofield's escape plan. Though Scofield could request what prison he was sent to, there was certainly no mechanism for requesting a specific cellmate. All research indicates that Scofield and Sucre did not know each other prior to their incarceration. It is interesting to note that soon after they were assigned as cellmates, Sucre requested a cell transfer. It is possible that Sucre was initially reluctant to join in Scofield's escape plan, but something must have occurred to change his mind, because the two cellmates were quickly reunited.

It seems unlikely that a prisoner serving time on a relatively minor count would attempt an escape with only a year and a half remaining before he was up for parole. Sucre may have come to this unwise decision as a result of a visit from his cousin, Hector Avila. Correctional Officer Keith Stolte reports that the usually even-tempered Sucre grew agitated during the visit.

Excerpt from C.O. Keith Stolte interview:

DOC: Do you know why this particular visit from the inmate's cousin, Hector Avila, caused him so much distress?

STOLTE: From what I understand, his fiancée Maricruz
    was supposed to come that day. Not Hector. She was a
    cute little philly—Maricruz.
DOC: He didn't know his cousin was coming to see him?
STOLTE: No sir. He was really looking forward to seeing
    Maricruz because his conjugals had just been revoked,
    and this was really the only time he was gonna have
    time with her for a while. I remember the look on his
    face when he saw Hector walk through that door. He
    was surprised to say the least.
DOC: Would you say he looked upset or angry when he saw
    his cousin?
STOLTE: Not really. I just don't think he was expecting it.
    But I think Avila must have known the visit wasn't
    going to go over well, because he made a specific
    request to speak with him in secured visitation—which
    basically means they had a locked metal grate separat-
    ing them.

DOC: Did you overhear their exchange?

STOLTE: Not the first part of their conversation. But then they started to raise their voices. Avila must have said something that Sucre didn't like. Sucre started yelling and banging on the cage. Everybody in the visitation area could hear him. We had to step in and subdue him. Even once we got him away from Avila, he was still mumbling to himself. I don't think I've ever seen Sucre so upset before in all his time at Fox River. Usually he's a good-natured, laid-back cat. But that day, he was pissed.

DOC: And do you know what it was that Avila could have said to upset him so much?

STOLTE: Turns out Avila came to tell him that Sucre's girl, Maricruz, was breaking up with him.

DOC: Do you think that was the motivation for Sucre to participate in the escape that Scofield was planning?

STOLTE: It is if you ask me. I mean the guy didn't have that much longer left on his bid. He could've waited it out. But after the visit—I don't know. I think he heard some bad news. He kept talking about Maricruz and how much he needed to see her and talk to her. He was obsessed.

Interviews conducted with the family after the escape indicate that Sucre and Maricruz were, in fact, having problems in their relationship. The couple seemed to be on the mend when Maricruz told Sucre that she was carrying his child. The happiness was short-lived when Maricruz broke off their engagement and told Sucre that Hector Avila had asked her to marry him. Avila's visit to Sucre must have been related to this affair.

After the escape, initial FBI attempts to place Maricruz Delgado under surveillance were complicated by her impromptu trip to Las Vegas, where she intended to marry Hector Avila. This was likely unknown to Sucre, as initial sightings had him heading for New York. It is unclear how Sucre learned of the wedding, but only days after the escape, Hector Avila alerted the Las Vegas Police Department that Sucre had shown up to try to stop the ceremony. Maricruz was kept from Sucre while he was there, and he managed to flee before police arrived.

Following Maricruz's return to New York, she was interviewed by the FBI and placed under surveillance in case Sucre tried to get in touch with her again. However, the surveillance plan was compromised when she decided to continue on her planned honeymoon trip, heading to Mexico with her sister, instead of her former fiancé Avila.

We believe that Fernando Sucre's cousin, Hector Avila, may be tracking Sucre's locations, and is seeking him to get retribution for disrupting Avila's marriage to Maricruz. While Avila's whereabouts are currently unknown, Kalinda Pumales recently filed a report with the NYPD, claiming that Avila threatened and assaulted her. The following is an excerpt from her statement to police:

> *. . . Hector showed up at my door, all red in the face. I could tell he was really angry. I thought he had stopped by to look for Theresa, but he just started yelling about Maricruz. I didn't know what to say when he asked me where she was. I mean . . . I know there's always been a weird love triangle between Maricruz, Hector, and Fernando, but . . . I didn't want to get anyone into trouble. Hector was so mad, and he said he had looked for Maricruz, everywhere—I think he even showed up at her job. Anyway, I didn't answer him right away, and he got really mad and grabbed my arm. He squeezed it really hard and shoved me against the wall. He called me a bitch and said, "You want problems?" I was scared so I told him the truth. I told him that Maricruz and Theresa went on the honeymoon to Ixtapa—the one that she was supposed to go on with him. He got so mad. I honestly thought he was going to hurt me or do something crazy. He just had this look in his eyes, like he totally lost it. . . . Thank God, he just turned around and left. But now I'm worried about Theresa and Maricruz.*

Sucre met up with several of the other fugitives at a private residence in Tooele, Utah, the day after he crashed Maricruz's wedding. The men were attempting to dig up money buried thirty years earlier by the famed hijacker, D.B. Cooper. Police Officer Anne Owens attempted to bond with Sucre when she and her mother, Jeanette Owens, were taken hostage. According to Owens, Sucre confirmed that he had indeed escaped for his girlfriend. Sucre was one of the first to leave the premises. At the time, it was unclear whether or not he took a share of whatever money was found by the fugitives.

Over the next couple days, the fugitive was reportedly seen alone and in the company of Michael Scofield. Sucre was last believed to be on a plane crossing the U.S./Mexico border. Air Force jets had been called in to intercept the plane or force it down. Somewhere over the Mexican desert, Sucre and the pilot bailed out. The pilot was later found dead after a parachute malfunction.

Though Bureau intelligence is not entirely sure how Sucre managed to survive the plane crash that transpired just after the "Bolshoi Booze" plane made it over the Mexican border, Sucre began to head down to Ixtapa. An anonymous tip called in to the command center identified it as the rendezvous point for him and his fiancée, Maricruz.

The following is a report from Mexican authorities, filed by Lt. Roberto Rodriguez. (Translated from Spanish.)

> *On the night of June 4, I pulled over a man driving an old Volkswagon beetle. I recognized the car as belonging to Jose Berradero, a man from town, recently widowed. The man driving the car was much younger, and I had never seen him before. I thought he had stolen the car. When I pulled him over, he told me that Berradero had lent him the car. I did not believe him, because I had never seen this man before, and our town is small. I know just about everyone who passes through—relatives and what not. I told the man that we were to return to Berradero's house, to prove if the car was truly lent to him. The man looked very worried when I told him this.*
>
> *When we arrived at the house of Jose Berradero, I was shocked. Berradero told me that, in fact, he had lent the man his vehicle, and that he was glad that I had brought him back. Apparently Berradero had wanted to give him some gas money, but had forgotten to do so. I left shortly after. Once I realized that the man was actually escaped convict Fernando Sucre, I was very upset that I did not arrest him when I had the chance.*

It appears that what transpired was this: while riding a local bus on his way to Ixtapa, Sucre became acquainted with an elderly man by the name of Jose Berradero. When Sucre was evicted for not having enough fare money to cover the ride, Berradero invited Sucre to have dinner with him and offered him his spare room, where he could spend the night. A Federale picked up Sucre that night in Berradero's vehicle, thinking that he had stolen it. However, when the Federale brought Sucre to Berradero's doorstep, Berradero confirmed Sucre's story and the suspect was released. Agents believe that Berradero might have more information about Sucre's whereabouts than he is telling.

The following is an excerpt from the interview with Mr. Berradero, conducted with the help of a translator.

> FBI: Mr. Berradero, would you please state for the record how it passed that you came to meet Fernando Sucre.
>
> JOSE BERRADERO: We were sitting in the same row on the bus. We were passing beautiful countryside on our journey. I made a comment about it.
>
> FBI: And how would you describe Mr. Sucre's disposition at this time?
>
> BERRADERO: He was friendly enough. But I could tell he had something on his mind.
>
> FBI: Did he tell you what that was?
>
> BERRADERO: Yes. Well, it was obvious. He was clearly lovelorn over a woman. I've been there myself.
>
> FBI: Did he discuss Maricruz Delgado with you?
>
> BERRADERO: Is that her name? It seemed as though he was hoping to marry her, but things had not quite worked out yet.
>
> FBI: Is it true that you invited Mr. Sucre into your home, to have dinner with you?
>
> BERRADERO: When he got kicked off the bus, I felt bad for him. I'm lonely myself. I lost my wife very recently, and I wanted some company for dinner. So I told him if he helped me cook he could dine with me.
>
> FBI: Did Mr. Sucre steal anything from your home? Did he threaten you in any way?
>
> BERRADERO: Oh heavens, no. I could tell he was a good soul. Troubled, but good. He just needs to work things out. Hopefully he will sooner rather than later.
>
> FBI: Why did you lend him your vehicle?
>
> BERRADERO: Like I said before, the kid needed some good luck, to help him get on the right path again. The path to grace.
>
> FBI: So you were unaware at this time that Mr. Sucre was on the FBI's most wanted list, and an escaped prisoner?
>
> BERRADERO: Correct.

Last updated on 6/6 by Agent Lang.

BENJAMIN MILES FRANKLIN

As a sergeant in the U.S. Army, Benjamin Miles Franklin was a member of the 117th, stationed at Al-Jabar Air Force Base in Kuwait. While serving as a prison guard, he was dishonorably discharged for engaging in illegal black market activity. However, the FBI investigation into the fugitive's history has unearthed documents that reveal his dismissal from the armed forces was not as simple as initially believed. The following deposition was taken from a witness whose identity is being kept highly classified.

Excerpt from John Doe deposition:

> Benny was the best. Much as he was in it for himself, you knew he'd always have your back. And, yeah, he was good at getting stuff for us. When you're out in the middle of Hell with hardly enough body armor to keep you alive, things like candy or a cool beer are real nice every now and then. Commander Meyers thought so, too. He used Benny's connections a bunch of times. This one time, Benny came through real good for Meyers and made himself one sweet deal out of it. Benny got himself prison duty. That kept him as far from the front as he could get. Man, was that good. Too good, sometimes.
>
> While Benny was on duty, he said he saw some prisoner being abused. I'm not proud of myself, but I told him to forget about it. They don't like it when we start raising trouble. Well, he goes and files a prisoner abuse report anyway. Went right to Commander Meyers and laid it all out for the guy. And you know what he got for it? Dishonorably discharged for engaging in illegal black market activity. And the whole thing got swept under the rug.

When Franklin returned to the states, he found it difficult to get a job with the dishonorable discharge on his record. After several attempts to find

FOX RIVER INMATE FILE

Name: Benjamin Miles Franklin

Prison Handle: C-Note

DEAL MADE

Age: 33

Back Number: 89416

Location: General Population, A-Wing, Cell 48

Crime: Possession of stolen goods

Sentence: Eight years

Time Left on Sentence: ~~Seven years, two months~~ ~~TBD~~ AT LARGE

Eligible for Parole in: ~~Three yeras, two months~~ TBD

Former Employment: First Sergeant, U.S. Army.
   Dishonorably discharged.

Next of Kin: Kacee Franklin

Relationship: Wife

employment netted nothing, Franklin took a job transporting stolen goods for an unknown accomplice. On what he admits was his first run, he was quickly apprehended by local police. The district attorney's office was willing to make a deal that could have knocked two years off Franklin's sentence, but he refused to give up the person he was working for. Though local police informants believed that Franklin was likely working with his brother-in-law, Darius Jones, without Franklin's testimony there was no proof.

Franklin was sent to Fox River Penitentiary, though interestingly, he did not tell his wife, Kacee, or their nine-year-old daughter, Dede, of his sentence. In fact, the fugitive never even told them that he had been discharged from the army. Ashamed to admit to his discharge, Franklin's initial story to his family was that he was on extended leave. When he was sent to Fox River, he told his wife that he was being sent back to the Middle East.

At Fox River, Franklin quickly used his talents to set himself up as the unofficial pharmacy for the Fox River inmates. He was known as the go-to man for hard-to-get items. Earning the prison handle "C-Note," Franklin used his procurement abilities to jockey for power and quickly became the unofficial leader of the African American contingent in A-Wing.

It is unclear how Franklin became part of the escape plan, as he had no known associations with any of the members of the crew or seemingly anything of value to add to the plan. (However, on the night of the failed escape attempt, correctional officers reported a broken down van parked suspiciously close to the prison. The driver matched the description of Franklin's brother-in-law.) It is likely that Franklin stumbled across the secret plot and forced his way into the group. Prison records show that he was not part of the initial P.I. crew working at the guard shack that was an integral point in the escape. In fact, Franklin only joined Prison Industries during the brief time that Abruzzi reportedly lost control of P.I., and the crew was reassigned. It is possible that during that time, he found the hole in the C.O. break room and threatened to reveal the plan if he was not brought on board.

The time Franklin spent working with the P.I. crew did hurt his standing in the Fox River hierarchy, particularly with regard to his relationship with known racist Theodore Bagwell. As Franklin was seen spending more time with the largely Caucasian work detail, members of C-Note's crew began to take notice. The prisoner known as Trumpet reportedly took control of the crew and C-Note's markers. There are rumors that Franklin was marked for death on the night of the successful escape.

Upon his escape from Fox River, Franklin's family was immediately placed under surveillance, and the family phone was tapped. Investigators later recorded Franklin calling to ask his wife, Kacee, to meet him one week

later. Kacee did not immediately agree. Special Agent Lang spoke with Kacee after the phone call, trying to confirm the location of this meet. It was clear that Franklin's wife truly had no idea that her husband had been incarcerated. In spite of the fact that he had been lying to her, Kacee remained loyal and refused to reveal the planned meeting point to Lang.

In the interim week, Franklin was spotted on a train traveling to Utah. To avoid capture, he jumped from the train, and was later seen by a Utah woman selling an RV. Franklin inquired about purchasing the RV and told her he would be back in a few days with cash. Franklin rendezvoused with most of the Fox River Eight in Tooele, Utah, where they unearthed Charles Westmoreland's hidden money. Franklin never returned for the RV.

As the date for Franklin's rendezvous with his wife approached, FBI investigators tightened their surveillance. On the day of the meet, Agent Lang approached Kacee again, reminding the mother that if she was charged as an accomplice, she could lose her child. Kacee told the agent where her husband was going to meet her, and the team set up a trap at the Fairgrounds Carnival. The capture went badly and Kacee escaped the team. At the same time, Franklin was successful at taking their daughter, Dede, out of school and going on the run. Their success ran out, however, when days later, Kacee was apprehended trying to fill a prescription for her daughter.

Kacee Franklin was charged with aiding an escaped convict and, if found guilty, is looking at considerable jail time. At her arraignment, Kacee claimed her husband was entirely at fault, and she had only gone along with him because he had left her no other option. The judge did not believe her claims of innocence. With ample evidence at his disposal, the judge considered her a flight risk and denied bail.

Days later, following a sighting at a Minneapolis-area hospital, a call was placed from a Minneapolis pay phone to an FBI switchboard in Washington, D.C. The call was then routed to the Fox River Eight manhunt command center in Chicago. On the phone was Franklin, who told Special Agent Mahone he was ready to turn himself in so long as his daughter received medical attention immediately. Franklin also agreed he would aid in the capture of Michael Scofield. During his interrogation, Franklin disclosed the website address of an internet message board Scofield allegedly set up so that the fugitives could stay in communication with each other. The site, www.europeangoldfinch.net, is currently being vetted by our analysts for hidden messages or clues that might disclose the fugitives' whereabouts. The owner of the site has been notified of the activity and control of the message boards has been turned over to Quantico. Below is one brief message posted on the site:

```
----------------------------------------------------------------
FROM: C-FINCH69

        Fish: Need help. My daughter's sick. —C-Note
----------------------------------------------------------------
```

JAIL REPORT ON ATTEMPTED SUICIDE

On June 6, Benjamin Miles Franklin attempted suicide while being held in a Chicago county jail cell, pending his cooperation with this investigation. At approximately 1:43 P.M., County Sheriff William Cammalleri found Franklin in his cell, hanging from a noose. Cammalleri immediately unlocked the cell door and attempted to lift Franklin up, to relieve pressure from the noose. After Franklin was cut down, he appeared winded and upset, repeatedly telling the sheriff to "help me die."

Franklin and his family have since been enrolled in the witness protection program in exchange for Franklin's testimony against Alexander Mahone in the Bureau's Internal Affairs investigation.

Last Updated on 6/14 by Agent Lang.

Prison Break
THE CLASSIFIED FBI FILES

To all angel Anjahi

Many thanks! from XOXO Robert Knepper

THEODORE BAGWELL

Some would say that Theodore Bagwell's life was doomed to tragedy from the start. The product of an incestuous rape between siblings, Bagwell was born to a mother with Down's syndrome. He was an outcast throughout his childhood and into adolescence, when he suffered the further indignity of a poor skin condition, which led to mocking from his peers. Bagwell's life did not change much as he entered into adulthood in his home state of Alabama. Always a loner, Bagwell's only true friend was his now-deceased cousin, James.

Theodore Bagwell was sought for years by the FBI for the rape and murder of a half dozen children, of both sexes. Bagwell managed to elude capture and fled the state, adopting a seemingly normal life in Tribune, Kansas, where he developed a relationship with single mother, Susan Hollander. It was Ms. Hollander who finally turned Bagwell in after seeing a report on him on *America's Most Wanted*. Though Ms. Hollander turned him in to the police, Bagwell claimed that he continued to love her. However, when it became clear to him that her love would never be returned, he grew angry and threatened her life. He repeatedly sent her letters from prison, but they were always bounced back to Fox River marked RETURN TO SENDER.

At Fox River, Bagwell was received with the kind of popularity he had never before experienced in his life, immediately earning the nickname "T-Bag"

FOX RIVER INMATE FILE

Name: Theodore Bagwell

Prison Handle: T-Bag

Age: 37

Back Number: 89632

Location: General Population, A-Wing, Cell 16

Crime: Six counts of kidnapping, rape, and first degree murder

Sentence: Life

Time Left on Sentence: The rest of his natural life

Eligible for Parole in: Inmate is not eligible for parole

Former Employment: NA

Next of Kin: James Bagwell

Relationship: Cousin (DECEASED)

from other prisoners. Though it is unusual for child predators to be treated well in prison, Bagwell's smooth and charming manner, combined with his racist beliefs, won him a following among the Aryans in the prison population.

It is reported that his proclivity toward younger men found multiple outlets at Fox River. He was linked with at least two younger men, whom he held onto through fear and intimidation. Both men, unfortunately, met tragic ends. The first, known as "Maytag" was killed during a prison riot. Though "T-Bag" mourned the loss, he quickly found a new victim in a prisoner he christened as "Cherry." Sadly, Cherry hanged himself after his rumored pleas for help from Michael Scofield went unanswered. Prison personnel report that Bagwell set his sights on newcomer David Apolskis

(whom Bagwell nicknamed "Tweener"), but Scofield managed to hold Bagwell off through some unknown means of intimidation.

Michael Scofield and Theodore Bagwell were at odds from the start of Scofield's incarceration. What initially began as an infatuation on Bagwell's part, quickly turned to animosity when his interest went unreturned. As far as investigators can tell, Bagwell brought nothing to the table to help in the escape plan. It is likely that he, like Franklin, stumbled across the plan accidentally and forced his way onto the team. He became a part of the P.I. crew shortly after the riot.

Prior to the escape, Bagwell's nearest relatives, James Bagwell and his young son, James Jr., were killed in a shooting. Witnesses report that a van pulled in front of Bagwell's home, and two men approached James. Suspicious of the men, James pulled a gun, and—to the horror of his neighbors—used his own son as a human shield. Both father and son were killed in the shootout, and the suspects escaped.

On the night of the escape, Bagwell's hand was completely severed in a farmhouse a few miles away from the prison. This was no accident, as an ax was found on the premises, lying in a pool of Bagwell's blood. It is at this point that Bagwell's trail diverged from the bulk of the group of escapees. Bagwell was on his own for several days, when he forced his way into the office of Dr. Marvin Gudat and forced the veterinarian to perform surgery to reattach the hand. As this was certainly outside of the veterinarian's field, it is unlikely that the reattachment surgery took. Upon completion of the surgery, Bagwell killed Dr. Gudat and stole his SUV. Zach Pushkarev, a camper, later came forward claiming he had been threatened by Bagwell while camping with his girlfriend, Tina O'Sullivan. The pair claim Bagwell stole their

Igloo cooler full of food and, wielding a screwdriver, threatened to return if they went to the police. It is likely that Bagwell used the cooler, which was found next to Dr. Gudat's body, to keep his hand on ice until he could find someone with the necessary skills and equipment to reattach it.

From there Bagwell met up with the fugitives in Tooele, Utah. As his useless hand would have prevented him from digging, he was assigned to keep the homeowner, Jeanette Owens, occupied while the other escaped convicts dug up her garage. In addition to the factual recounting of her time as a hostage, Ms. Owens also provided great insight into the fugitives, particularly Bagwell.

Excerpt from Jeanette Owens interview:

FBI INVESTIGATOR: You said that, for the most part, you were in the kitchen with Theodore Bagwell when the digging was going on?

JEANETTE OWENS: The man with the southern accent? Yes, he claimed to be the boss of those boys. But I guess his real job was to keep me busy and away from my garage and what they were really doing.

FBI: How did he keep you busy?

OWENS: We was just talking. He was smooth, a ladies man really. After being locked up for that long with just boys, I don't blame him for trying. Wasn't my type, though.

FBI: Before your daughter came home, did you feel that you were in any danger?

OWENS: No, that's the scariest thing about it. One minute he's Mr. Friendly, seems he couldn't hurt a fly, and then he's got that damned hammer up to my throat threatening to kill me. I don't think he's stable. He seemed like a real sick person.

Jeanette and her daughter were later tied up and held hostage, while the inmates fled the premises. Shortly afterward, Bagwell returned and picked up a large backpack, slipping a hundred-dollar bill into Jeanette's bra to cover the damages to her home. It is believed that Bagwell wound up with D.B. Cooper's money after swindling the other fugitives.

From there, Bagwell seemed to go in search of Susan Hollander, the

woman who had turned him in to the police. Former Correctional Officer Brad Bellick claimed he saw Bagwell in Tribune, Kansas, at the former home of Ms. Hollander. This sighting was later substantiated when Bagwell's severed hand was found on the premises. Neighbors report that Ms. Hollander had packed up her family and moved to an undisclosed location the moment she heard that Bagwell had escaped Fox River.

In Tribune, Bellick blamed Bagwell for the death of Roy Geary, but after questioning the hotel staff, those accusations were found to hold no merit. The only disturbance at the hotel that day was from three "professional" women who demanded to be let up to Mr. Geary's room after being stopped by security. Bellick ultimately plead no-contest to the crime.

Bagwell, however, has continued his violent trail across the country. His latest victim was U.S. Postal employee Denise Gummerson. It's believed that Bagwell seduced her to gain Susan Hollander's forwarding address. According to Postmaster Juvonen, Hollander's records were the last thing Denise accessed on her computer before she was murdered.

Bagwell used this information to kidnap Ms. Hollander and her kids. Bagwell forced his way into their house, threatening them with a pistol. From then on he tried to mold the four of them into the picture-perfect family Bagwell never had as a child. He sequestered Susan Hollander and her children, Zach and Gracey, hoping they would eventually stop resisting and become a happy family. To the unknowing eye, a happy family is exactly what they seemed to be. The following excerpt was taken from our interview with Patty Wallace, head of the local Welcome Wagon Committee:

> FBI INVESTIGATOR: Was this the first time you had met the entire Hollander family?
> PATTY WALLACE: Yes, it was. I had told Susan that I wanted to make them feel welcome in the neighborhood, and let them know what our community has to offer.
> FBI: And nothing seemed odd or strange?
> WALLACE: No. I mean, I didn't think so at the time in. But in hindsight, I guess it was a bit. Susan didn't speak much, the kids either, now that I think of it. Teddy was doin' most of the talkin'. He was very charming, and a good cook to boot. Susan seemed like a very lucky woman to land a man like that.
> FBI: According to Ms. Hollander, Bagwell had a gun with him the entire time. Were you aware of this?
> WALLACE: No. If I would have seen a gun, I would have lost my mind. He really had a gun that whole time? I find that shocking.

After the brunch with Patty Wallace, Bagwell took his "family" to a new home; his boyhood home. The building was in shambles, and Susan pointed out that no one could live in such a place. In response Bagwell locked her and her children in the basement. An anonymous phone call was placed to local law enforcement shortly thereafter and the Hollanders were rescued; however, Bagwell had already fled the scene. The following excerpt was taken several hours after Susan Hollander's return:

> FBI INVESTIGATOR: Ms. Hollander, you received dozens of letters from Theodore Bagwell. . . .
> SUSAN HOLLANDER: I never opened them, not a one. But going by the amount of them and what he said to me at Fox River, I knew I had to get out of town when I heard of the escape.

FBI: And what was discussed during your visit at Fox
    River?
HOLLANDER: I told him how my shrink thought it was a
    good idea for me to tell him how I felt, for closure. But
    he threatened me. His eyes glossed over and he said,
    he said that he would "remember what my front steps
    look like."
FBI: How did you manage to evade Bagwell?
HOLLANDER: I'm not sure. He did mention that I brought
    out the good man and suppressed the evil one within
    him. Theodore just wanted everything to return to
    what it used to be. That couldn't happen, obviously, but
    I know this for sure, the good man that he was when
    he decided to let us live, that man's gone forever and I
    hope you find him and put him back behind bars before
    he can hurt anyone else.
FBI: Is there anything you could tell us, anything you saw,
    or heard that can help us in his capture?
HOLLANDER: Not that I can recall right now. I'm just
    grateful that my kids are all right, and he's out of our
    home.

On June 6, Dr. Eric Stamel, a psychiatrist, was found bludgeoned to death
in his office. Eva Bol, one of his longtime patients, was in his waiting room
for over forty-five minutes. Mrs. Bol eventually became worried for her doctor and entered his office after knocking repeatedly. She found Dr. Stamel
splayed across the floor bleeding from a head wound and promptly called
the police. Police arrived and called in federal agents to the crime scene after
dusting for prints and finding a match for Theodore Bagwell. The doctor's
glasses and wallet were missing, and it is believed that Bagwell took Stamel's
forms of ID to use as his own.

Last updated on 6/16 by Agent Lang.

DAVID APOLSKIS

The youngest of the fugitives, David Apolskis was seemingly a typical kid who put up an exaggeratedly strong front. His aggressive side combined with nimble hands helped him secure a starting position as a wide receiver on the football team at Woodrow Wilson Junior High School. Throughout his life, academics always proved to be his downfall, especially when in the ninth grade he was deemed academically ineligible to continue on the team. As football had provided Apolskis with his first true outlet for his youthful energy, he was naturally devastated when he could no longer play. He unfortunately then turned his talents to shadier pursuits, becoming an expert pickpocket.

Apolskis approached his new interest with a kind of intensity that he had never given his schoolwork. He studied up on jewelry design, particularly clasp manufacturing on watches and necklaces, in order to become a better thief. Though he was impressively skilled in petty theft, Apolskis did spend eight months in juvenile hall on two separate occasions, when he was caught stealing from tourists in Chicago. During his time in lockup, he was known to brag to anyone who would listen about his success in stealing over 200 wallets and 150 watches. It was also during that time that Apolskis's vocabulary was known to have changed dramatically, and he began using heavy street slang almost exclusively in his day-to-day interactions.

FOX RIVER INMATE FILE

Name: David Apolskis

Prison Handle: Tweener

Age: 18

DECEASED

Back Number: 95012

Location: General Population, A-Wing, Cell 88

Crime: Grand larceny

Sentence: Five years

Time Left on Sentence: ~~Five years~~ TBD ~~AT LARGE~~

Eligible for Parole in: ~~Two years, six months~~ TBD

Former Employment: Unemployed

Next of Kin: Kathy and David Apolskis Sr.

Relationship: Mother and Father

Apolskis's two stints in juvenile hall apparently did nothing to curb his desire for petty theft. This interest continued into adulthood, when he inadvertently ran a bump and switch on an off-duty police officer. Apolskis managed to get away, but he was later found in his apartment, where a search revealed a baseball card collection he had recently stolen from a family in the neighborhood. Unbeknownst to Apolskis, the collection included an incredibly rare Honus Wagner card from 1910. At the time, the card was estimated at $300,000, though a similar card has since sold for considerably more. The possession of that card bumped Apolskis's charge to grand larceny. He was found guilty and sentenced to Fox River.

From the moment Apolskis arrived at Fox River, he had trouble fitting in. Unaware of the racial tension in the prison, Apolskis first tried to befriend the black inmates in A-Wing, but was quickly shunned. His street slang vocabulary also put him at odds with a considerable part of the prison's white population. Reportedly, this earned him the nickname "Tweener," as he was considered in between both groups and welcome in neither. Theodore Bagwell quickly took a liking to the young inmate, but it is rumored that Michael Scofield intervened to protect Apolskis.

Captain Brad Bellick capitalized on Apolskis's loner status and tried to use the young inmate to find out information on Scofield. Bellick was suspicious of Scofield's activities—though he did not suspect an actual escape attempt—and managed to gain Apolskis's assistance through a combination of rewards and intimidation. When this initially failed to produce results, Bellick moved Apolskis to Cell 88, where he became the cellmate of Avocado Balz-Johnson. Balz-Johnson reportedly sexually abused Apolskis, until an unfortunate accident resulting in the near severing of Balz-Johnson's penis. Though it was widely assumed that Apolskis had attacked the inmate, Balz-Johnson did not report the incident, presumably so he could take his own revenge when he got out of the infirmary.

Apolskis continued to aid Bellick, but his initial attempts to join the P.I. group were denied, until Bellick placed him in the unit himself. The young inmate did then manage to ingratiate himself into the group.

Prior to the escape, Apolskis reported to Bellick that something was happening in the C.O. break room, but he was unclear of what it was at the time. Upon inspection of the shack, Bellick located the hole the P.I. crew had been digging, but he was incapacitated before he could report it. At the same time, Balz-Johnson was about to be returned to his cell so he could exact his revenge. Guards noted that Apolskis had been asking about Bellick on the day of the escape. It is likely that, seeing no other option, Apolskis chose to escape with the crew before his cellmate could return.

Once outside, Apolskis was almost immediately separated from the rest of the group. He turned up in St. Louis where, posing as Scott Kolbrenner, he hitched a ride with a college student named Debra Jean Belle after seeing

DRIVING HOME TO UTAH.

"DON'T LAUGH"

Looking for someone to share ride/split expenses.
-Debra Jean Belle
801·555·0199

her posting on a school bulletin board. The pair grew close over the course of the drive, until Apolskis stole her car and took off on his own. Though Belle claims that she did not know Apolskis's identity, evidence suggests that she did learn who he was during the trip and allowed him to take her car.

Apolskis was apprehended in Tooele, Utah, when he went into town to get gas for the fugitives' escape vehicle. Once taken into custody, the former snitch refused to reveal the location of the other escaped convicts. After a time, it appeared that he had come to a plea deal with Agent Mahone and Apolskis was willing to give up his associates. Apolskis brought FBI agents and police to what they believed was the home where the fugitives could be found. Instead, Apolskis used the agents to take him to see Debra Jean, where he told her his real name and promised that he would write her from prison.

Agent Mahone took the unusual step of returning to the local FBI field office alone with Apolskis. During transport, Apolskis reportedly went for Mahone's gun and made a break for it. Mahone was forced to defend himself by shooting the young man at point blank range, killing him. Questions have been raised over the legitimacy of the shooting.

The following interview was conducted in the home of Debra Jean Belle, before the death of David Apolskis was reported.

Excerpt from Debra Jean Belle interview:

FBI INVESTIGATOR: Why did you give a complete stranger a ride across the country?

DEBRA JEAN BELLE: Students do it all the time. That's what the Ride Board is for. I needed someone to split the cost of gas with.

FBI: Did you think to ask for any identification? A student ID maybe?

BELLE: No. I mean, he seemed so nice, and my father kept telling me to have someone ride along with me. Though I think he was hoping that it was going to be one of my girlfriends, as opposed to a guy.

FBI: Did anything out of the ordinary happen during the trip?

BELLE: Not really. It was kind of fun, actually. We got to talking . . . sang along with the radio. That kind of thing. Nothing that made me nervous about riding alone with him. He was actually kind of sweet.

FBI: A local police officer went to the motel room you and Apolskis shared and showed you a picture of David. Why didn't you turn him in then?

BELLE: I was confused. I didn't know if it was David in the picture and it just didn't seem to fit. He doesn't look like a criminal. He's so nice.

FBI: How did he steal your car? With force?

BELLE: No, I had to clear my head so I went for a walk. He must have known something was up, because when I came back, my keys and car were gone.

FBI: Any thoughts as to why Apolskis would come to your home just to tell you his name?

BELLE: I don't know. I guess he thought we were friends or something.

FBI: Were you?

BELLE: Yes.

Last updated on 6/2 by Agent Wheeler.

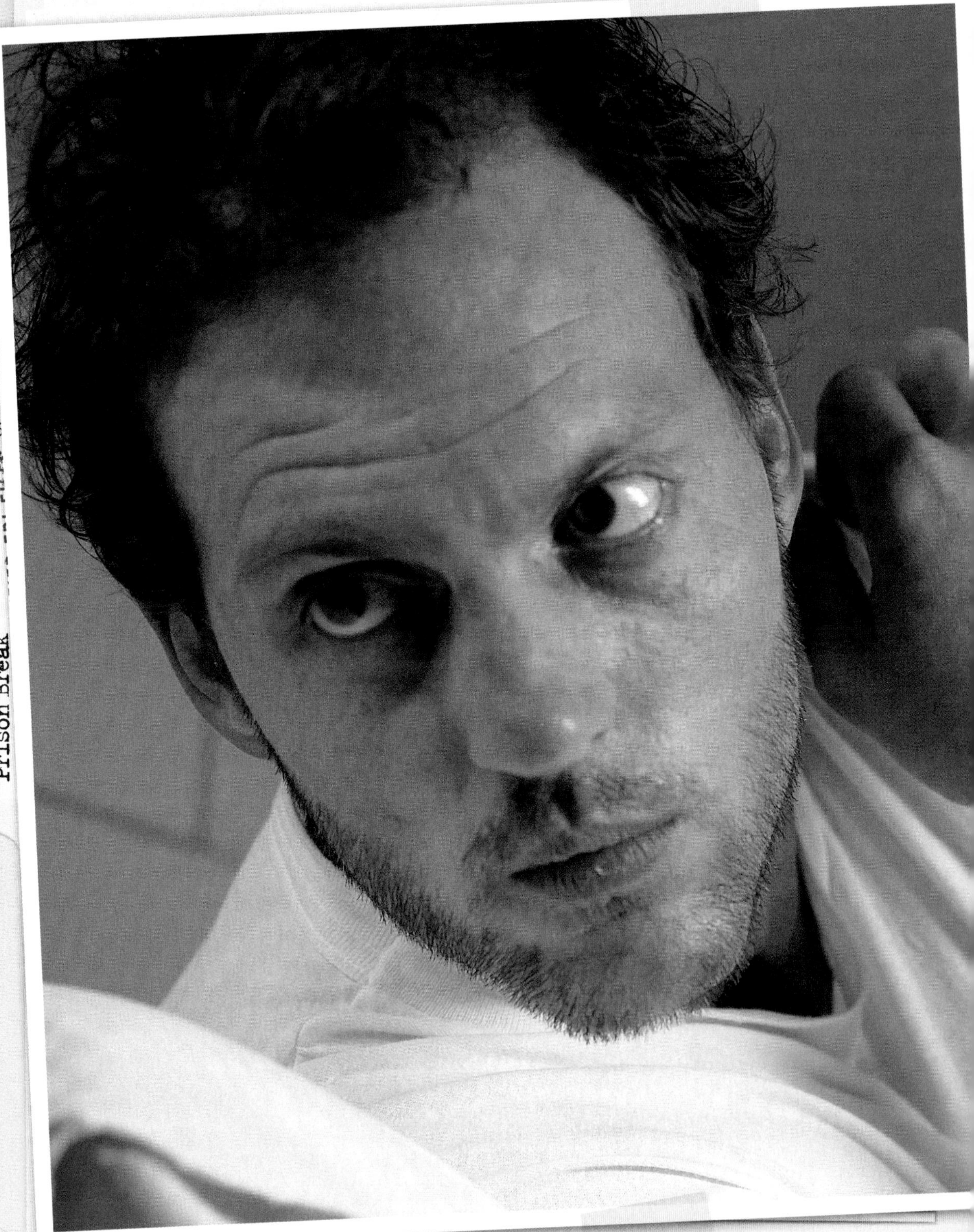

CHARLES PATOSHIK

C harles Patoshik displayed an astounding intellect for most of his life. While studying for a doctorate in mathematics with a focus on fractals, he began to experience noticeable symptoms of mental illness. Though concerned about the changes in his own mental state, Patoshik did not feel the need to seek a formal medical evaluation. If he had, it may have saved his family from the resulting devastation when the full force of his mental illness took hold. One night, following a typically long day of research, Patoshik returned to his parents' home. Despite his father's drinking problem, and indications that Patoshik was severely punished once or twice as a child, no one could have predicted that he would enter their bedroom with a shotgun on this particular evening and kill both his parents while they slept.

In court, Patoshik claimed to have no memory of the crime and offered no explanation for his motive. Patoshik was convicted of two counts of second degree murder and sent to Fox River Penitentiary, where he was committed to the psychiatric ward, known around the prison as the "Whack Shack." Patoshik was ultimately diagnosed as having schizoaffective disorder with bipolar tendencies. He was put on medication to manage the disorder. Further evaluation revealed that he also suffered from a neuro-anatomic lesion that caused profound insomnia.

After four years of careful observation, it was determined that Patoshik, who had earned the nickname "Haywire," was finally ready to be moved

FOX RIVER INMATE FILE

DECEASED

Name: Charles Patoshik

Prison Handle: Haywire

Age: 29

Back Number: 72864

Location: Psychiatric Ward, Cell 25

Crime: Second degree murder (two counts)

Sentence: Sixty years

Time Left on Sentence: Fifty-six years ~~TBD~~ AT LARGE

Eligible for Parole in: Twenty-six years ~~TBD~~

Former Employment: Doctoral student

Next of Kin: Family deceased

in with the general population. The decision came after it was observed that Patoshik's meds in combination with his newfound hobby of drawing, seemed to calm him considerably. When Fernando Sucre requested to be transferred out of Michael Scofield's cell, Captain Bellick assigned Patoshik to replace Sucre in what many of the prison personnel felt to be a personal form of punishment for Scofield.

During the brief period in which they shared a cell, Patoshik took a noticeable interest in Scofield's intricate tattoo. Patoshik's sketchbook, which was filled alternately with geometric designs and nightmare images, soon began to contain images found in Scofield's extensive tattoo work.

Patoshik's time in gen pop was short lived. He reportedly attacked Scofield in an incident that seemed to happen just as suddenly and without warning as his attack on his parents. Prison guards report that Patoshik was heard screaming about a "pathway to hell" as he was returned to the psychiatric ward. We now suspect that Patoshik had recognized the hidden map within Scofield's tattoo and turned violent when his mind was unable

69

to process the information. (Either that, or the attack was a ruse by Scofield to get Patoshik sent back to the psych ward so that Sucre could return to the cell.) Once he was back under observation, blood tests revealed that Patoshik had not been taking his medication.

According to an interview with Manche Sanchez—the only surviving member of the team not to make it over the wall—Patoshik was never intended to be a part of the escape plan. Scofield's secondary escape route required the fugitives to go through the psych ward to access the pipes below. Patoshik saw the escapees and was cognizant enough to connect the dots and realize what they were up to. He followed them to the infirmary and forced his way in on the escape. Once outside the prison walls, Patoshik immediately split from the group.

One of the earliest fugitive sightings came that night from a young girl who claimed that a "weird man" came into the family's garage and stole her bicycle. Oddly enough, he also stole a football helmet, presumably to wear as protective gear. Amazingly, the fugitive managed to evade the police while on the girl's bike, and wearing a football helmet and a psych ward uniform.

Charles Patoshik was the sole fugitive who did not reunite with the others at the house in Tooele, Utah. Instead, he was spotted in Wisconsin at a camping store, where he stole a bevy of outdoor equipment including MRE's, maps, and a tarp.

A teenage girl and boy named Sasha Murray and Matt Feytek in Algoma, Wisconsin, later stumbled upon Patoshik in a wooded area. The fugitive told them he was building a raft to travel to Holland. The pair asked if he would buy them beer and Patoshik complied. Later that evening, Patoshik made unwanted advances toward the young woman, prompting the pair to leave. It is believed that Patoshik then followed Sasha Murray home and subsequently murdered her stepfather while the teenager slept upstairs. Below are excerpts from each of the statements given by Feytek and Murray.

Excerpt from Feytek interview:

SPECIAL AGENT AKINYELE: After Patoshik made his move
    on Sasha—what did you do?
MATT FEYTEK: I grabbed her away. Called him a freak.
    And we bolted.
AKINYELE: And how did Mr. Patoshik react?
FEYTEK: He just stood there, like a guy who knows he
    can't back up his actions.

AKINYELE: You intimidated him?

FEYTEK: No doubt. He didn't want to fight.

AKINYELE: But then he followed you two.

FEYTEK: That's what they say. We both looked back a few times, just to make sure he and some buddies weren't heading our way, but we never saw him again.

AKINYELE: Why do you think he killed Sasha's stepfather?

FEYTEK: Probably jealousy. Revenge. He knew he was never gonna get with Sasha. So he lashed out.

Excerpt from Murray interview:

AKINYELE: I know it's hard to talk about what happened, Ms. Murray, but it's important to find out everything we can as soon as we can so we bring this criminal to justice. You told Agent Davis that you recognized Charles Patoshik.

SASHA MURRAY: He's a homeless guy who hangs around Hancock Square. Hittin' up college kids for change. He's down there all the time. If he ain't there, I don't know where to find him.

AKINYELE: Has he ever made advances toward you before, prior to the other night?

MURRAY: No. He's quiet. He just keeps to himself.

AKINYELE: We've canvassed Hancock Square, but so far can't find anyone who remembers ever seeing him there. Is there a chance you've confused that location with somewhere else?

MURRAY: He's always there. At least, that's where I remember him from. I'm sorry I can't think of anything else.

After the murder, police investigators uncovered a surveillance videotape from the liquor store where Patoshik had purchased the beer. Special Agent Mahone then tracked Patoshik to a grain silo in Wisconsin. In his attempt to talk Patoshik down, the fugitive leapt to his death.

Last Updated on 6/5 by Agent Lang.

CHARLES WESTMORELAND

One of the senior inmates at Fox River, Charles Westmoreland had been incarcerated there for twenty-eight years prior to his death on the night of the escape. Westmoreland had been tried and convicted of vehicular manslaughter in Douglas, Arizona. He served the first two years of his sentence at the Arizona State Prison in Florence, before budgetary restrictions forced the state to outsource some of its inmates to facilities in other parts of the country. He had been imprisoned at Fox River since the early 1970s.

Throughout his time at Fox River, Westmoreland was an exemplary prisoner with very few incidents filed against him. Early on, rumors of his being the legendary hijacker D.B. Cooper—a man who had successfully ransomed a plane full of passengers for one and a half million dollars—did cause some friction. Being suspected of having over a million dollars stashed away can lead to harassment from other prisoners. His files indicate that in the 1970s he had been routinely threatened and assaulted. On one occasion, an inmate trying to extort money from Westmoreland even broke his nose.

Over time, the rumors diminished to mere folk story, and Westmoreland became a model inmate. His near spotless record had earned him "trustee" status, giving him permission to work prison jobs with the highest security clearance, often considered to be the cushiest assignments. One of the other "perks" of being at Fox River for a long stretch was that Westmoreland was allowed to keep a pet cat

FOX RIVER INMATE FILE

Name: Charles Westmoreland

Prison Handle: None

Age: 60

Back Number: 21562

DECEASED

Location: General Population, A-Wing, Cell 13

Crime: Aggravated vehicular hijacking, vehicular invasion, involuntary manslaughter, and reckless homicide

Sentence: Sixty years to life

Time Left on Sentence: ~~The rest of his natural life~~

Eligible for Parole in: NA

Former Employment: Unknown

Next of Kin: Anna Westmoreland

Relationship: Daughter

named Marilyn. Westmoreland had adopted Marilyn prior to Illinois law making it illegal for prisoners to have such creature comforts, and she was grandfathered in so that Westmoreland would not have to give her up. Unfortunately, Marilyn died shortly before Westmoreland's escape. Circumstances surrounding the cat's death remain unclear. Some prisoners insist that the cat was murdered by Captain Brad Bellick as revenge for Westmoreland refusing to provide the name of the inmate who killed rookie C.O. Bob Hudson during the Fox River riot.

Being incarcerated for half of his life clearly took an emotional toll on the man, though he rarely showed it inside prison walls. Ann Westmoreland, the inmate's wife, died while he was in prison, and he recently learned that his daughter, Anna, had been diagnosed with esophageal cancer. The cancer was in its advanced stages, and she had been committed to Sacred Heart hospital in Indianapolis with seemingly little time left. Warden Pope vigorously petitioned the DOC to allow Westmoreland to visit his daughter before it was too late. However, the DOC stood firm on the position that prisoners can only be released for visits in the event of funerals, and Westmoreland was considered a flight risk. The request was denied. It is believed that Westmoreland's desire to see his daughter is what prompted him to join Scofield's escape team. As for why Scofield would want Westmoreland on the team, the answer is fairly obvious. Scofield believed that Westmoreland was, in fact, famed hijacker, D.B. Cooper. Recent events seem to indicate that Scofield was correct in his suspicion.

The story of D.B. Cooper began in Portland, Oregon on November 24, 1971, when a man matching Charles Westmoreland's description took a 727 full of passengers hostage at the local airport. The airport standoff of Flight 305 lasted for hours with local authorities, and the airline company, finally giving in to Cooper's demands by delivering $5 million in unmarked bills to the plane. (It should be noted that authorities informed the press that the ransom was only one and a half million dollars in order to avoid embarrassment.) Cooper then demanded the plane be cleared for takeoff. Citing concern for the hostages, authorities allowed the plane to escape while they tracked it on radar. An hour into the flight, D.B. Cooper parachuted out of the

plane at ten thousand feet somewhere over Utah. He managed to elude the ensuing manhunt and escape with the money, and it has always been assumed that he roamed free to this day.

Meanwhile, days after the hijacking, Charles Westmoreland was picked up for vehicular manslaughter in Arizona and ultimately sentenced to sixty years to life for his crime. The sentence would have been only twenty years, but he was in a stolen car at the time, and the felony murder rule multiplied his sentence by three. Local police never made the connection that they might have D.B. Cooper in custody due to the fact that, on November 24, Charles Westmoreland was in Folsom Prison finishing up a thirty-day stint for a drunk and disorderly charge. A simple administrative error overlooked the fact that Westmoreland and his father shared the same name and that it was actually the senior Westmoreland who had been incarcerated at Folsom.

In recent years, bloggers obsessed with the mystery have made interesting connections between Cooper and Westmoreland. Special Agent Alexander Mahone made the same correlation that we suspect Michael Scofield did: having what he believed to be one and a half million dollars available to him when he broke out of prison would be a great way to finance a life on the run. What follows is the chain of conclusions that led Agent Mahone to determine that Westmoreland was indeed D.B. Cooper.

Going back to the crime for which Westmoreland was incarcerated, it

'D.B. Cooper' Myth Still Alive Despite Conviction

JOHN MUIR, Correspondent

Bloggers and self-proclaimed experts maintain to this day that the infamous skyjacker--who parachtued out of a 727 over a quarter century ago with a million and a half dollars--is still alive and out there enjoying his windfall to this very day, despite the fact that a man is serving out a life sentence for the crime in Illinois...

Conspiracy theorists across the country refuse to put the D.B. Cooper myth to bed despite the fact that this man serving time for the last two decades for the crime in an Illinois penitentiary. No less than 10,777 results come up when the name was recently entered into a search engine on the internet. As many as twenty websites are dedicated solely to the man who parachuted out of a 747 in early 1972 with more than a million dollars in cash.

Some claim to know the true whereabouts of the still-missing cash. One thing's for certain, however: if 59-year-old Charles Westmoreland was rightly convicted of the crime, he'll likely never get to spend a penny of it, as he's currently serving a life sentence without possibility of parole for the two killings linked with the hijacking.

is unclear why he was even in the state of Arizona in a stolen car in the first place, unless one factors in that he was only ten miles from the Mexican border at the time he was caught. Two days prior to his arrest, Westmoreland's wife received a phone call from someone in a motel in Portland that was within one mile of the airport where the D.B. Cooper hijacking took place. In the time between those two events, records from a free clinic in Brigham City, Utah, show that a Charles Westmoreland was treated for an injury to his left knee; the kind that could have been sustained from a skydiving accident.

It is assumed that D.B. Cooper would have had a car waiting for him at a specific drop point. According to DMV records, in 1971, Charles Westmoreland owned a 1965 Chevy Nova. As it turns out, a car of the same make and model, with a blown gasket and the registration number scraped off, was found abandoned along the Arizona border only a mile or two from where Westmoreland accidentally hit the woman with his stolen car. During the course of the investigation, Agent Mahone made further inquiries into the case and learned where the money could have been buried. (For more on this, see the file on the FBI manhunt.)

Prior to the Fox River escape attempt, it is believed Charles Westmoreland happened across Captain Brad Bellick as Bellick was uncovering the hole in the C.O. break room. Westmoreland attacked the guard to keep him quiet. During the fight, Westmoreland received what was to become a fatal injury when a piece of glass from a coffeepot tore into his stomach. Westmoreland managed to incapacitate Bellick, tie him up, and drop him into the pipes below. Not wanting to jeopardize the escape plan, Westmoreland refused to have his injury tended to and continued to lose precious amounts of blood as the hours ticked away. By the time the escapees reached the infirmary that night, Westmoreland knew that he was not going to make it. He presumably shared the location of the money with Scofield and then expired.

The following letter was found during a search of Charles Westmoreland's cell after the escape. These would ultimately be his last words to his daughter, Anna, who is currently living in Schaumburg, Illinois, as a patient at St. Mary's Hospital, where she is undergoing chemotherapy. A copy of the letter was delivered to Anna, and the original is being kept with the other evidence from the escape.

Dear Anna,

If you're reading this letter, I guess something must have gone wrong. I doubt the warden would have delivered it unless I was gone. It was a crazy plan, I know. But when Warden Pope told me that you were sick, I just had to see you. I know you wouldn't have wanted me to do this, but there was just no other way. I'd already lost your mother while I was stuck inside. I couldn't stand the thought of not having the chance to hold you in my arms to give you my strength.

I know it's been hard having a father in jail for pretty much all your life. But I want you to know how proud I am of you. To know all you've done in spite of my being gone. To hear about the woman you've become made my mistakes seem somehow lessened. Like I didn't mess everything up. I know I have no right to claim any part of your success, but knowing you were out there living your life always gave me hope for myself. You will never know how much you kept me sane and walking the straight and narrow in here. I guess I always wanted to make you as proud as you made me.

Now, don't you cry for me and don't doubt for a second that I wasn't doing the right thing in trying to see you. Sure, it may not have worked out the way I intended, but I hope I'm with your mother now. And we're both together looking down at you. You should also know that I'm probably making whatever deals I can to see to it that you get through this okay.

With undying love, Dad

Last updated on 5/30 by Agent Lang.

MANCHE SANCHEZ

Manche Sanchez was the last member of the escape team officially invited to participate. Sanchez was assigned P.I. in the prison laundry. His cousin, Fernando Sucre, initially went to Sanchez for help with the escape by asking him to provide them with a guard's uniform. When the uniform was returned damaged, Sanchez complained to his cousin, but let the matter drop. He did not bother to investigate the situation any further. However, when Sucre came to him for help a second time, Sanchez insisted the inmates tell him what was going on. Burrows ultimately brought Sanchez in on the escape, which was beneficial since Sanchez was able to put in an order for extra psych ward uniforms. These would have been integral to the escape plot, had the crew not been forced to move up their timetable.

On the night of the escape, the prisoner suggested that he should be last to cross the cable to the exterior wall, fearing that it would not support his weight. His suspicion proved accurate when the alarm sounded and he started across the cable while Scofield was still on it. The combined weight snapped the cable, sending Sanchez to the ground. Guards found him trying to scale the wall.

Sanchez refused to provide any details of the fugitives' plans once they were outside of the prison walls. FBI interrogators believe that this had more to do with the fact that Sanchez knew very little of the plan rather than a willful attempt to withhold information. He did, however, provide many useful details regarding how the fugitives managed to escape in exchange for some time being taken off the five years that were added to his sentence for the escape attempt. Much of the information provided by Sanchez, combined with extrapolations from Special Agent Alexander Mahone, was used to compile the report on the escape in the following section.

Last updated on 5/30 by Agent Lang.

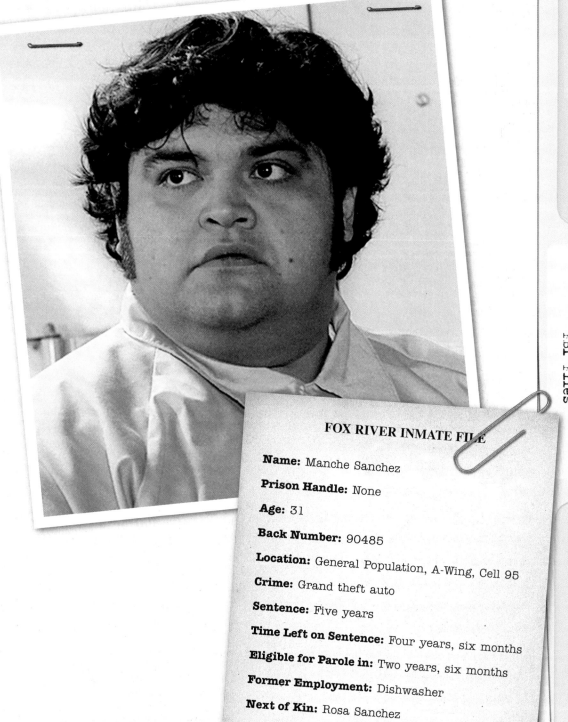

FOX RIVER INMATE FILE

Name: Manche Sanchez

Prison Handle: None

Age: 31

Back Number: 90485

Location: General Population, A-Wing, Cell 95

Crime: Grand theft auto

Sentence: Five years

Time Left on Sentence: Four years, six months

Eligible for Parole in: Two years, six months

Former Employment: Dishwasher

Next of Kin: Rosa Sanchez

Relationship: Mother

CAPTAIN BRADLEY BELLICK
(FORMER) SENIOR CORRECTIONS OFFICER

Current Status: Working as FBI consultant

Brad Bellick was hired as a correctional officer shortly after graduating high school and has worked at Fox River Penitentiary his entire adult life. As a rookie correctional officer, Bellick was said to be wide-eyed and innocent. Having never moved out of his mother's home, the young officer had a naiveté that he quickly found had no place inside prison walls. Immediately hardening himself to the harsh realities of working inside a prison, Bellick steadily worked himself up the C.O. ranks. Three years prior to the Fox River escape, he had been promoted to Captain of Correctional Officers, and the day-to-day operations of the Fox River general population was placed under his command.

While Warden Pope was widely known as a major proponent of rehabilitating prisoners, Captain Bellick subscribed more to the "spare the rod, spoil the inmate" school of thought. Several allegations of prisoner abuse dogged the C.O. during his time at Fox River, but no corroborating evidence was ever found. His hard stance on inmates was what initially impressed the DOC into expediting his promotion. In fact, Bellick has held the title Correctional Officer of the Month numerous times during his tenure at Fox River. It was widely suspected that, in

FOX RIVER INMATE FILE

RELEASED

Name: Bradley Bellick

Prison Handle: Boss / Fish

Age: 40

Back Number: 452857

Location: General Population, A-Wing, Cell 22

Crime: First degree murder

Sentence: Twenty-five years

Time Left on Sentence: ~~Twenty-five years~~ NA

Eligible for Parole in: ~~Twelve years, six months~~ NA

Former Employment: Correctional Officer, Illinois DOC (Employed at Fox River)

Next of Kin: Ruth Bellick

Relationship: Mother

spite of their philosophical differences on the treatment of prisoners, Warden Pope was grooming Bellick to replace him when he retired.

During the Fox River riots, Captain Bellick was clearly opposed to the warden's by-the-book handling of the situation. The C.O. much preferred action over negotiation, an opinion he boldly shared with the governor. The governor agreed and had officers storm the prison. Though the police action managed to subdue the riot, the fact that Bellick had secretly gone over Pope's head contributed to a growing distance between the two men. Warden Pope clearly reevaluated his plan to support Bellick for warden after the riot.

Still, Bellick was placed in charge of the investigation into the death of rookie C.O. Bob Hudson, who was killed during the riot. In typical fashion, Bellick used fear and intimidation in his attempt to get the prisoners to talk. Rumors around the prison even suggest that he may have gone so far as to kill the cat belonging to Charles Westmoreland in an attempt to force the inmate to admit what he had seen. Eventually, another inmate came forward with a claim that Christopher Trokey had killed Hudson, though it is now suspected that Theodore Bagwell was, in fact, the guard's murderer.

For reasons unclear to FBI investigators, Bellick was immediately suspi-

cious of Michael Scofield, as early as the inmate's first day. This was possibly due more to the C.O.'s jealousy over Scofield's prior success and position in life than any specific event. It is almost a testament to the brilliance of Scofield's plan that, even with Bellick's watchful eye always on the lookout for questionable activity, the escape was ultimately successful. In the end, Captain Bellick was able to locate the escape route in the guard shack, but Charles Westmoreland subdued him in a fight. Bellick was tied up for hours and left hidden in the tunnel beneath the break room. He was not found until after the prisoners had escaped.

The DOC investigation into

the escape unearthed a side of Bellick always hinted at, but never seen outside the prison walls. The DOC conducted the following interview with former C.O. Roy Geary prior to the formal hearing into the escape. It should be noted that Geary had previously been fired from Fox River under his own cloud of suspicion; however, his testimony was key in the decision to dismiss Brad Bellick.

Excerpt from DOC pre-interview of Roy Geary:

DOC INTERVIEWER: Mr. Geary, what is it that you felt was so important that you needed to speak to us first thing in the morning after the escape?

ROY GEARY: I just want to make sure that the blame goes to the right place.

DOC: And where would that be?

GEARY: Captain Brad Bellick.

DOC: Not Warden Pope?

GEARY: Hey, the warden ain't perfect, but he tries. Nope. This one rests squarely with Bellick. I heard it from my buddies on the inside. Those prisoners went through the guard shack, right?

DOC: We can't confirm the details of the escape at this time.

GEARY: Yeah? Whatever. Thing is, they couldn't have gotten out if Abruzzi didn't have the run of the place. And that's all thanks to Bellick.

DOC: How do you mean?

GEARY: He was being paid to look the other way. Abruzzi had control of P.I. thanks to the monthly contribution Bellick got from Philly Falzone. Abruzzi picked who was on P.I. and what they did. He was the one who put them in the guard shack in the first place.

DOC: Are you suggesting that Captain Bellick was in on the escape?

GEARY: Nope. Not at all. He ain't that bright. But I will tell ya that it was his incompetence and his greed that let it happen.

Following his dismissal from the correctional system—which included the loss of his pension—the few people close to Bellick feared that he would become suicidal, considering that working at Fox River had basically been his life. On the day of his termination, several people, including his mother, had commented on how despondent he had become. His mood, however, changed shortly after the reward was announced for the capture of the Fox River Eight.

Several of their former coworkers at Fox River have mentioned that Bellick and Geary teamed up to search for the fugitives themselves, like many other bounty hunters and persons peripherally associated with the law. Though they would seem an unlikely pair, they apparently got together after Bellick ran into his accuser at the convenience mart where Geary worked security after being fired from Fox River. Geary lost his job at the convenience mart after a brief tussle that laid waste to part of the store. The two men were shortly thereafter seen back at Fox River, where they were permitted to interview Manche Sanchez about the escapees. It is unclear why this was allowed or, more important, what the two men learned, but they soon took off on a cross-country trek in search of the escaped convicts.

The partnership seemed like a bad idea from the start, but took an unexpectedly dark turn in Tribune, Kansas. Detective Kathryn Slattery conducted an interview with Brad Bellick in a local hospital after he was admitted for a blow to the head. He claimed that an unknown assailant had attacked him as he was traveling through town. Though the detective was suspicious of the story, the investigation would have gone no further, but for the fact that the body of Roy Geary was brought in just as Bellick was being discharged. When Bellick admitted to knowing the dead man, he was brought to police headquarters for questioning.

The report from local police indicates that Det. Slattery opened up the interview in a friendly manner, but the tone changed as the night wore on and Bellick's story continued to shift. Bellick ultimately claimed that he and Geary had been hunting for Fox River fugitive Theodore Bagwell under the impression that the convict was carrying five million dollars that had been dug up in Utah. Bellick admitted to finding the fugitive and forcing Bagwell to reveal the location of the money to him and Geary. Then, Geary supposedly double-crossed his partner and attacked him, stealing the money while Bellick was unconscious. Bellick claimed that that was the last time he saw Geary alive.

Slattery did not believe that story any more than she had the others. When Geary's body was found in the Fauntleroy Hotel, he was clutching a credit card receipt with his finger, pointing to the name Brad Bellick. But the truly damning evidence was the voicemail message Bellick had left on Geary's phone, swearing that he would "gut [Geary] from bow to stern." Geary had been found dead of a knife wound straight down his torso.

Bellick was placed under arrest for murder in the first degree. In spite of the fact that he had no prior record, bail was denied. Fearing life in prison or the death penalty, Bellick cut a deal, so long as he got to choose where he was incarcerated. Naturally, Bellick chose Fox River, where he probably thought he would have been placed in Ad Seg. However, the new warden, Ed Pavelka, had other plans. In an attempt to make an example of the corrupt former C.O., the warden had Bellick placed in gen pop where he shared a cell with Avocado Balz-Johnson.

As one might expect, mixing the former C.O. in with the inmate population was a powder keg waiting to explode, and Bellick was alternately threatened and attacked by the other prisoners. Though he feared his life was in danger, his requests to be transferred to Ad Seg were denied.

Bellick's stay at Fox River was cut short when Special Agent Mahone visited Bellick and asked for his help in decoding the videotape that Scofield and Burrows had made proclaiming Burrows's innocence. With his knowledge of Dr. Sara Tancredi and his experience with Alcoholics Anonymous, Bellick was able to ascertain that the tape contained a coded message to Sara. Using the AA guide to decipher Scofield's words, Bellick turned Mahone on to St. Thomas Hospital in Akron, Ohio. Convinced Bellick could be a major help to the investigation, a deal was struck that enabled Bellick to leave Fox River, under the jurisdiction of Special Agent Mahone and the FBI.

Last updated on 6/5 by Agent Wheeler.

Prison Break
THE CLASSIFIED FBI FILES

(FORMER) WARDEN HENRY POPE

Current Status: Retired

Warden Henry Pope had worked in corrections for forty years prior to the escape of the Fox River Eight. Until the breakout, his career was marked by a stellar performance in an often unforgiving job. Pope's philosophy on incarceration was focused on rehabilitation. In the eighteen years he had been at Fox River, he developed numerous programs oriented toward helping prisoners prepare to be released back into society. The two cornerstones of his plan were the educational program and Prison Industries. P.I., as it came to be known, helps inmates gain real world experience in a variety of fields, ranging from landscaping to office work. Though both programs have been largely successful, P.I. is now coming under criticism in light of the way former C.O. Brad Bellick used it to supplement his pay. Additionally, the access P.I. allowed prisoners to have in certain areas of the prison was instrumental in Michael Scofield's escape plan.

Warden Pope's professional career was largely marked by successes, but his personal life was another matter. He married Judith Warner in the same year that he began his work in corrections. As his reputation steadily rose in his chosen career field, his marriage was a far bumpier ride. While working for the Toledo Department of Corrections, Pope engaged in an extra-marital affair that produced an illegitimate child. The child's mother did not want Pope in her son's life unless he left his wife. When Pope refused to honor that request, he was cut off from his son. The warden did manage to keep tabs on the boy, though it was done largely from a distance.

Pope's son, Will Clayton, spent much of his childhood lashing out at authority figures. As a teen he was a thief and eventually turned to drugs. Will's path to destruction ended at the age of twenty-two, on July 15, 1998. He was found dead on a Toledo street after suffering blunt force trauma to the head and torso. He had been last seen exiting a nearby convenience store. Little evidence was found at the scene, and the investigation is still unresolved. It is unclear whether or not Pope's

Accident Claims Life of Toledo Man

By ERIC KRAUSE
STAFF WRITER

Will Clayton, age 22, was found dead in the street yesterday. He suffered blunt force trauma to the face and torso. The youth was last seen leaving a nearby convenience store. Police at the scene had little evidence to go by and asked the public for any information regarding his death.

involvement with his son could have altered the boy's tragic path.

Pope eventually told his wife, Judy, about the affair, but he kept the secret of his son from her until recently. Throughout their forty years of marriage, they had their ups and downs, but, according to those who know him, Pope never stopped loving her. To make up for the long hours at work, Warden Pope wanted to plan a special gift for their fortieth anniversary. Pope was in the process of building her a model of the Taj Mahal, a favorite place of Judy's, in spite of the fact that his abilities in model construction were limited. When Pope learned that new inmate Michael Scofield was a structural engineer, he asked for the prisoner's help on the project. At first Scofield refused, but eventually he agreed as a way to avoid solitary confinement, following an altercation in the yard. This highly unusual level of access to the warden and his office proved instrumental in Scofield's escape.

The time Pope spent with Scofield seemed to engender a close bond between the two men. Upon learning that Scofield was brothers with death row inmate Lincoln Burrows, Warden Pope saw to it that the two men had the opportunity to spend time together before Burrows's death. And when a mysterious request came through for Scofield to be transferred to Statesville Prison, Pope was instrumental in seeing that the prisoner's Motion for

Interlocutory Injunction was properly handled so the brothers could remain together at Fox River, at least until the execution. The warden would eventually grow to regret that decision.

Scofield took Warden Pope hostage in his office on the night of the escape. He then forced Pope to cover for the missing Captain Bellick. He also ordered Pope to have Lincoln Burrows transferred to the infirmary, where Burrows could join in the escape. Scofield then tied up the warden, knocked him unconscious, and hid him in the warden's closet. It was over an hour before the warden was located and freed. At that point, Pope alerted the correctional officers to sound the escape alarm and took control of the situation.

The next morning, Pope and Bellick were taken off the search and commanded to appear before a Department of Corrections Inquiry Board. During the inquiry, Pope defended his actions to the best of his abilities, but was caught entirely off guard when he learned that Captain Bellick had been accepting payoffs in exchange for offering inmates control of Prison Industries. In light of this evidence, the DOC terminated Bellick's employment, effective immediately. Warden Pope, however, was only docked two weeks pay and placed on probation for three months. Pope, however, immediately resigned his position and left the proceedings, stating that although he was not proud of Bellick's actions, he had no intention of turning his back on

one of his men. It is rumored that he then returned to his office to clear out his things, and destroyed the model of the Taj Mahal that he had built with the help of Michael Scofield. Pope went into retirement and was replaced by D.O.C. Administrator Ed Pavelka.

Pope was later spotted at the downtown Chicago Corona De Oro Club, a private cigar club, in the company of Michael Scofield and Sara Tancredi. According to the manager of the club, Pope accessed the private humidor belonging to the late former governor Frank Tancredi. It is uncertain what, if anything, Pope may have removed from the humidor.

Last updated on 6/5 by Agent Lang.

DR. SARA TANCREDI

Current Status: Missing

Sara Tancredi, daughter of Illinois governor Frank Tancredi, seemed to have the perfect home life. As the man who would become known as "Frontier Justice" Frank Tancredi worked his way up through party ranks, he and his wife and daughter projected the appearance of a traditional American family. Sara was not particularly close to her father though, as his work often took him out of town, causing him to miss many holidays and family gatherings. Behind the scenes this seemingly happy family was a perfect example of how the pressures of politics can adversely affect a home.

Sara's parents reportedly had a strained relationship for years before Mrs. Tancredi's tragic death. Rumors of alcoholism on Mrs. Tancredi's part were always gossiped about in whispers among the other politicians' wives, but it was never formally substantiated. The rift between Sara and her father had been growing long before her mother's death, but it only intensified in the years that followed.

In addition to the familial strain, Sara and her father had dramatically divergent political opinions. Frontier Justice Frank held strongly conservative views and often clashed with his liberal daughter, until the two of them simply stopped talking about certain issues. This was particularly difficult considering how active Sara was in humanitarian causes while at school. Sara was a Phi Beta Kappa at Northwestern University, where she studied medicine. Always one for a cause, Sara even took several months off from her education to work abroad.

The strain of keeping up appearances, along with the loss of her mother, clearly began to overwhelm Sara. It is unclear when she turned to drugs to cope with her issues, but as she grew older, it became increasingly obvious that her growing addiction was having a deleterious affect on her life. It was even suspected that she was stealing drugs from her workplace at a Chicago hospital. Her father was forced to use his influence on several occasions to keep her or a boyfriend out of jail, which exacerbated their already troubled relationship.

Sara's problems came to a head one winter afternoon in the city, when she was out walking with her boyfriend, Colin. The pair witnessed an accident in which a car was unable to stop on the ice and hit a child on a bike. Sara was

Governor's Daughter Wins Humanitarian Award

Sara Wayne Tancredi was honored by the Kiwanis Club in Aurora last Thursday night for her philanthropic efforts both in India and here in Illinois. Tancredi, the second eldest daughter of Frank Tancredi, spent 9 months in Calcutta last year setting up an orphanage with money raised through a non-profit organization she put together a half dozen years ago as a student at Northwestern. Upon her return, Tancredi opted to work with what she deems "America's disenfranchised": the million-plus incarcerated men and women throughout the country. Tancredi's plan is a bold one, and one, she admits, is going to take a lot more effort than she alone can sustain. With the widespread

'She is attempting to lobby local and state government reps to bring the programs back.'

cancellation of Pell Grants and other educational programs for prisoners already taking place throughout the U.S., Tancredi is attempting to lobby local and state government representatives to bring the programs back, under a work-and-learn program in which inmates, if they so choose, can finance their own educations through the meager earnings they make from prison employment.

"My initial passion for the issue of working conditions in prisons stemmed from a realization that my closet was filled with clothes made by women, more or less my age, sewing rather than studying," she wrote.

Tancredi, a senior Phi Beta Kappa, Morehead Scholar and N.C. Fellow at the University of North Carolina at Chapel Hill, has worked to fight unfair labor practices worldwide. On July 13, she will receive a national Howard R. Swearer Student Humanitarian Award in recognition of her efforts.

The award, created in 1987, is given by Campus Compact, a group of more than 600 college and university presidents who promote public service in and out of the

classroom. The late Chancellor Michael Hooker served as a member of the group's board of directors.

The award recognizes students who have "connected service with academic work, developed systems to ensure long-term support for their service projects and linked their service with its larger social context through policy work and awareness-raising."

Hannah Richman, who coordinates the award program, said: "Sarah is really incredible in that she did all of these in her project. She was not only looking at issues of economic justice, but she also brought the local issues to this global emphasis. She saw an issue, and she translated that into concrete activism. She really raised campus concern about this and brought local, as well as international issues, to the forefront."

Tancredi, 22, founded the Humanitarian Awareness Campaign at UNC-CH in 1997 to question Nike Corp. labor practices abroad, as well as a licensing contract between the company and the university. The campaign eventually grew into the ongoing Students for Economic Justice, which fights unfair labor practices and

Erin Taber
Gamma Phi, Drama Club
[...] with temptation by yielding to it"

Jane Tachara
Women's Fencing

Sue Tamarack
Drama Club
"Make the audience suffer as much as [...]

Silvie Talliard
[...]hi-O, Poetry Club

Sara Tancredi
Phi Beta Kappa, Spanish Club
"Be the change you want to see in the world"—Gandhi

John Tapord
Phi Kappa Psi, Math Club

too strung out on morphine to render aid to the victim. This had a sobering effect on Sara, who immediately joined Narcotics Anonymous after the event. While in the group, Sara was partnered with her sponsor, Shelley, and set about straightening out her life. This began with her severing her relationship with Colin as well as leaving her work at the hospital, not trusting herself to be around patients until she was able to get a handle on her own drug problem.

After being clean for eighteen months, Dr. Tancredi was ready to get back to work. She was looking to give back to the community in a more hands-on way, and a fellow member of her N.A. therapy group, Captain Brad Bellick, suggested that she work at Fox River Penitentiary and recommended her for a position in the prison's medical unit. It is also believed that early on Bellick was infatuated with Sara, but she did not return his affections.

As the primary doctor in the medical unit, Dr. Tancredi was responsible for all measures of care for the prisoners, including everything from performing physicals to emergency surgeries. Her position at the prison led to further distancing between father and daughter. Aside from the fact that the two continued to differ over the treatment of prisoners, Governor Tancredi was also concerned for her safety. He felt that she continued to work at the prison and place herself in danger largely because she knew he was opposed to the job.

In her position, Dr. Tancredi interacted with most of the prisoners in Fox River. This was especially true of Michael Scofield. Based on files found in Scofield's recovered hard drive, he had determined that the infirmary was the weak point in prison security prior to his incarceration. To make the necessary preparations for escape, he would need to make repeated visits to the main examination room. Upon his incarceration, Scofield reported that he had type-1 diabetes, a condition that required him to go to the infirmary daily for shots. During his many visits, it is reported that he and Sara began to develop a personal relationship. Though Sara initially justified her interest in the prisoner as his being someone she could help rehabilitate, it soon became clear that there were more intense feelings involved.

During the Fox River riot, Dr. Tancredi was trapped in the sickbay in B-Wing with a small group of prisoners. She had managed to protect herself

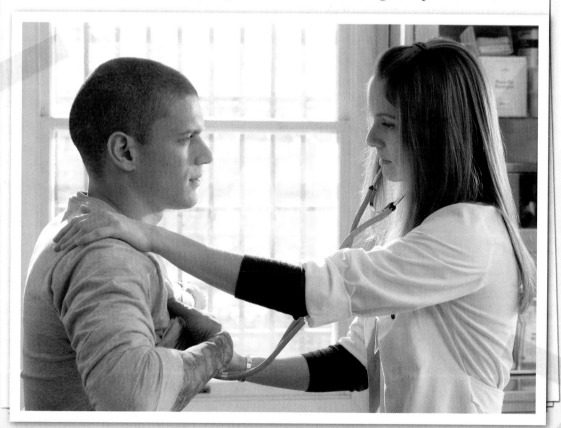

by locking herself in an examination room, but she knew that the door would not hold back the prisoners for long. As Dr. Tancredi searched for an alternate exit, Scofield came to her rescue, providing her with a way out of the room and escorting her to an exterior door to the prison so she could escape. In subsequent interviews regarding her experience, Dr. Tancredi was vague on the details of how she did manage to leave the prison safely. It was thought that the trauma of the event had clouded her memory, though now it seems possible that she was trying to downplay Scofield's knowledge of the prison design.

As Scofield's brother, Lincoln Burrows, approached his date of execution, Dr. Tancredi was required to give the condemned inmate weekly physicals. She deliberately scheduled those physicals to end just as Scofield was coming in for his insulin shots so the brothers could spend a few moments together. Dr. Tancredi's involvement with the brothers did not end there. On the day of Burrows's initially scheduled execution, Sara reluctantly approached her father, asking him to consider granting Burrows a pardon. She gave him a file of information that had been given to her by Veronica Donovan, hoping—though not expecting—that he would intercede. Sara's expectations of her father were proved correct when he did nothing, even though she had felt there was more than enough information in the file to warrant further investigation into the case. What she did find suspicious was that soon after her father denied granting Burrows a pardon, he was placed on the short list for consideration as then-Vice President

Reynolds's running mate. Sara had a hushed, but very public argument with her father over that very subject in a Chicago restaurant on the night of the Fox River escape.

Dr. Tancredi's attempt to have Burrows pardoned was not the last time she would help the brothers. On the night of the escape from Fox River, Scofield's revised plan required him to access the infirmary through a locked door. After the escape, it became clear to the prison staff that the only way that door could have been accessed was with a key. Nurse Katie Wech reluctantly admitted that she suspected Dr. Tancredi had left the door open for the escapees. When members of the Chicago PD went to question Dr. Tancredi, they found her in her apartment suffering from a drug overdose.

Excerpt from DOC interview with Nurse Katie Wech:
(The following is a portion of the transcript from an interview conducted with Nurse Katie Wech, who worked at the Fox River infirmary alongside Dr. Sara Tancredi.)

DOC INTERVIEWER: Do you suspect that Dr. Tancredi helped the inmates escape?

NURSE KATIE WECH: No, I don't. All I said was that she seemed to be close to one of the prisoners, Michael Scofield. I don't believe she intentionally did anything wrong.

DOC: But someone in here had to have opened the door for them.

WECH: All I can tell you is that it wasn't me.

DOC: Can you describe the nature of Dr. Tancredi's relationship with Michael Scofield?

WECH: I wouldn't call it a relationship. They were friends, I guess. Friendly. Michael was here every day for his insulin shot. It's natural that they would get to know each other. I think Sara saw him as someone she could have a positive effect on. I think she wanted to reach out to him, help him rehabilitate and all that.

DOC: Did Dr. Tancredi always take such an active interest in her patients?

WECH: To varying degrees. She wanted to help people— that's why she became a doctor. She believed that peo-

ple could rise up after hitting rock bottom. What
with her history and all, I think she saw a little bit
of herself in Michael. She made her own mistakes
in the past.

DOC: Would you categorize Dr. Tancredi's behavior with
Scofield as inappropriate?

WECH: What? Sara was always professional. Just because
they got along, it doesn't mean anything. She got a second chance when she came to work here. She was just
trying to show Michael that he could have a future, too.

DOC: You know by now that she was found in her apartment suffering a drug overdose.

WECH: Yes.

DOC: Had you seen any signs of abuse at work?

WECH: Absolutely not. This had to have been a one-time
thing.

DOC: How can you be so sure?

WECH: Listen, I'm a nurse and I work at a prison. I
know what drugs do to people, I recognize the signs.
Sara was clean.

Tancredi was released from Chicago County Hospital after recovering
from her overdose, and taken directly into police custody for questioning
about the Fox River escape, and under suspicion of being an accessory to
said escape. He father paid her bail and arranged for her representation. He
reportedly even suggested to her that she could place the blame on the warden
for Scofield having access to the keys. Sara refused to implicate an innocent
man, and was set to stand trial for her alleged crime of aiding and abetting.
Sara began attending daily Narcotics Anonymous meetings in an attempt to
move on with her life.

Though his political advisers suggested that the governor distance himself from his daughter, her troubles instead seemed to be bringing them closer
together. The governor was recently seen visiting her at her apartment, and he
called her three times on what turned out to be the last day of his life.

The newly inaugurated President Reynolds was in the process of nominat-
ing Governor Tancredi to fill her vacated vice presidential position when she
abruptly withdrew the nomination. Seemingly distraught over losing the nod,
Tancredi returned home and committed suicide. Sara was the one to find the
body. She tried to revive her father, but it was too late.

Excerpt from Chicago Police Department Report:

On the evening of June 1, a civilian woman by the name of Kelli Foster was shot and killed at the corner of Third Street and Harper Boulevard. The woman had been standing at a public payphone when a black unmarked vehicle turned from Third onto Harper and opened fire through the rear passenger window. Eyewitness accounts confirm that the windows were tinted black and no ID was made on the perpetrator. Ms. Foster received four gunshot wounds, and ballistics have shown that the weapon fired was a semi-automatic Bristol Faber 809.

The following is an eyewitness account from a pedestrian at the scene:

I was coming out of the grocery store over on Harper Boulevard when I heard this horrible noise—I guess it was the sound of gunshots. I'd never heard a gunshot before so I wasn't sure. A big dark SUV zoomed past me and I remember I looked over at it and noticed it didn't have a license plate on the back. I saw a woman lying on the ground a few meters in front of me and I ran over to her. There was another woman kneeling down by her. She looked up at me and yelled for me to call 911. I was so shocked though, for a second I just stood there. But then it hit me that this woman was probably about to die. So I went to the phone booth to call an ambulance. I remember I could hear the woman who was kneeling by her, tell her that she was a doctor and to hang on. But by the time I finished making the phone call, the woman—the doctor, was gone. I bent down to look at the woman on the street, and it looked like she was dead. Some other people had crowded around and I heard a man say he recognized the doctor—she was Sara Tancredi, daughter of the govenor, who worked at Fox River and has been all over the news for letting those prisoners out.

Shortly thereafter, Special Agent Alexander Mahone discovered a key piece of evidence, indicating that Michael Scofield had planned a rendezvous with Dr. Tancredi in New Mexico. He was able to track down the pair, but they managed to elude him. When Scofield was captured, Sara Tancredi was not in the area. It is assumed that they split up for a time, but have since reunited as they have been spotted together making their way to Chicago. Tancredi is currently wanted for skipping out on bail in addition to the other charges against her.

Last updated on 6/7 by Agent Lang.

VERONICA DONOVAN

Status: Missing

Veronica Donovan and Lincoln Burrows had been friends for most of their lives. Following the death of their mother, Burrows and his younger brother moved in with Donovan's family for a short time. However, the combination of her abusive father and Burrows's protectiveness toward her complicated the situation and the brothers were forced to move out. Unlike Burrows, Donovan never let the street life of Cicero, Illinois, get in the way of her dreams. Her interest in law was clear at an early age, and probably grew out of the need to help her friend, Lincoln, who had spent so much of his adolescence in trouble with the law. During their teen years, Donovan's and Burrows's relationship moved beyond friendship, though their romance was ultimately short-lived.

Donovan knew that the only way out of her family situation was to take control of her own life. Diligent studies earned her a full academic scholarship to the University of Illinois at Urbana-Champaign, where she graduated with a B.A. in political science. Afterward, she attended Baylor University, graduating in the middle of her class with a juris doctorate.

While away at college, Donovan tried to stay in touch with Burrows, but her studies—and Burrows's attitude—made communication difficult. When Donovan found out that Burrows had fathered a child, with another woman, she was devastated, but managed to maintain their friendship. After college, she attempted to rekindle their relationship. By that time, Burrows's problems kept him so far out of reach that she eventually had to remove herself from his

IN THE SUPREME COURT OF THE UNITED STATES

LINCOLN BURROWS

Petitioner

vs.

STATE OF ILLINOIS

Respondent

PETITION FOR WRIT OF CERTIORARI

CAPITAL CASE

EXECUTION DATE: MAY, 11, 2005

Veronica Donovan, Esq.
Project Justice
Illinois Bar No. 31a060161c43
15 West Superior St.
Chicago, IL 60610

COUNSEL FOR PETITION

life in order to keep from being hurt any further. The two lost contact for a few years prior to Burrows being charged in the murder of Terrence Steadman.

After college, Donovan was hired by the legal firm of Glazer and Ross, where she specialized in real estate law. While employed by the firm, she met and began a relationship with Sebastian Balfour. When she heard of Burrows's legal troubles, she tried to be there for him as a friend, but could not assist him with his legal problems as she was not qualified to defend a death penalty case. Again, Burrows reportedly kept her at arm's length, which is likely why she did not do more to help with his legal woes at the time.

When Burrows's brother, Michael Scofield, was charged with armed robbery, Donovan did step in to aid in his defense. Scofield, however, pled no contest to the charge and ignored her advice to allow the case to go to trial. It is now clear that Scofield wanted to be incarcerated and would not have taken Donovan's advice in any case. Her inability to help Michael clearly opened old wounds, and she attempted to reconcile her friendship with Burrows before he was to be executed. During this time, she learned of the inconsistencies in Burrows's case and apparently took it upon herself to dig further into the growing mystery.

Donovan's investigation into the Burrows case began to wear on her relationship with Sebastian. At the time, the two were engaged, but Donovan's work kept her from important appointments with her fiancé. Eventually, when she admitted that she wanted to postpone the wedding, Sebastian countered by ending the relationship. Though Donovan was upset by the decision, she was now on a dedicated mission to clear Lincoln Burrows's name.

At Burrows's suggestion, Donovan approached Project Justice—an organization that specializes in providing legal assistance for the wrongly convicted—for help with additional appeals for the death row case. Though her initial inquiries were rejected, junior associate, Nick Savrinn, found merit in the case and offered his assistance. Shortly after they began investigating the circumstances surrounding Terrence Steadman's murder, Donovan's apartment exploded, resulting in the death of the building's maintenance man, Lucasz Peshcopi. The official investigation into the explosion listed the cause as a gas leak, but questions have been raised as to whether it was actually an attempt on Donovan's life.

Fearing for their safety, Donovan and Savrinn went into hiding at an undisclosed location. It is assumed that during this time they reunited with Burrows's son, L.J., who was on the run after being suspected in the death of his mother and stepfather. Again, questions have been raised about the events

surrounding these deaths, as well as the death of Sebastian Balfour, Donovan's former fiancé, who was found murdered during this time.

As the date for Burrows's execution approached, Donovan came out of hiding and spoke to the press outside Fox River Penitentiary. During a brief interview, she rattled off a long list of deaths she believed were related to the Burrows case. She also laid out a theory that highly placed people in the government had set Lincoln Burrows up for the death of Terrence Steadman. Though all her evidence was circumstantial, she promised that an insider was about to come forward and provide the truth behind this seemingly outlandish theory. That witness never materialized. Donovan later claimed that he had been murdered, although no body was ever produced.

On the day of Lincoln Burrows's execution, Donovan and Savrinn managed to secure time with Judge Randall Kessler to present all the circumstantial evidence they had collected regarding the Burrows case. They hoped that it would be enough to convince Judge Kessler to grant a stay of execution;

however, with no real evidence available, the judge's hands were tied. Lincoln Burrows was scheduled to die that night.

Donovan and Michael Scofield were the only witnesses Burrows had requested to be at his execution. Holding back tears, Donovan bid the man she loved farewell and waited to witness his death. But that death did not come. Judge Kessler eventually did grant a stay of execution in the eleventh hour, when additional evidence mysteriously came to light. Donovan used that evidence to get an injunction to exhume the body of Terrence Steadman, who she suspected was actually still alive. However, Steadman's dental records did match that of the body and Burrows's execution was rescheduled.

Donovan used the additional time to conduct a deeper investigation into the mystery surrounding Terrence Steadman's death. Airline records show that she boarded a flight to Montana on the same night that Burrows escaped from prison. She rented a car at the airport and drove to an unknown location and has not been seen since.

Last updated on 6/1 by Agent Lang.

NICK SAVRINN

Current Status: Deceased

Nick Savrinn fought for lost causes his entire life. When Savrinn was a child, he could only watch as his father defended himself against a false accusation of criminal activity. In the end, the elder Savrinn was convicted, but never stopped trying to prove his innocence. As a result, Nick decided at a young age to dedicate himself to the law.

Savrinn attended Duke University for undergraduate studies and later graduated with honors from Columbia Law School. He received offers from all the prestigious Manhattan law firms, but returned home to Chicago to join Project Justice, where he did pro bono work for the wrongly convicted. During his eleven years with the firm, Savrinn successfully cleared thirteen clients, facing a combined 300 years in prison, five of whom were on death row. His job at Project Justice also ensured that he could continue working on clearing his father's name.

Though Project Justice, Savrinn's boss, Ben Forsik, officially refused to assist in the Burrows case, Savrinn realized that it had merit. He requested a short sabbatical so that he could devote his time to the cause. He quickly discovered that what he had initially thought was merely a case of false charges, was possibly just the beginning of a deep and intricate conspiracy.

Shortly after accepting the Burrows case, Savrinn went missing when Veronica Donovan's apartment was destroyed in what was reported to be a gas explosion. It is believed that he and Donovan fled to safety at an undisclosed location. Later, a man matching Savrinn's description was admitted to a local hospital, suffering what was clearly a gunshot wound. The unidentified woman with him insisted that it was a household accident, but doctors were skeptical. Although the bullet had been removed from the wound prior to Savrinn's admittance, the hospital reported the incident to local authorities. The patient, however, fled the premises before the police could arrive to question him.

Savrinn continued his work, using his connections to ensure that Burrows's case was heard. Despite mounting circumstantial evidence, Savrinn and Donovan were unsuccessful in getting Burrows released, only managing a brief stay of execution. During this time, Savrinn experienced a personal victory when his father was quietly released from prison when a member of the Falzone crime family, who was already serving a life sentence for murder, came forward and confessed to the crime. Their reunion, however, would ultimately end in tragedy.

On the day after the Fox River escape, investigators went to Nick Savrinn's apartment hoping for his help in apprehending his client, Lincoln Burrows. When the investigators arrived, they found Savrinn's front door unlocked. They announced themselves and entered to find the bodies of Nick Savrinn and his father. They had both been shot. Their murders remain unsolved.

**Last updated on 6/1
by Agent Lang.**

L.J. BURROWS

Current Status: Missing

Lincoln Burrows Jr. was born into a difficult situation. He was the result of an unexpected pregnancy, and his unmarried parents were never truly a couple. Though both his mother, Lisa Rix, and his father, Lincoln Burrows, did their best to raise L.J., circumstances seemed to conspire against them to make their lives more difficult. L.J.'s parents had agreed that Rix would have sole custody, although no legal documents were ever drawn up formally to establish the arrangement. Burrows was allowed to see his son on most weekends. In spite of his hardships growing up, L.J. was a stellar student for most of his childhood.

L.J. was very close to his mother in his early years. Though Burrows clearly loved his son, he was not always dependable. L.J.'s uncle, Michael

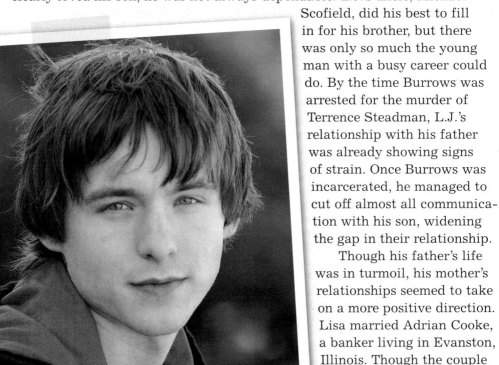

Scofield, did his best to fill in for his brother, but there was only so much the young man with a busy career could do. By the time Burrows was arrested for the murder of Terrence Steadman, L.J.'s relationship with his father was already showing signs of strain. Once Burrows was incarcerated, he managed to cut off almost all communication with his son, widening the gap in their relationship.

Though his father's life was in turmoil, his mother's relationships seemed to take on a more positive direction. Lisa married Adrian Cooke, a banker living in Evanston, Illinois. Though the couple seemed happy, there were rumors that Lisa married Adrian more for the security that he could provide for her and her son than out of love. Between his father's legal troubles and his mother marrying a man L.J. never connected with, it was little surprise when L.J.'s grades began to slip, and he withdrew from his friends and family. By the time he was fifteen, L.J. was arrested for possession of two pounds of marijuana with intent to sell. His parole officer, Jenae Collins, was concerned about the anger she saw in the boy. In an attempt to help him deal with that anger, she signed him up for the Scared Straight program at Fox River Penitentiary, where his father would serve as his mentor. At the time, the parole officer could not have anticipated the tragedy that was about to occur.

On the afternoon of April 24, police were called to the family home where they found the bodies of L.J.'s mother and stepfather. Both had been shot and left for dead at the scene. The weapon was recovered onsite with L.J.'s fingerprints on it. His bloody footprints were also found near his mother's body. In addition to the evidence, neighbors admitted to hearing screaming in the household the day before.

L.J. was sought on suspicion of the murders, but he managed to evade capture. It is believed that during this time his father's friend and lawyer, Veronica Donovan, was helping him to hide from the authorities. The attached document was found among Lincoln Burrows's possessions after his escape from Fox River. It came to the prison under the guise of an official legal document, but by reading the last words of each line of the first paragraph, it is clear that this was actually a secret communication from the convict's son.

Shortly after Burrows's execution was delayed, his son found himself in even more trouble. A neighbor of Owen Kravecki, a Chicago buffalo jerky salesman, reported the teen breaking and entering the Kravecki home. Police arrived to find L.J. with a gun trained on Kravecki.

unable to seek the death penalty under Illinois Penal Code No. 19.03.05(a)(1). It's appropriate to give access of the viewing to the son of Mr. Burrows, LJ, who has accepted the invitation to attend. He has expressed an interest; therefore I'm inclined to support it. Per our procedure, minors must have a parent/guardian attend with them at the event. It has been proposed that the defendant's lawyer, Ms. Veronica Donovan would accompany Lincoln Burrows Jr. (LJ) and act as his chaperone. I'm inclined to support this as well. In light of LJ's recent and tragic situation this is okay. It is not the normal condition that a non-parent and non-legal guardian would attend. I allow that this is an unusual event. It is right that someone should be there to show love and support to this child in a trying time. As we have supported this exception, only you can negate the decision by barring him from the event.

The approach taken in this situation is decidedly untraditional. However, the extenuating circumstances justify this unprecedented solution. LJ has suffered a terrible heartache in watching his father's many unsuccessful appeals and eventual sentence of death, though his most formidable years. During this time he has been supported by his mother and step-father, who, in an unthinkable turn of events, were murdered in their home, an event to which LJ was a witness. Without any other family available, Ms. Veronica Donovan is and exceptional choice. Aside from being Mr. Burrow's lawyer, she is a close family friend and has known the defendant since childhood. She has volunteered for this position and it has been agreed to by both LJ and Mr. Burrows. We believe that granting this inmate his dying wish is important to the closure and healing of his young son. Please consider this compassionate measure, not just for Lincoln Burrows but also for his son, who has suffered a great deal.

He had already fired once at the man, grazing him in the neck. L.J. dropped his weapon and was taken into custody. He was promptly charged with attempted murder on top of his prior charge for double homicide.

Excerpt from transcript of interview with Parole Officer Jenae Collins:

FBI INVESTIGATOR: According to your files, you cited that L.J. Burrows was suffering from anger issues.

PAROLE OFFICER JENAE COLLINS: Well, that seemed pretty clear, considering his sudden decline in grades and his lashing out at authority figures. Obviously, there was a lot of anger associated with his dad's situation. I just never imagined it would escalate so quickly. He didn't strike me as a danger to his family.

FBI: Don't often hear about kids convicted of pot possession moving up to murder like that.

COLLINS: Oh, it happens. But as much as L.J. was acting up, I could see he still had a close bond with his mother. And that's really all it seemed at the time: acting up. I thought some time with his father would straighten him out.

FBI: I guess the opposite happened?

COLLINS: I really don't think they had enough visits together to really affect L.J. one way or the other. Besides, all reports that I received indicated that L.J.'s father was having a positive influence on him.

FBI: Then how do you explain the sudden murder of his mom and her husband?

COLLINS: I can't. You know, L.J. insists that he's innocent. I mean, they all insist that they're innocent, but there's something . . . L.J. really believes it. I'd be inclined to believe him, but there's no doubt that he broke into that Kravecki man's home and shot him.

FBI: What do you think about L.J.'s claim that he's been set up? That it's some kind of government conspiracy?

COLLINS: That's the real tragedy in this. I hear his father's lawyers were pushing that story, too. I think L.J. is just confused. He's grasping at whatever straws he can find.

I suggested that he speak with a counselor before his trial. I think his father's situation is clearly having an affect on him.

FBI: So you don't believe in this conspiracy?

COLLINS: Do you really have to ask? Look, I'm not so naive as to think that the government is looking out for us all. I've been in this job long enough to know who I can and can't trust. I just don't see any conspiracy in the deaths of L.J.'s family or an attack on some buffalo jerky salesman, you know?

The day after his father escaped from Fox River, L.J. was scheduled to be transported to a holding facility in Arizona. His father and uncle attempted to break L.J. out of custody, but they were thwarted by Special Agent Alexander Mahone. Only a few days later, however, L.J. found himself released from prison when crucial blood and fingerprint evidence in his case suddenly disappeared. Upon his release, L.J. was kept under surveillance in case his fugitive father came for him. Burrows did indeed make contact with his son, but the pair managed to slip away together unnoticed.

L.J. traveled with his father for a short time before they were briefly apprehended at a train station in Arizona. They managed to escape from the custody of local law enforcement and disappeared. When Burrows was captured again in New Mexico, L.J. was not with him. His location is still unknown.

Last updated on 6/3 by Agent Wheeler.

Official FBI Investigation
into the Fox River Escape

What was initially believed to be merely a useful tool for identification has proven to be of much greater value to the investigation into the Fox River escape and the ensuing manhunt. Prisoner Michael Scofield, believed to be the mastermind behind the breakout, is distinguished by an intricate tattoo encompassing his entire torso and both arms. Upon closer examination of these unique markings, Special Agent Alexander Mahone made the connection that integral clues to understanding the escape, and Scofield's plan to flee the country were buried within the artwork of the tattoo.

Scofield's familiarity with the design of Fox River Penitentiary was not simply the result of research into the facility. Through a fortuitous set of circumstances, Scofield was one of the structural engineers involved in the recent redesign of the correctional facility. Initially, Chapparal Associates was awarded the contract to retrofit Fox River in 1999. The job proved to be too complex for the company, so they subcontracted it out in an under-the-table deal with Middleton, Maxwell, and Schaum, the architectural firm where Scofield worked. Scofield was brought in to ghost write the plan for the redesign. When his brother, Lincoln Burrows, was incarcerated in Fox River, Scofield recognized the unique opportunity, removed the prison blueprints from his company files, and used his knowledge to devise an escape plan to free the brother he insists is innocent. Once that plan was in place, Scofield designed key components of the plot into his intricate tattoo.

The following is the FBI analysis of said tattoo in an attempt to reconstruct the complicated escape plan devised by Scofield. This report will incorporate photos of the tattoo taken by prison personnel upon Scofield's incarceration; interviews with, among others, the tattoo artist responsible for the application; and files pulled off the hard drive of Scofield's computer after it was retrieved from the Chicago River. Please be advised that much of this report is speculation, though it is based on extensive research.

Escape Plan: Phase 1

Evidence Item #1: Schweitzer / Allen / 11121147 Tattoo

The success of Michael Scofield's escape plan was largely dependent on his ability to have unsupervised access in three main locations in the prison: his cell, the infirmary, and the guard's break room. The primary location for the initial stage of Scofield's plan was, obviously enough, his cell. Once he was able to exit his cell freely, he could access almost any point in the prison unsupervised. As all cells in the general population area of A-Wing were constructed with the exact same design and equipment, his plan was not entirely dependent on his cell assignment.

Following the escape, a search of Scofield's cell netted a small tool created from a metal bolt that was hidden in a copy of the book *Primitive Machines*. The part number on the bolt (**11121147**) matched the number seen in the tattoo pictured here. Information from Scofield's hard drive revealed that these bolts were used in the construction of the bleachers in the prison yard. Scofield used the part number to locate this specific type of bolt and surreptitiously removed it from the bleachers so that he could use it to make an appropriately sized tool.

The tip of the bolt was shaved down to a hexagonal shape to fashion a makeshift **Allen** wrench. The wrench was then used to remove the 1/4" **Allen** bolt in the sink assembly and toilet located in the cell. The fixture was made by the **Schweitzer** Plumbing Company. To make sure that he created the proper instrument, Scofield included an exact match to the 1/4" hexagonal shape of the Allen bolt in the tattoo. Once the bolt was filed down to the proper size,

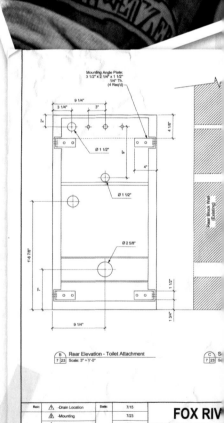

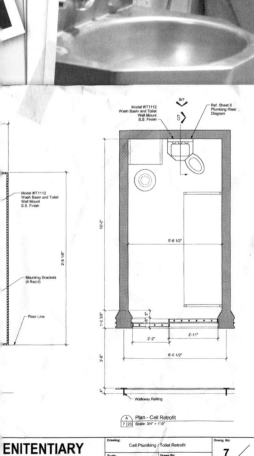

Model #IT1112
Wash Basin and Toilet
Wall Mount
S.S. Finish

Ref. Sheet 6
Plumbing Riser
Diagram

B/7

C7

Model #IT1112
Wash Basin and Toilet
Wall Mount
S.S. Finish

10'-0"

5'-6 1/2"

Mounting Brackets
(4 Req'd)

2'-6 1/8"

1'-0 3/8"

3'-8"

Floor Line

2'-2"

2'-11"

6'-0 1/2"

4"

Walkway Railing

A
7 23   Plan - Cell Retrofit
Scale: 3/4" = 1'-0"

ENITENTIARY	Drawing: Cell Plumbing / Toilet Retrofit	Drawing No: 7 / 23
idual Cell Retrofit	Scale: As Noted	Drawn By: C Jackson	
	Date: 7/14	Approved: G Baugh	

Scofield used it to remove the screw from the sink so that the entire sink and toilet assembly could be pulled away from the wall.

With the assembly out of the way, Scofield proceeded to chip out a hole in the mortar in the cell's cinderblock wall. It is likely that he did most of this work at night, though it is unclear how long the process took. What is clear is that it would have been almost impossible for him to make any progress unless his cellmate was in on the plan. It is assumed that he experienced some delays in his plan when Fernando Sucre requested a cell reassignment. Considering that his second cellmate, Charles Patoshik, was an insomniac, little progress was likely made during that time. Once Sucre was reassigned to the cell, Scofield would have been able to proceed at will.

It should be noted that several prisoners have reported that Scofield and Sucre's cell often had a sheet hung up for privacy. Traditionally, this is a sign that the prisoners are engaged in sexual activity, but in this case it was presumably related to the escape. Once Scofield was able to chip away at the mortar, he broke through the wall and into the catacombs of the prison. The sink and toilet assembly could easily be replaced to cover the hole and removed again when needed. Scofield was then free to exit his cell and essentially come and go as he pleased.

Evidence Item #2: Cute Poison Tattoo

Another essential objective of Scofield's plan was to find a way to access the infirmary on the night of the escape. At first, it was unclear to investigators what this Cute Poison tattoo on Scofield's arm represented. Due to the fact that the "poison" in the tattoo was being poured into a drain, investigators suspected that it had something to do with the extensive network of pipes inside the walls of the prison. It wasn't until the information from Scofield's hard drive was recovered that Special Agent Mahone was able to make the correct connection.

Among Scofield's files was a list of chemical equations with the following equations highlighted: $CuSO_4$ (copper sulfate) and H_3PO_4

Periodic Table
the Elements

(phosphoric acid). By removing and reordering the letters in the chemical equations, these periodic elements, with the exception of H for hydrogen, could all be found in the words: **Cu**te **PO**i**SO**n. When combined, these chemicals form a corrosive that, in time, can eat away at even the thickest metal. Though highly volatile when mixed, both chemical formulas are stable separately and can be found in commonly available products. Copper sulfate is a component in solutions often used to remove roots from sewers, while phosphoric acid is found in most industrial masonry cleaners. Both of these items can be located on the grounds of Fox River Penitentiary in the storage areas of the toxic control center and the gardening shed. All it would take was for Scofield to negotiate access to either storage area with another prisoner, likely for little more than the cost of a carton of cigarettes.

The rest of the tattoo implies that Scofield poured this solution into a drain at some location in the prison. It is likely that the drain used is the one under the sink in the main examination room in the prison infirmary.

Citing that he suffered from type-1 diabetes, Scofield was required to make daily trips to the infirmary for insulin shots. In point of fact, Scofield's prior medical records show no evidence of the disorder. However, a stash of the insulin blocker, PUG-NAc, was found during a search of his cell after the escape, shedding light on how he was able to feign the disease. During his trips to the infirmary, Scofield likely poured the copper sulfate and phosphoric acid down the drain beneath the infirmary sink to corrode the metal pipe beneath. This would have required two containers—such as simple tubes of toothpaste—to keep the chemicals separate until Scofield poured them down the drain where they would combine. Repeated visits would have been necessary to ensure that the metal pipe beneath the drain was completely corroded so that on the night of the escape, Scofield's crew could enter the infirmary through the pipe.

Evidence Item #3: English, Fitz, Percy Tattoo

This piece was one of the first connections that Agent Mahone made in realizing that Scofield's tattoo was not merely decorative. **English, Fitz,** and **Percy** streets border the grounds of Fox River Penitentiary. Prior to the escape, the local law enforcement response protocol called for cruisers to take the most direct route from the precinct headquarters to the prison. This had cars traveling along English and Percy, but not Fitz. In emergency drills, estimated time for travel to the prison was four minutes from the initial call. As there was no way Scofield could access this information from outside the local police department, he would have needed the prison to run a drill. He would then be able to establish which road would be safe for his escape route and what he could expect in terms of police response time. Since he couldn't just hope that the prison would run a drill when he wanted one, he needed to create an escape scenario on his own. The following incident report suggests that he arranged for just such a situation.

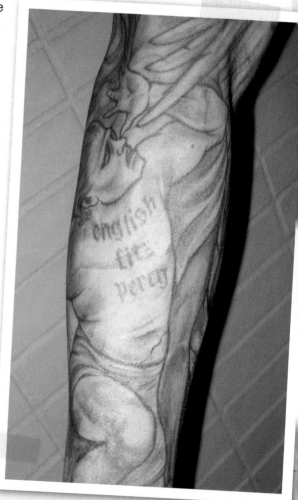

FOX RIVER INCIDENT REPORT

INMATE: Michael Scofield
INCIDENT: Escape Attempt False Alarm
REPORT PREPARED BY: Rebecca Gerber

SUMMARY OF EVENTS: At the time of 7:00 P.M. count, inmate Michael Scofield was reported missing from his cell. An escape alert was immediately issued over the walkie-talkies. C.O. Louis Patterson, who was stationed in the warden's outer office along with myself, reported that Scofield was in the warden's office working on a personal project for Warden Pope. When C.O. Patterson checked the warden's office to confirm that Scofield was still there, the C.O. did not see the inmate. This was due to the fact that, after several hours of standing while working on a project for the warden, the inmate took a seat on the floor beside a large object that obstructed the guard's view.

C.O. Patterson reported back to Captain Bellick that the prisoner was missing. The escape alarm was sounded, putting all guards on alert. While the guards gathered the dogs, a call was made to the police as per protocol. At the same time, Warden Pope was alerted to the alarm and returned to his office within minutes. At that time, the misunderstanding was resolved, and a second check of the office revealed that Scofield had been there all along. It would have been impossible to leave the warden's office without either going through the outer office past C.O. Patterson and myself or through a secondary door, which is always kept locked.

In light of what the FBI has learned about the escape, it seems clear that Scofield was able to make his way out the locked door. One possible explanation for his possessing a key comes from a minor incident that was reported in the yard several hours earlier. According to the report, an inmate, reputed to be a member of John Abruzzi's crew, got into a minor scuffle with one of the guards. It is possible that the inmate either stole or made an impression of the guard's key during the commotion. A duplicate key could have been fashioned that would open the outer door, allowing Scofield access to the roof, where he could watch for the approaching police vehicles.

Evidence Item #4: Devil Tattoo

Once Scofield was successfully through the wall of his cell and working steadily on a way into the infirmary, the next step was to find a way to link the two destination points. To do that, he began to make his way through the catwalks and access halls in the inner workings of the penitentiary, searching for the best spot to break through a wall that would give him access to the main drainage pipe for the prison's old sewage system. It was initially unclear how two men without equipment managed to accomplish this. Although Scofield and Sucre were both members of P.I., all tools were accounted for at the end of each shift. It is possible that they were able to sneak a tool out with them, but unlikely. A more probable solution was revealed during the interrogation of Manche Sanchez.

Excerpt from interview with Sanchez:

SANCHEZ: You ever heard of hookers law?

DOC INTERROGATOR: Can't say that I have.

SANCHEZ: Sucre told me about it. It's like this process where you drill a whole bunch of holes into the wall to weaken it. That makes it weak. Then all you gotta do is push your way through. Scofield had this devil tattoo that he copied onto some paper and projected on the wall with a light. Then he just drew the devil on the wall. Once they had that, they drilled holes on, like, the horns and teeth. It sounds like it took them a while to do the whole thing and Sucre and Abruzzi did most of the work.

DOC INTERROGATOR: Why was that?

SANCHEZ: 'Cause that was happening during the riot—and Scofield was off trying to get Dr. Tancredi out of the infirmary before those goons could get to her.

We suspect that Sanchez is referencing Hooke's Law of Elasticity, in which drilling holes at specific points in a wall can compromise the load carrying capacity. Professor of Engineering Nathan Schumer confirmed that if the demon image seen in the attached photo was projected at the proper size onto the wall, the points at the tip of each horn, the eyes, the end of the nose, the bottom of the fangs, and the ends of the braids would make a perfect X design that would be able to knock a considerable size hole in the wall.

Two pieces of evidence were found in the tunnels near the hole: an egg beater, showing much wear, and an Allen bolt filed to a sharp point. (This is presumably the same Allen bolt that was used to access the sink.) These two items, when combined, could have been used to create the makeshift drill necessary to burrow into the wall.

Professor Schumer concurred with Sanchez's comment that it would have been a time consuming process. The drilling needed to be carefully performed so as not to hit a gas line. Such a lengthy procedure would have been impossible to pull off because of guard rotation in the cell-block. Neither Scofield nor Sucre could be out of their cell for any extended length of time. During his interview, Sanchez let slip the phrase "to piss off the meat in concrete, turn up the heat." He seemed to realize immediately that he had said too much and shut down on that line of questioning. However, it is possible to extrapolate that, having already accessed the climate control section of the prison, Scofield then disabled the air-conditioning unit, hoping to rile up the inmates and force a lockdown. In a lockdown situation, guards do not circulate to perform the count, leaving the prisoners confined in their cells for a minimum of twenty-four hours. It is unlikely that Scofield intended for the lockdown to turn into a full-scale riot.

FOX RIVER INCIDENT REPORT

INMATE: Prisoners in A-Wing/Prisoners in B-Wing Sickbay
INCIDENT: Full-Scale Disturbance
REPORT PREPARED BY: Rebecca Gerber

SUMMARY OF EVENTS: The prison climate control unit malfunctioned, causing A-Wing to grow increasingly hot and uncomfortable for the prisoners. The inmates began to complain about the heat. In an attempt to restore order to the wing, C.O. Roy Geary had the cells opened and ordered the inmates to line up. Inmate Theodore Bagwell refused to comply, causing a minor disturbance. Bagwell encouraged other prisoners to act out as well, forcing Geary to issue a lockdown. Most of the inmates returned to their cells, except for Bagwell and about twenty other prisoners. The angry inmates advanced threateningly on officers Geary and Mack, forcing them into the guard station. Geary instructed Mack to close the cells, believing it would be easier to control two dozen prisoners than the full 300 that reside in A-Wing.

Captain Bellick was called to the guard station, where the inmates were growing increasingly agitated. They began hanging on the cage between the cellblock and the station, attempting to gain access. When the guards realized that the inmates were going to make their way into the station, Bellick ordered them to fall back to his office. From that point, surveillance cameras show the prisoners taking control of the guard station and opening up all the cells in A-Wing. As the prisoners in the wing flooded out to the common area, the inmates in the guard station discovered that C.O. Mack had dropped a set of keys in the commotion. Those keys would give the prisoners access to all of A-Wing.

Captain Bellick issued an alert, announcing that A-Wing had been breached and ordered an immediate evacuation of the area, including cutting off all access to B-Wing. Inmates in the B-Wing sickbay heard this order over C.O. Green's radio and became unruly. They subdued Green and tried to attack Dr. Sara Tancredi. The doctor managed to lock herself in the exam room, as the inmates fought to work their way in. C.O. Green was forced to report that everything was under control in sickbay when a call came in to confirm the status of the area.

Warden Pope set up a staging area in the yard outside sickbay as police were called in to assist. In accordance with protocol, Warden Pope had the water to A-Wing shut down, with the objective of making the inmates uncomfortable and forcing the situation to a peaceful conclusion. After an hour, one of the prisoners called out from a window with a list of demands. The inmate informed authorities that they had hostages, including C.O. Tyler Robert Hudson and Dr. Sara Tancredi.

Shortly after that contact was made, Governor Tancredi arrived and took control of the situation.

At 6:00 P.M. Governor Tancredi declared a state of emergency and called in the National Guard. After determining that the Warden's negotiations were not sufficient, Governor Tancredi ordered that the guardsmen be prepared to move in. Meanwhile, inside the prison, Dr. Tancredi's situation had become increasingly precarious. The doctor reports that inmate Michael Scofield came to her aid and helped her get out of B-Wing, exiting through the visitation area. As she fled the prison, a sniper fired on the prisoners chasing her. Once the doctor's safety was confirmed, the governor ordered the guardsmen to move in.

An alert was sounded as the guard troops lined up in full riot gear, preparing to enter A-Wing. The inmates scrambled as gas canisters were thrown into the area. Most of the prisoners returned to the cells, but the guardsmen were forced to subdue the rest. Within minutes, order was restored to A-Wing. In the end, two inmates died during the disturbance, several guards were injured, and C.O. Hudson was murdered by one of the prisoners. Captain Bellick has launched an investigation into the guard's death.

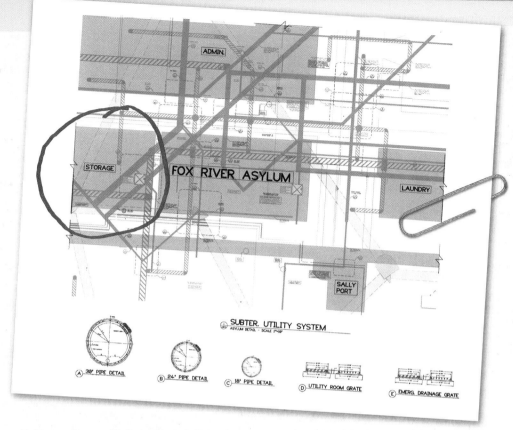

Evidence Item #5: Location: C.O. Break Room

Once Scofield had access to the tunnels, he and his cellmate had a direct line to the infirmary, the key point in the escape plan. However, that would not provide for their accomplices and, most notably, Scofield's brother, Lincoln Burrows. During DOC interviews with other prisoners in A-Wing, several inmates commented on suspicious activities and conversations that the correctional officers apparently missed. However, this could simply be a case of hindsight being twenty-twenty.

Excerpt from prisoner interviews:

CHRISTOPHER TROKEY: Yeah, we knew they was up to something. They kept talking about [expletive] "New York" and "California" and "Route 66." That's when they started spending all that time on P.I. in the [expletive] guard shed.

DEXTER JACKMAN: C-Note [Franklin] was spending too much time with Snowflake [Scofield] and them white boys. Had to be up to something. Didn't take no genius to know that.

GUS FIORELLO: 'Course I'm [expletive]! Damn Abruzzi gave me this! [Motions to eye patch covering left eye.] When I took over P.I., we were in that guard shack for hours. Never had no clue there was an escape route right under our feet.

The "guard shack" the prisoners refer to was the C.O. break room. Records recovered from Scofield's hard drive list the building as a storage facility, though clearly at some point following the prison's retrofit, the space was converted to a break room as well. It is likely that Scofield did not anticipate this change in his plan. He probably suspected that the P.I. crew could have nearly unlimited access to the storage shed, but a C.O. break room would require a new approach. Shortly after the riot, the guard shack was damaged in a small fire. An investigation revealed that an unattended cigarette, allegedly left by Captain Bellick, had been

the cause of the blaze. It is now believed that the fire was intentionally set so the inmates could have access to the room on P.I.

Once the crew was assigned to make repairs in the shack, they began widening the drain underneath the floor in the center of the room. Four feet down into the ground, the drain met with the mainline tunnel. On the night of the initial escape attempt, the P.I. crew would enter the tunnels at that point, as they could not all get access through Scofield's cell.

Evidence Item #6: Playing Cards Tattoo

The numbers on this run of cards was suspected to be a telephone number. When dialed, investigators reached a voicemail with the following message:

> *Hello, only one person has this number, so Michael, I hope you're okay. If you're getting this message then it might mean that I'm not. When this is over, you still have one more thing left to do. I'm trusting you, Michael, to do it. Be safe.*

The voice on the message matched that of Michael Scofield's wife, Nika Volek. Ms. Volek was immediately interviewed following the escape. Volek refused to explain the cryptic comment that her husband "still [has] one more thing left to do," but did provide other information valuable to the investigation, which is detailed elsewhere. Shortly after the interview, the phone number was disconnected. Though Ms. Volek was placed under surveillance, investigators have since lost track of the woman.

The circumstances surrounding the marriage of Michael and Nika are suspicious, particularly since the ceremony took place the day before Michael committed the bank robbery that led to his incarceration in Fox River. Though it is reasonable to assume that the marriage was set up at least in part to provide Nika with American citizenship, it is unclear what Scofield got out of the arrangement. Nika visited Fox River prison on three occasions, the first of which was an unsupervised conjugal visit. Shortly after that visit, Captain Brad Bellick insisted that Nika had slipped Scofield a credit card during their time together. No such card was ever found.

Excerpt from Nika Volek interview:

FBI INVESTIGATOR: Our investigators have already established that you married Michael Scofield to gain U.S. citizenship and while he was incarcerated that you brought him a credit card.

NIKA VOLEK: Neither of those things are true.

FBI: Ms. Volek, we've got Captain Bellick's statement confirming our suspicions, and if you lie to us we can press charges against you for attempting to thwart our investigation.

VOLEK: Captain Bellick? That pig came to my workplace and threatened me. He's as bad as a criminal himself. I wouldn't trust him if I were you.

FBI: So then you maintain that you married Scofield because the two of you were in love?

VOLEK: Yes. Michael is a very attractive man, with many good qualities. I was lucky to find him.

FBI: How lucky could you be? Your husband was arrested the day after your wedding.

VOLEK: It was a very unfortunate situation, but I am still happy to have him as part of my life. He is a good man. Better man than most.

FBI: If he was such a good man why did you have to sneak in contraband for him?

VOLEK: I did not—

FBI: We know you must have had some kind of arrangement. All we want to know is what Scofield got out of it.

VOLEK: I was only visiting him . . . we missed each other—

FBI: Do I really need to threaten your citizenship to get a straight answer? Did you or did you not sneak a credit card to Scofield?

VOLEK: No.

FBI: Let me put it to you this way, Ms. Volek. You could be tried as an accessory to this escape. Do you understand that?

VOLEK: Yes. And I'm telling you, I had no idea that Michael was up to such a plan.

It is unclear why Scofield would need a credit card in prison, but current belief is that the card served some other purpose. One possibility is that the item was not actually a credit card. Most of the doors in Fox River have traditional key locks, but there are several high security areas in the prison that require keycard access. An unauthorized access to Fox River's Receiving and Discharge was logged the day after Nika's first visit to the prison. A keycard was used to access the room, so no alarm sounded. At the time, it was assumed that the unauthorized entrance was a glitch in the system, but it is reasonable to assume the area was actually accessed by Scofield.

Following the escape, all of the fugitives' possessions were re-logged, but the contents of Scofield's box were missing. Interviews with prison staff revealed that it is not entirely unusual for items to go missing from Receiving and Discharge. Former C.O. Roy Geary was suspected of being the worst offender in this area. He was ultimately discharged for extort-

ing money and personal items from the prisoners. However, in this case, it is believed that Scofield was the one who accessed his personal effects packet and removed items that were integral to his escape plan.

See the attached list of Michael Scofield's personal effects. All items listed were missing from the packet.

The question then becomes, if Michael Scofield did take these items from his personal effects packet, what did he do with them? Manche Sanchez supplied the answer for investigators during the hours of interviews he underwent with the FBI and Illinois DOC following the escape. Though Scofield was reportedly tight lipped on the details of his plan, he did explain many facets of his plan to his cellmate, Fernando Sucre, once each facet had been executed. Sucre, in turn, was considerably more free with his stories, bragging about Scofield's plan to his cousin, once Sanchez was brought in on the escape. The following was Sanchez's response when investigators showed him Scofield's Receiving & Discharge paperwork.

Excerpt from Sanchez interview:

MANCHE SANCHEZ: What's this?

DOC INVESTIGATOR: A list of Michael Scofield's personal effects. They were missing at the time of the breakout.

SANCHEZ: I bet.

DOC: Do you know what happened to all of the missing items?

SANCHEZ: Scofield did. Well, except the watch. One of the bulls stole that first and Michael had to get Tweener [Apolskis] to steal it back.

RECEIVING & DISCHARGE

PERSONAL EFFECTS LIST

Items confiscated at the time of incarcerat...
will be returned upon release.

NAME: Scofield, Michael
ADMISSION DATE: April 10th

CONTENTS:
1 Suit: Black
1 Pair of Socks: Black
1 Pair of Shoes
Shoelaces
1 Small tape recorder
1 Gold watch

Michael Scofield
Inmate

T. Abromsky
R&D Officer

Inmate's signature and C.O. Countersignature confi...
that the list of contents is complete and accurate.

DOC: Guards often steal from the prisoners?

SANCHEZ: They wouldn't call it stealing, but yeah. Scofield got the rest himself. Don't know how he got into R and D, but he made off with all of those things. Did some crazy [expletive] with it too.

DOC: Such as?

SANCHEZ: Right here on the list where it says tape recorder. Scofield used his know-how to hook that thing up to the watch. Then he buried it out in the yard to record when the guards passed by so he could clock how much time he had to get out the infirmary window and across the phone cable.

DOC: So, he scheduled his escape based on the rotation of prison personnel?

SANCHEZ: Exactly. But that was before I was cut in on the escape. It was only supposed to be Scofield, Linc, Sucre, Abruzzi, C-Note [Franklin], T-Bag [Bagwell], and West- moreland that were making it over the wall. It turned out they had too many guys and not enough time. That's why Abruzzi got cut.

DOC: Scofield slit Abruzzi's throat?

SANCHEZ: He's not a killer.

DOC: So who was it then?

SANCHEZ: I might be talking but I'm no snitch.

DOC: What about the other items?

SANCHEZ: Sucre told me they had to climb a rope up this big ol' shaft under the storage room to get up to the infirmary. [Note: Inmate is referring to a twenty-foot access pipe.] Scofield sewed the rope into his suit. Then he blocked off the shaft with his suit and let the shaft fill up with water. From there, he just swam to the top and tied a rope to the grate. Then he emptied the water, and no one's the wiser.

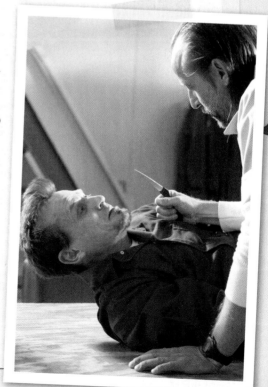

Once the rope was tied to the grate and the pipe beneath the infirmary drain had been broken through, all the prisoners needed to complete their plan was to finish digging the hole in the guard shack. Upon completion of that task, they would be able to escape. However, they ran into a major stumbling block when Burrows was placed in solitary for hitting a guard one day prior to the planned escape. As with almost every part of his plan, Scofield clearly had a contingency in place to ensure that his brother would be in position for the escape attempt. But unfortunately for the prisoners, it was simply impossible for Scofield to anticipate and plan for every moment on that night.

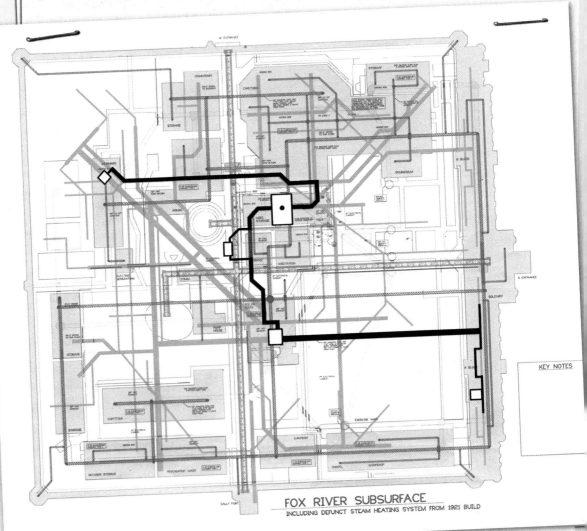

KEY NOTES

FOX RIVER SUBSURFACE
INCLUDING DEFUNCT STEAM HEATING SYSTEM FROM 1921 BUILD

Timeline of Events on the Night of the Initial Escape Attempt

The following timeline was constructed based on evidence gathered and interviews conducted with prison personnel. Most times are approximate.

4:48 P.M. The P.I. crew intentionally busts a pipe in the C.O. break room, soaking the walls and floor. Captain Bellick is prepared to send them back to A-Wing, when Scofield mentions that mold will be a concern if the room is not dried properly. Believing that he is punishing the crew, Bellick insists that they remain in the room to ensure the process is done correctly. The crew is left largely unattended for the rest of the evening.

8:20 P.M. In solitary, Lincoln Burrows reports being ill. His initial calls are thought to be made merely for attention and are ignored.

8:35 P.M. After repeated pleas for assistance, C.O. Patterson opens Lincoln's cell to find the prisoner doubled over in pain, lying beside a pool of his own vomit.

8:36 P.M. Orderlies receive an emergency summons to solitary.

8:52 P.M. It is determined that Burrows cannot be properly treated in his cell and needs to be rushed to the infirmary.

9:00 P.M. Scofield and the P.I. crew descend into the hole in the C.O. break room and begin to make their way underground to the infirmary.

Dr. Sara Tancredi, still on duty, is called to render aid to Burrows.

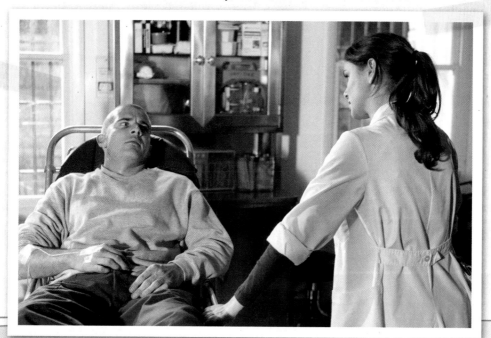

Though it is possible that Burrows was faking his illness to get himself to the infirmary, all reports indicate that he was, indeed, violently ill at the time. It is more likely that he had somehow managed to take something to induce his condition.

9:15 P.M. Perimeter guards report two African-American males experiencing car trouble in a large black SUV parked on Fitz Street. The guards help fix the vehicle and send the men on their way.

9:26 P.M. Burrows is left unattended in the infirmary. Due to the immediate nature of his emergency, guards have forgotten to handcuff him to the examination table.

9:30 P.M. All five members of the escape crew have made their way up the rope into the storage area beneath the infirmary. At that point, they would have noticed that the corroded pipe, through which they intended to access the infirmary, had been replaced that very afternoon after a janitor noticed that the metal had rusted through.

9:34 P.M. C.O. Rudy Spenser hears a noise from the storage unit. He goes to investigate and finds a broken metal tube on the floor. It is likely that the prisoners had been using the tube in an unsuccessful attempt to pry the new pipe loose. Considering the timeline, it is also likely that the prisoners were hidden in the room when the guard entered. Spenser leaves the storage room to ask C.O. Keith Stolte to join him in the storage unit.

9:35 P.M. Dr. Tancredi returns to the examination room to find Burrows has removed his I.V. and is sitting by the drain. Inmate claims that he was sick again and moved to the drain to vomit. When the guard returns, he realizes the previous oversight and handcuffs Burrows to the examination table.

9:42 P.M. Both correctional officers return to the storage room to examine the scene. Presumably, by that time the inmates would have all made their way back down the vertical drain pipe.

10:00 P.M. Captain Bellick clocks out for the evening. He notices that the lights are on in the C.O. break room and learns that no one has checked on the P.I. crew in hours. Bellick investigates and finds the door to the room jammed shut. He wrenches the door open to find the P.I. crew right where he left them. Their initial escape plan has failed.

Escape Plan: Phase 2

Lincoln Burrows was set to die in little more than twenty-four hours after the failed escape attempt. At 6:00 P.M. on the evening of May 10, Burrows was taken to Final Visitation, where he was reunited with his brother and his lawyer, Veronica Donovan. An eleventh hour appeal requesting the exhumation of Terrence Steadman's body had been refused, exhausting all avenues of legal recourse for delays. The execution was to proceed as scheduled unless Governor Tancredi stepped in. Burrows spent the next few hours with his loved ones while he picked at his last meal of blueberry pancakes.

Excerpt from C.O. Louis Patterson interview:

DOC INTERVIEWER: You were the one who prepared the
    paperwork for Burrows's execution, correct?
LOUIS PATTERSON: Yes.
DOC: Is it true that he initially didn't want a last meal?
PATTERSON: I don't think he didn't want it. He just didn't
    seem to care.
DOC: Or is it possible he thought that he wasn't going to
    be around to eat it, so why bother?

PATTERSON: I doubt it. Why couldn't he just write anything down then? Just to get rid of me. No. He knew
that requesting a last meal meant this thing was going
forward. I just don't think he was ready to deal with it.

DOC: But if he escaped, he wouldn't have to deal with it
at all.

PATTERSON: I don't think he was hanging all his hopes on
that escape plan. Linc was pretty torn up over everything. Didn't want anyone to witness the execution.
Acting out . . . hitting Geary only a day before. As cool
as that guy is, you could tell he was messed up beneath
the surface.

DOC: Sounds like you were friends with the prisoner?

PATTERSON: I didn't hate the guy. Look, most cons are
troublemakers. And, yeah, Linc could raise his share
of ruckus, but usually only when his back was to the
wall. That's why his sudden attack on Geary was such
a surprise.

DOC: So, Burrows hadn't been any trouble before that event?

PATTERSON: Oh, sure he'd been trouble. You don't get a
name like "Linc the Sink" by sitting back and taking
things. But he had never been the cause of the trouble.
He just reacts. Word is, he even did everything in his
power to keep one of our guys safe during the riots. I
have to give him props for that.

DOC: So, you don't have a problem with him being back on
the streets?

PATTERSON: Didn't say that, did I? No, he belongs in jail.
But I will admit, I don't think he deserves to be dead.

As the hour approached midnight, Burrows was walked to the execution chamber. A last-minute call from the governor's office alerted
the staff that no pardon was forthcoming. Burrows said his farewells to
Donovan and Scofield and was taken to the death chamber, where he was
strapped into the electric chair. As the clock ticked down to midnight, a
phone call came in from Judge Kessler's office with a last-minute delay.
New evidence had come to light raising further questions about Terrence
Steadman's death. The court needed to postpone the execution in order
to exhume the body of the victim.

While Burrows's legal team went back to work attempting to prove his innocence, Scofield and his crew began work on a second escape plan. With the new pipe in place, they would need to find another way to reach the infirmary, which was still the crucial exit point.

The Fox River Psychiatric Ward is the only other building that shares a subsurface line with the infirmary. Scofield's backup plan would call for the crew to go down the hole in the guards' room and travel forty yards through the pipes until they reached a grate in the ceiling. At that point they would have to go aboveground and cross the yard to the psych ward. Once inside the psych ward, there was an alternate route of tunnels that would take them to the infirmary. Unfortunately for the inmates, that was the point where the plan became truly complicated.

Evidence Item #7: Full Back Tattoo

As seen in the blueprints on page 138, the pipework beneath the Fox River asylum is a labyrinth of twists and turns. When the prison was originally built in 1858, the pipes running beneath the facility were lead. A century later, when the health risks of lead were discovered, prison administrators switched everything over to copper piping. In a cost saving measure, they left thousands of yards of lead pipes underground instead of removing them. Then, during the retrofit that Scofield helped design, the planners switched to industrial plastic for the pipes. Again, it was cheaper to lay the pipes over the old ones instead of removing them.

Without a map, it would be impossible to negotiate these serpentine catacombs beneath the prison, but Scofield was able to design just such a map into the tattoo on his back. But first, he needed to do a test run to ensure that he could get to the pipes under the psych ward before they made their escape attempt. The only problem was that the attempt would require him to be out in the yard at night without being noticed. It was at this point that Manche Sanchez was first approached for assistance.

Excerpt from interview with Manche Sanchez:

DOC: So it was at this point that you were brought in on
   the escape plan?
SANCHEZ: Nah. They were just using me because I worked
   laundry duty. Sucre needed a guard's uniform but he
   wouldn't tell me why.

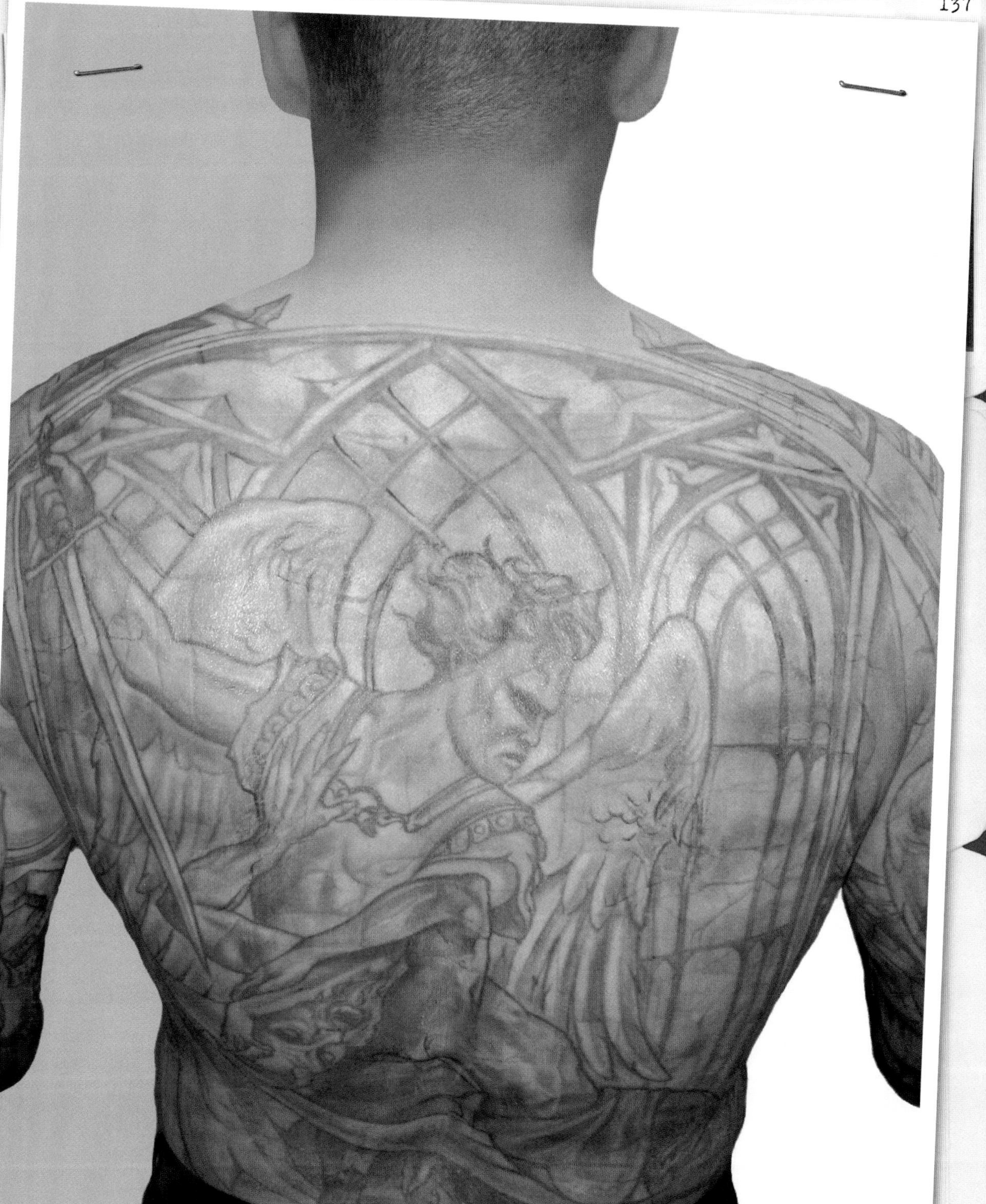

ADMIN.

STORAGE

FOX RIVER ASYLUM

LAUNDRY

SALLY PORT

SUBTER. UTILITY SYSTEM
ASYLUM DETAIL - SCALE 1"=10'

DOC: Were you able to get one?

SANCHEZ: Yeah, but it got all burned up.

DOC: How did that happen?

SANCHEZ: After they brought me in on everything, Sucre told me Scofield used the uniform to sneak into the psych ward. But he almost got caught creeping, and got himself between a steampipe and a hard place. Burned him real bad.

DOC: This was the incident that was later charged to C.O. Geary?

SANCHEZ: Geary got what was coming to him.

From what investigators can piece together, Scofield's burn was serious. The material of the guard's uniform shirt was burned right into his skin. When Sucre removed the shirt from Scofield's back, the scream that the inmate let out woke the entire cellblock and alerted the correctional officers. By the time they arrived, Scofield was unconscious. He was rushed to the infirmary, where Dr. Tancredi tended to him and found pieces of fabric embedded in the wound. When she determined that the fabric was from a guard's uniform, she reported the incident to Warden Pope. The warden immediately launched an investigation, but ran into a wall when Scofield refused to admit what had happened to him, claiming that he could not remember. The warden placed Scofield in solitary until he agreed to talk. Scofield, however, had other concerns on his mind. The burn had destroyed a portion of his tattoo. Without it, he could not negotiate his way through the pipes underneath the psychiatric ward.

Evidence Item #8: The Drawings of Charles Patoshik

During his time in solitary confinement, Scofield became nonresponsive. Lincoln Burrows, also in solitary at the time, alerted the guard to check on his brother. Dr. Tancredi was called in, and she diagnosed Scofield as suffering trauma-induced delusions with self-destructive tendencies as a result of all that he had experienced since being incarcerated. Scofield was moved to the psych ward for a brief period of time. It is likely that his goal for being committed was so he could be reunited with his former cellmate, Charles Patoshik [a.k.a. Haywire]. Among the anomalies in Patoshik's mental workup was his photographic memory. If taken off his medication, the inmate's mind was not only volatile, but incredibly systematic.

Scofield must have convinced Patoshik to re-create the tattoo that Patoshik had been so interested in when they were cellmates. Once Scofield had Patoshik's sketches of the tattoo art, he effectively had a reproduction of his original map. He was clearly unaware that Patoshik had made numerous copies of his drawings as several additional versions were found among Patoshik's possessions after the escape.

As soon as Scofield had obtained the necessary sketches, he would have wanted to be removed from the psych ward. However, that would have only landed him back in Ad Seg. Again, Manche Sanchez sheds some light on that situation.

Excerpt from interview with Manche Sanchez:

SANCHEZ: That's how I got in on the plan. Once Scofield was done in the psych ward, we had to get him out. We also had to find a way to pin that burn on someone—otherwise none of us were going anywhere. Geary was shaking down prisoners for Sucre and Scofield's cell. Takin' pay and not ponying up the prime real estate. He even took Westmoreland's watch. The crew thought he needed payback, so they pinned the crime on him. We burned one of Geary's uniforms and put it back in his locker. Worked out for everyone.

DOC: Except for Officer Geary.

SANCHEZ: Like I said, he got what he deserved.

It should be noted that Scofield refused to press charges against the C.O. At the time, he cited his reasoning as wanting to protect Warden Pope, since a corruption charge on the warden's watch would look bad on his record. But Scofield was clearly feeling some remorse. Even though Geary wasn't entirely innocent, he also wasn't guilty of the crime Scofield claimed had been commited.

Final Planning

With everything in place, the new escape route would take the crew into the second floor of the infirmary. However, to access the main examination room, and their route out of the prison, they would need a key to the door. As the room was locked and alarmed, there was no way to get in unless they had a key, or the door was left unlocked. It is believed that Scofield attempted to make a copy of the infirmary key, as Nurse Katie Wech reports that Dr. Tancredi's key was missing for a portion of the day prior to the escape. The key was recovered, but Tancredi still had the lock changed as a security measure. At that point, investigators believe that Scofield approached Dr. Tancredi and asked for her help.

Several other events were taking place as the final escape plans came together. Among the more interesting developments was the surprise return of John Abruzzi from the hospital. This ensured that the convicts would have a plane waiting for them when they got out.

One potential glitch in their plan occurred when new carpeting was scheduled to be laid down in the C.O. break room. The prisoners needed to cover up the hole they had dug to ensure that it was not found. Scofield had planned to do this by pouring a light layer of plaster into the hole that they could easily break through later. However, his plan was thwarted when he was sent to solitary confinement. Presumably, Sucre went out through the hole in their cell to do the job, as he was later found in the yard at night. He claimed that he was receiving a special gift from his girlfriend and was sent to Ad Seg as a result. But he apparently accomplished his mission, as the carpet was laid without anyone finding the hole. Once Scofield and Sucre were out of Ad Seg, the plan was set for three days hence.

Timeline of Events on the Day of the Fox River Escape

The following timeline was constructed based on evidence gathered and interviews conducted with prison personnel. Most times are approximate.

9:10 A.M. Apolskis alerts Captain Brad Bellick that Scofield's P.I. crew is planning to escape, and that the guard shack is an integral part of the plan. Bellick tears apart the C.O. break room and finds a hole in the floor under a couple inches of freshly laid plaster. Before he can report the discovery, Westmoreland enters the shack behind the captain and attacks him. A fight ensues and Westmoreland gets the upper hand, though he is critically injured in the process. He ties up Bellick and hides the guard in the tunnel beneath the break room, replacing the carpeting and placing a table over the area so no one finds the hole.

9:30 A.M. Westmoreland informs the crew that they need to push up the escape immediately. Since the extra psych ward prisoner uniforms Sanchez was going to obtain from the prison laundry will not be coming for another day, Scofield makes alternate preparations.

Noon C.O. Stolte begins to raise questions regarding Bellick's whereabouts. During lunch, the prisoners take items from the cafeteria to help disguise their scents when they return to their cells. This is done in the hopes of slowing down any pursuit by trained dogs.

1:30 P.M. During his regularly scheduled insulin shot, Scofield presumably tells Dr. Tancredi that he intends to break out that evening. He asks for her help, telling her that he needs her to leave the door to the infirmary unlocked.

2:40 P.M. Dr. Tancredi leaves the prison early and without explanation.

3:00 P.M. P.I. and yard time ends. Drops of blood are found in the P.I. locker room afterward. Scofield claims that he injured his hand, but it is more likely that the blood came from Westmoreland's still-open wound. The P.I. crew returns to their cells with their regular uniforms over their P.I. uniforms.

3:05 P.M. Scofield is taken to Warden Pope's office to finish his work on the Taj Mahal model intended to be an anniversary gift for the warden's wife. While alone in the office, Scofield removes a key component from the model.

3:35 P.M. With his work complete in Pope's office, Scofield is permitted to visit his brother in Ad Seg.

At Scofield's request, Franklin fills several plastic bags with hydrogen peroxide while on kitchen duty. He reportedly has a brief scuffle with the inmate known as Trumpet. Franklin wins the fight, though Trumpet swears his revenge. Franklin exits the kitchen with the bags of peroxide under his clothing. The individual bags are later distributed to the other escapees.

4:05 P.M. Stolte questions Apolskis, who earlier claimed to have seen Bellick that morning. Apolskis changes his story, telling the guard that he had been mistaken about the day.

It is estimated that, at the same time, the rest of the prisoners begin to bleach their uniforms with the stolen peroxide.

6:15 P.M. Warden Pope attempts to move the model Taj Mahal. As the model is being lifted, it collapses in the middle. Scofield is summoned to the warden's office to help fix the problem.

6:30 P.M. Warden Pope is alerted to the fact that Captain Bellick has not been seen all day, and did not even sign in to work that morning. A call is made to Bellick's mother, who confirms that her son did go to work that day, and called her once he arrived.

6:35 P.M. Scofield, who had been sitting in the waiting area, is shown into the warden's office. He produces a knife and takes the warden hostage.

Captain Bellick's truck is found in the parking lot. When the warden is

contacted over walkie-talkies, Scofield forces Pope to tell the guards that he heard from Bellick and lie about the captain's whereabouts. Then, Scofield ties the warden to a chair and orders him to have Burrows transferred from Ad Seg to the infirmary. Scofield gags the warden, knocks him unconscious, and hides him in the closet. Then, Scofield places a call from the warden's phone, leaving the phone off the hook. When the prisoner exits the office, he informs the warden's secretary that the warden is on a call with the DOC and does not wish to be disturbed.

6:55 P.M. Scofield returns to his cell.

7:00 P.M. Tier Time: The cells in A-Wing are opened and the prisoners are free to mingle. Abruzzi, Franklin, Bagwell, Westmoreland, Sanchez, and Apolskis make their way to Scofield and Sucre's cell with their bleached uniforms.

7:05 P.M. Scofield removes the sink assembly in his cell, and the crew begins to make their escape by going through the wall.

7:10 P.M. Captain Bellick, still in the tunnel beneath the C.O. break room, manages to remove his gag and screams for help. The prisoners find him and silence him. Scofield takes Bellick's uniform jacket and hat and separates from the group while the others put on their bleached uniforms.

Dr. Tancredi returns to Fox River.

7:20 P.M. Scofield accesses the utility box connected to the psychiatric ward. By using foot powder on the keys, he locates the oil left behind from peoples' fingerprints and begins to work out the code. He sets off the fire alarm in the psych ward, forcing an evacuation.

7:25 P.M. The alarm is determined to be false, and the psych ward inmates are returned to the building. The escapees climb up through a grate in the yard and follow the inmates into the psych ward. Scofield is still wearing Bellick's uniform jacket and hat.

Upon their entrance into the psych ward, Orderly Sklar recognizes that Apolskis's uniform—which had not been entirely bleached—is not standard issue. When he raises a question, Scofield subdues Sklar, taking the orderly's supply of emergency sedative and using it on Sklar, rendering him unconscious. As the inmates make their way to the tunnels beneath the psych ward, Scofield's former cellmate, Patoshik, sees them and follows them to the infirmary.

7:35 P.M. Dr. Tancredi exits the infirmary, leaving the door unlocked for Scofield. She has also removed a bottle of morphine. Within moments, the prisoners access the infirmary, where they find C.O. Roszkos guarding Burrows in an examination room. They force Roszkos to remove Burrows's handcuffs, then Bagwell knocks the guard unconscious. (When Roszkos woke later, he reported that his handcuffs had been stolen.)

Warden Pope's assistant, Rebecca Gerber, grows so concerned over the length of the warden's phone call that she surreptitiously picks up the extension. She hears that the open line has been connected to a pay number, Jokeline, the entire time. Gerber enters the warden's office to find that he is missing.

7:40 P.M. The prisoners discover that the main examination room door has been left unlocked. To remove the bars from the infirmary window, they tie a fire hose to the bars and attach the other end to the elevator, making sure to pad the window first to cut down on any noise. Apolskis takes the elevator down one level, pulling the bars free of the window.

Psych ward inmate Patoshik reveals himself to the team, forcing himself in on the escape plan.

7:45 P.M. The inmates make their way across the cable leading to the outer wall, beginning with Burrows and Abruzzi. When Burrows reaches the wall, he throws the discarded bleached uniforms over the razor wire to protect the escapees from injury.

Gerber alerts C.O. Stolte that the warden is missing.

7:50 P.M. Westmoreland collapses due to the loss of blood from the wound he had suffered in his altercation earlier in the day. It is now believed that he may have revealed the location of the money he stole as D.B. Cooper in his final moments, which would explain why the prisoners later converged on a spot in Tooele, Utah (see file on FBI investigation into the manhunt).

7:58 P.M. Still unable to locate Warden Pope, Gerber calls his cell phone. She and the guards hear the phone ringing in his closet. Gerber opens the closet to find Warden Pope bound and gagged inside.

Westmoreland dies.

7:59 P.M. At Pope's command, the escape alarm sounds. Scofield is making his way across the cable, with only Sanchez still in the infirmary. The metal coupling holding the cable is loosening due to the weight.

The dogs are released as the prison goes into full lockdown. Sensing the impending danger, Sanchez climbs onto the cable, while Scofield continues to make his way across. The combined weight pulls the cable from the metal coupling, sending Sanchez to the ground, while Scofield slams into the outer wall, with several feet to climb to the top.

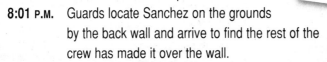

8:01 P.M. Guards locate Sanchez on the grounds by the back wall and arrive to find the rest of the crew has made it over the wall.

Westmoreland's body is found in the infirmary, along with the unconscious guard.

8:05 P.M. Captain Bellick is discovered in the tunnel beneath the C.O. break room.

8:10 P.M. Warden Pope addresses the correctional officers and local police. The official manhunt begins.

9:07 P.M. Search teams find a bloody handprint at an old mill on Fitz Street. A local resident reports seeing a blue van parked there for most of the afternoon. Smashed bits of the taillights from the van are found in the dirt. A set of footprints is discovered, heading in the opposite direction from the van's tire tracks. It is believed that one of the prisoners has split off from the group. This was most likely Patoshik, who was probably deliberately abandoned by the others.

9:15 P.M. It is determined that the door to the infirmary was not forced open. While being interviewed by Warden Pope, Nurse Katie Wech reluctantly admits that Dr. Tancredi was romantically interested in Scofield. Pope suspects that Tancredi intentionally left the infirmary door unlocked for Scofield's escape. An APB goes out to locate Tancredi, who is now considered an accessory.

9:28 P.M. A call comes in to police from Goose Field Airstrip, reporting an unidentified plane with a tail number of 986D sitting on the runway.

9:40 P.M. Search teams locate the blue van, stuck in the mud on Renwick Road, a quarter mile west of Weber Street. It is determined that the prisoners traveled on foot from that point. The dogs pick up scents leading in two different directions. Footprints show one lone prisoner splitting off from the group. Most likely, this was Apolskis.

9:42 P.M. Police receive a call from a man reporting that his daughter's bicycle was stolen, along with a child's football helmet. The thief's description matches that of Charles Patoshik.

10:05 P.M. A local farmer hears a scream coming from his barn and calls the police. Later, investigators find a large pool of blood in the barn and a dent in the hood of the man's car. They determine that another member of the team broke off from the main contingent at this time, clearly after suffering a major accident. Later witnesses in the investigation reveal that Bagwell's hand had been severed, presumably at this location, and later reattached. What motivated this violent act is still unknown.

10:22 P.M. Under an emergency warrant, Chicago police enter the residence of Sara Tancredi and find her unconscious from a morphine overdose.

10:30 P.M. Scofield, Burrows, Abruzzi, Sucre, and Franklin are seen heading toward Goose Park Airstrip as the plane that was presumably intended to be their escape vehicle takes off in the midst of increased police presence. Left on their own, the escapees flee across the field and into the night.

Official FBI Investigation into the Manhunt for the Fox River Eight

The Federal Bureau of Investigation took control of the manhunt on the morning following the escape. Special Agent Alexander Mahone launched the investigation by distributing pictures of the Fox River Eight to the press to make sure the convicts were in the national consciousness. Under different circumstances, this would have been extremely difficult, as it was only one day after the death of President Mills, and the news cycle was understandably full. However, because one of the escapees was the man convicted of killing the brother of the newly installed President Reynolds, the two stories became intertwined.

After the press was alerted, Mahone embarked on a thorough review of the inmates' records. Upon seeing photos of the intricate tattoo worn by Scofield, Mahone had the tattoo artist brought in for questioning. The artist revealed that Scofield had designed the tattoo himself and was very specific about its application. Mahone quickly made the connection that the art in the tattoo was related to items in and around Fox River Penitentiary.

A search of Scofield's home revealed no additional clues to the fugitive's plans. However, one wall was filled with holes that seemed to have been made by dozens of push pins. Mahone concluded that Scofield had made extensive plans for the escape prior to his incarceration and then designed them into the tattoo. Since Scofield's home was close to the Chicago River, Mahone ordered that the river be dredged, suspecting that it was a prime location for Scofield to have dumped the evidence. A hard drive was recovered from the river, and the serial numbers matched an order that Scofield had placed with Dell a few months before he was incarcerated. Files found on the hard drive revealed additional information important to the investigation, as detailed elsewhere. It took some time to recover all the data.

The day after the escape, it was announced that the reward for information leading to the fugitives' capture was set at $300,000 for Lincoln Burrows and $100,000 for each of the other escapees. At that time, calls to the FBI hotline reporting fugitive sightings tripled, although most of them were false leads. It is believed that bounty hunters and assorted other interested parties all over the country are currently on the lookout for the Fox River Eight, which is both an aid and a detriment to the ongoing investigation.

DAILY HOROSCOPE PAGE 17

CHICAGO HERALD

LUCKY LOTTO NUMBERS

.... $1.00

Hazy sunshine, warm and more humid. 87 / Weather: Page 40

MANHUNT FOR FOX RIVER EIGHT

SEE MANHUNT: PAGE 41

HORSE RACING SELECTIONS   PAGE 54   LAST WEEKS WINNING LOTTO

CHANGES IN BOILER HOUSE
LLEGE, LIAMSTOWN, MASS

215 H.P H.R.T BOILERS.

PRISON

PLAN AND SECTION
PLAN N°
MORE, CEDAR BINS
ARCHITECTS & ENGINEERS
PARK 36 BLDG 3 ST ...sh Av Boston
SCALE
1/8 - 1'0   DRAWING N°
COMPLETED   981-405

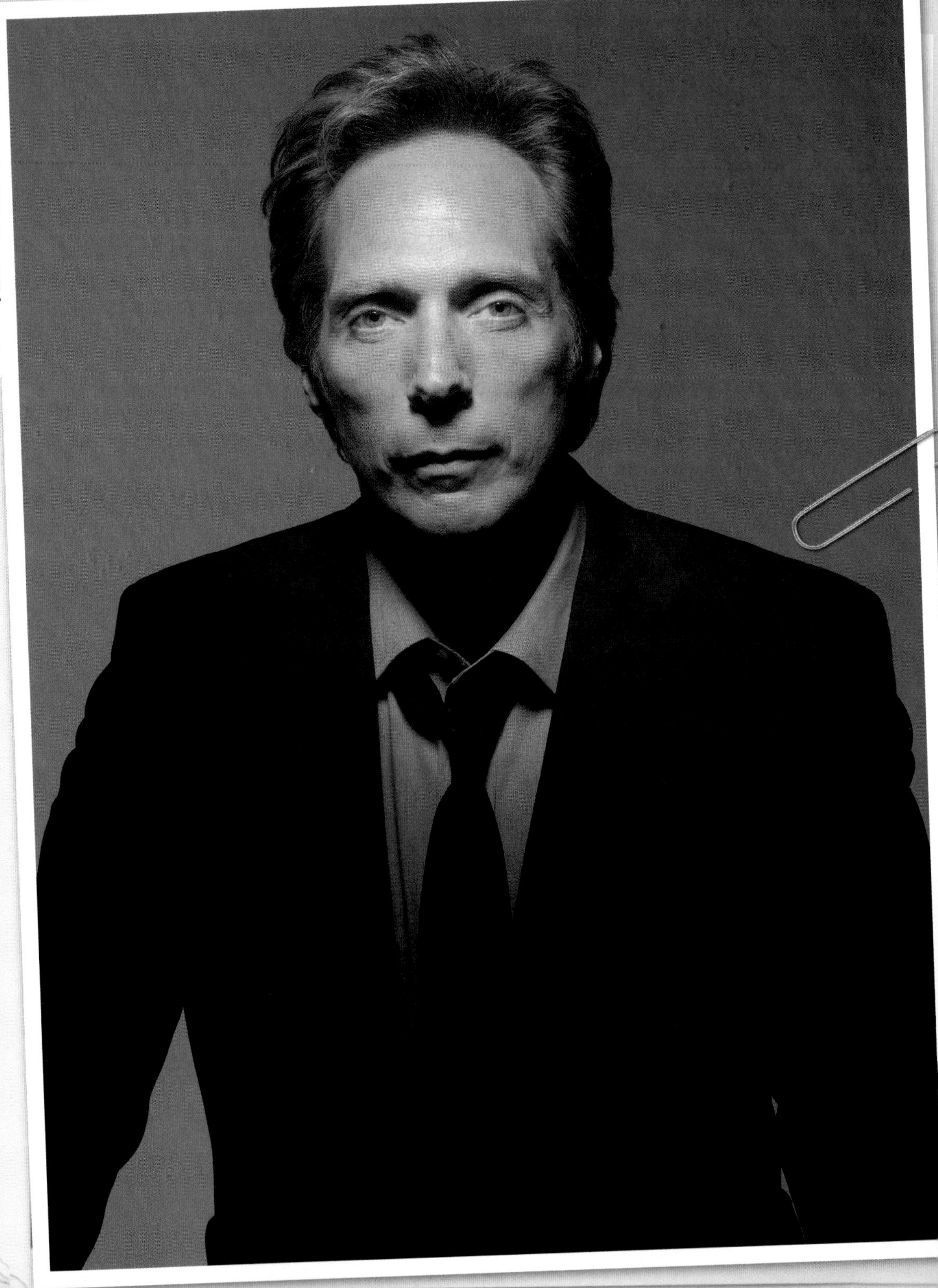

FBI FILE ON MANHUNT
LEAD INVESTIGATOR

SPECIAL AGENT ALEXANDER MAHONE

Alexander Mahone's life is a complicated one, highlighted by unanswered questions and unexpected twists. Born into a family struggling with poverty, his mother filed for divorce when Alex was a teenager. Although she cited spousal abuse in her divorce papers, her husband managed to retain sole custody of their son. A review of Mahone's pediatric medical reports leads one to suspect that he was systematically beaten for years before he joined the army as a means of escape. There, he made a surprising move from low-ranking infantry soldier with less-than-stellar marks to a member of Special Ops during the first Gulf War. Upon his discharge from the military, he was immediately accepted by the FBI.

An accomplished agent, the manhunt for the Fox River Eight is Mahone's largest investigation to date. Prior to this investigation, Mahone headed up numerous searches for criminals charged with everything from murder to crimes against the government. His most high-profile case was the still unsolved search for fugitive murderer Oscar Shales.

Mahone tracked Shales across the country as the fugitive left a trail of bodies in his wake. Many people close to Mahone felt that the agent was consumed with finding Shales. It was the only case he worked on for a solid year. It was officially marked as a cold case on June 15, when Shales went off the grid. Reports from those who know him indicate that Mahone's entire attitude changed on that day.

OSCAR SHALES

Excerpt from Pamela Mahone Interview:
(Note: This interview took place on October 31, 2004, after Pamela and Alex Mahone had divorced. It was conducted as part of Mahone's clearance for his upcoming promotion.)

FBI: During your last recorded interview for a background check on your ex-husband, you had nothing but praise for the man.

PAM MAHONE: Yes. I did.

FBI: And now? Would you still give him the same glowing recommendations?

PAM: Well . . . things are a little different now. We've since divorced.

FBI: Yes, I see that in our records. I'm sorry to hear that. Not to pry into your personal affairs too deeply, but what happened?

PAM: I wish I knew myself.

FBI: According to our records, your marriage ended shortly after the investigation into Oscar Shales went cold.

PAM: I guess that's right.

FBI: Some of Agent Mahone's coworkers have remarked that they noticed dramatic changes in his behavior and attitudes after he lost Shales's trail. Did you notice the same?

PAM: Alex devoted his life to that case. Of course he was devastated when he lost Shales. But it was more than that. It was like a switch went off somewhere inside him. He just changed on a dime. He cut himself off emotionally from both myself and Cameron, our son.

FBI: Does Mahone still see his son?

PAM: Often enough, I guess.

FBI: So you still speak to him then?

PAM: We speak every couple weeks to arrange his visitation with Cameron.

FBI: And how does his behavior seem to you? Stable? Erratic?

PAM: Well, he didn't seem stable when he told me he wanted the divorce. But he seems calmer now.

FBI: It seems natural a divorce would upset anyone.

PAM: Well, yes. He was definitely upset. He gave me almost no warning before ordering me and Cam to leave the house. But now he's gotten over it a bit. Still though, he is a changed man. Chasing that man—Oscar Shales—it turned him into a different person, a man I didn't recognize.

Since taking over the manhunt for the Fox River Eight, Mahone has alternated between moments marked with brilliance to highly suspicious behavior. Internal Affairs has already opened up an inquiry into Mahone's involvement in the deaths of John Abruzzi and David Apolskis, though certain government officials have been pressuring Internal Affairs to drop the investigation.

At the moment of what looked to be Mahone's greatest success—the capture of Burrows and Scofield—a series of inexcusable DOC oversights allowed the prisoners to escape again while en route to Fox River Penitentiary. Illinois DOC officer Captain Tuggle found Mahone in an area of the desert above the tunnel. Agent Mahone had been shot.

Mahone was rushed to a hospital in Albuquerque, where he was treated for his injuries to the collarbone and rotator cuff. While in the hospital, Mahone learned that his son, Cameron, had been struck by a car and broke his leg in two places and was currently in surgery. Mahone immediately left the hospital against doctor's orders and resumed command of the manhunt. Internal Affairs has initiated an investigation and instructed that all of Mahone's orders be cleared through their office.

WANTED BY THE FBI

FOR UNLAWFUL FLIGHT TO AVOID CONFINEMENT

Apolskis, David

Alias: Tweener

Crime: Grand Larceny

Franklin, Benjamin Miles

Alias: C-Note

Crime: Possession of stolen goods

Patoshik, Charles

Alias: Haywire

Crime: Second Degree Murder

Bagwell, Theodore

Alias: T-Bag

Crime: Six counts of Kidnapping, Rape and First Degree Murder

Burrows, Lincoln

Alias: Linc the sink

Crime: First Degree Murder, Aggravated discharge of firearm

Abruzzi, John

Alias: None

Crime: Murder, Conspiracy to commit Murder

Sucre, Fernando

Alias: None

Crime: One Count of Aggravated Robbery

Scofield, Michael

Alias: None

Crime: Armed Robbery

FOX RIVER EIGHT

Above individuals are wanted for the escape from the Illinois State Penitentiary at Fox River.

SHOULD BE CONSIDERED ARMED & DANGEROUS

If you have any information concerning these persons; Please contact your local FBI office or the nearest American Embassy or Consulate.

Director, Federal Bureau of Investigation

FBI FILE ON MANHUNT FOR THE FOX RIVER EIGHT

Reported Fugitive Sightings

Location: Will County, Illinois

Fugitives Sighted: Scofield, Burrows, Abruzzi, Sucre, and Franklin

Captain Bellick and local law enforcement were at their closest to catching five of the convicts shortly after daybreak on the morning following the escape. Dogs picked up the fugitives' scents by train tracks only a few miles west of the Goose Field Airstrip. The escapees were able to hop through the empty car of a passing train to cut themselves off from their pursuers.

Later that same day, investigators interviewed a hunter and his daughter about a sighting of the same five fugitives. When the hunter realized the identity of the men, he raised his shotgun and threatened them. In retaliation, Abruzzi produced a handgun and took the man's daughter hostage. They stole the man's shotgun and his vehicle, a 1978 Jeep Grand Cherokee, leaving him and his daughter unharmed.

The witness reported that the fugitives were heading north toward Oswego. Using Michael Scofield's credit card transaction history, Bellick learned that Scofield had spent a large sum of money in Will County before he was incarcerated. Among those purchases was a storage unit at Allen's Self Storage in Oswego. The lead turned out to be a dead end, as the space showed no signs of ever being occupied by Scofield.

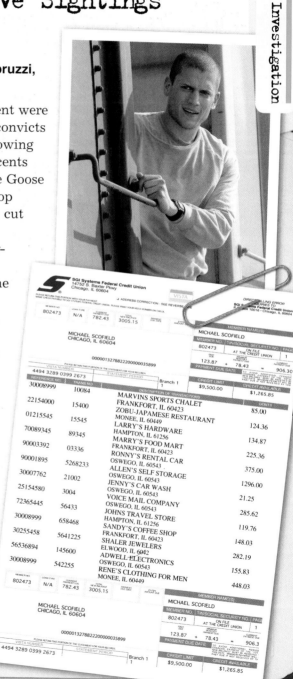

Location: Veterinary Clinic of Dr. Marvin Gudat. Will County, Illinois

Fugitive Sighted: Theodore Bagwell

Theodore Bagwell took Dr. Gudat hostage in the early morning before the clinic was open for business. Evidence shows that the doctor was forced to operate on Bagwell's hand, which had been severed the night before. It is assumed that Bagwell would not have allowed himself to be sedated for the painful operation. Since Dr. Gudat was a veterinarian and not a trained surgeon, it is likely that the reattachment did not go well.

Investigators found evidence of a struggle in the facility. Dr. Gudat was stripped to his underwear and tied to an examining table.

Bagwell injected him with a deadly dose of chemicals and left the body behind. He then stole the doctor's vehicle. Records from Autostar, the vehicle's GPS service, note that Bagwell called in asking for directions to Utah immediately following Gudat's estimated time of death.

Location: Oswego, Illinois

Fugitives Sighted: Scofield, Burrows, Abruzzi, Sucre, and Franklin

Once Special Agent Mahone made the connection between the tattoo art and Scofield's plan, he concluded that the **Ripe * Chance * Woods** tattoo held an important clue to the fugitives' plan of flight. When an internet search of those words failed to determine a location in any Illinois county, Mahone suspected that Woods was not a place, but a name. After pulling up all available census records for Will County, Mahone directed the search to the local cemetery. There, he found a recently dug grave with the epitaph: R.I.P. E. CHANCE WOODS. It is assumed that Scofield had buried supplies in the grave prior to his incarceration.

While at the cemetery, Mahone heard what he believed was the sound of convicts fleeing the area. He gave chase into town, where he lost all sign of the men. Shortly after Mahone lost them, it is believed that the five fugitives parted ways, heading off individually, except for the two brothers, Scofield and Burrows, who remained together. At this point, the investigation was formally handed off to the FBI.

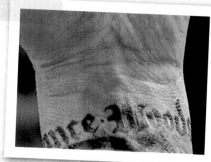

Location: St. Louis, Missouri

Fugitive Sighted: David Apolskis

A call came in at a bus station in St. Louis, reporting a possible sighting of David Apolskis. The caller said that the man matching Apolskis's description was attempting to buy a ticket to Utah. Apolskis quickly left the station without a ticket after learning that the bus was not scheduled to depart until the next day. Police were dispatched to the location, but the suspect had already fled the area. While police were at the station, a man named Scott Kolbrenner reported his wallet missing. Considering that Apolskis was an accomplished pickpocket, it is likely the events are connected.

Location: Orson's Hardware. Chicago, Illinois

Fugitives Sighted: Scofield and Burrows

A local resident flagged down police to report seeing Lincoln Burrows standing outside the hardware store near the corner of Hancock Street and 15th Street. Burrows then entered the store and met up with his brother, who had an armload of purchases. Police entered the premises, but the brothers exited through the back and escaped.

Location: Cook County Courthouse. Chicago, Illinois

Fugitives Sighted: Scofield and Burrows

L.J. Burrows was scheduled to appear at a hearing at the Cook County Courthouse at 3:00 P.M. in the afternoon. Prior to the hearing, a call was logged from one of L.J.'s attorneys. Using Nick Savrinn's bar number, Burrows posed as Savrinn over the phone to pass a message to his son. (The call was recorded and Burrows's voice was matched to the caller's. Nick Savrinn had been found dead in his apartment an hour before the call was made.)

Transcript of the call between Lincoln and L.J. Burrows:

L.J. BURROWS: Hello?

LINCOLN BURROWS: Know who this is?

L.J.: Yeah. Yeah. Nick Savrinn.

LINCOLN: How you holding up?

L.J.: Doing what I can do. How about you?

LINCOLN: I'm worried about you. Sorry about what you're going through.

L.J.: Thanks. Word is after this hearing, cause of my dad being so high-profile, they're shipping me to an adult facility in Kingman, Arizona.

LINCOLN: Yeah, well, hopefully that ain't gonna happen.

L.J.: You hear from Veronica [Donovan] today? She didn't show up. They gave me some court appointed clown.

LINCOLN: No. I haven't heard from her.

L.J.: Hey, this, uh, this Fed came by and talked to me today.

LINCOLN: Yeah?

L.J.: He wanted me to help try and get my dad to turn himself in.

LINCOLN: Well, knowing your dad, I doubt that's gonna happen. Listen up, L.J., this is real important.

L.J.: All right.

LINCOLN: On the third, look out for Otis Wright. Got that? On the third, look out for Otis Wright. Until then, keep your head up.

L.J.: What?

LINCOLN: Just remember that. I'm gonna do everything I can to get you out.

L.J.: Hey, Nick. If you talk to my dad, tell him, no matter what, I love him.

Special Agent Mahone questioned L.J. about the call, but the boy claimed not to know any Otis Wright. Later, as L.J. was being escorted through the building, he stopped to tie his shoes at the elevator on the third floor, causing them to miss the first available car, the car on the left. Once the elevator car had bypassed the floor, the elevator on the right opened. Mahone noticed that the elevator bore a sign from Otis Engineering and made the connection that something would happen in "Otis, right." He offered to escort L.J. into the elevator, dismissing the police officer.

Within moments, the elevator access hatch slid open, revealing L.J.'s father and uncle. Burrows pointed a gun at Mahone and instructed L.J. to press the elevator stop button. Once that was done, Scofield told L.J. to hand him Mahone's gun while Burrows put his own weapon down. While Scofield covered Mahone, Burrows attempted to lift L.J. through the access hatch.

During the attempt, Burrows's gun fell, and Mahone grabbed on to L.J. to keep the boy from escaping. When Scofield refused to shoot the agent, Mahone managed to restart the elevator. Burrows was forced to let go of his son to ensure his own escape.

Officers spotted Scofield and Burrows outside the courthouse and gave chase, firing several shots. The fugitives hopped into an idling delivery truck and escaped with Scofield behind the wheel. The truck was later recovered several miles away. Blood was found on the passenger's side of the truck, indicating that Burrows had been shot. Mahone instructed that all the hospitals in the area be notified to keep an eye out for the fugitives. At that point, Burrows went off the grid for several hours.

Location: Brewster's Towing

Fugitive Sighted: Michael Scofield

Local police brought in a vagrant who was carrying a backpack that had belonged to Scofield. Assorted items were found in the pack, including money, a cell phone, calling cards, and passports showing Scofield as Phineas McClintock and Burrows as Archie Ryan. The vagrant admitted to stealing the bag from a gray Honda Accord that had been parked near the corner of Hancock Street and 15th Street. The vagrant explained that he had no time to get anything else from the car because a tow truck arrived to pick up the Accord, which had been parked at an expired meter.

Local police confirmed that Brewster's Towing held the city contract for impounds and would have been the first lot notified to pick up the vehicle. Mahone called the tow yard to inquire about a car matching the description and the employee, Chuck, confirmed that a person had come in and that he was on the premises at that moment. During the call, Scofield grew suspicious and grabbed his keys. He fled the lot in the car while the police units were still minutes away.

Location: Downtown Chicago, Illinois

Fugitive Sighted: Benjamin Miles Franklin

While phones were being monitored at the family homes of all the escaped convicts, Franklin was recorded contacting his wife, Kacee. The call originated from a pay phone in downtown Chicago. During the call, Franklin tried to set up a meeting with his wife in the following exchange:

> BENJAMIN: In the rainbow room. Do you remember that beautiful spot where we took that picture? The one by the window?
> KACEE: Um-hum.
> BENJAMIN: I am going to be waiting in that spot one week from now. And that's all that I want in this whole world is for my two girls to be waiting there for me. Do you understand what I'm saying?

Kacee ended the phone call without indicating whether or not she would meet her husband. As a precaution, Franklin's photo was sent to the NYPD and to employees at the Rainbow Room restaurant in Rockefeller Center. Special Agent Lang interrogated Kacee in an attempt to determine the meaning of the cryptic message. When Kacee refused to provide any information, Lang ordered extra surveillance on her and her daughter over the coming week.

Location: Defiance, Ohio and Latrobe, Pennsylvania

Fugitive Sighted: Fernando Sucre

A call came in from a witness in Defiance claiming that he saw Fernando Sucre stealing a car. Shortly afterward, a motorcycle officer in Latrobe stopped Sucre for having expired tags, unaware at first that Sucre was a fugitive and the car was stolen. Sucre claimed to have lost his wallet, but he pulled the registration from the glove compartment, which belonged to a Mrs. Miller. This raised a red flag with the officer and prodded him to recognize Sucre as one of the Fox River Eight. When the officer went to call in the car, he reported that he had identified Sucre and requested backup. While the officer was confirming the details, Sucre slipped out of the car unnoticed and disappeared.

Location: Route 38 North, 12 miles past the turnoff from the interstate. Illinois

Fugitives Sighted: Scofield and Burrows

The FBI surveillance station intercepted a call to a voicemail number that Scofield had purchased before he left for prison. Scofield left a message for an unknown individual and cited a phone number. Investigators noted that the number Scofield indicated had a cell phone prefix. Once the FBI had that number, they were able to track the cell phone in question as long as it was still on.

The cell phone signal stopped moving at Route 38 North, 12 miles past the turnoff from the interstate. When Agent Mahone arrived at the location, he saw that Scofield's car had crashed through a bridge and into the dry riverbed below, where it had exploded. Charred human remains were found inside the vehicle, believed to be the bodies of Scofield and Burrows. Initial tests showed that blood found in the vehicle was B-negative, matching the brothers'

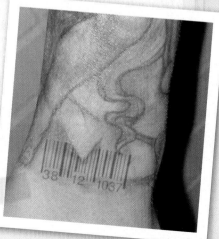

blood types. Special Agent Lang was prepared to alert the media, but Mahone stopped her. He was concerned that the other fugitives would become more vigilant if they learned their friends had died. He insisted that it was not FBI policy to announce deaths until they were confirmed.

Tests later determined that the body parts did not belong to Scofield or Burrows, and the blood had been taken from a pig. A forensic examination of the car revealed that an explosive device was linked to the radio. When the radio reached station **103.7**, the bomb exploded. It was not determined until hours later that these numbers matched the bar code tattoo on Scofield's wrist.

Location: Friend, Nebraska

Fugitive Sighted: Theodore Bagwell

Police found the SUV stolen from Dr. Marvin Gudat at a gas station in Friend, Nebraska. When Bagwell exited the lavatory, he found police waiting around the SUV. When questioned, Bagwell claimed that his name was Clyde May and spun an intricate story about being a wandering war veteran whose hand had been injured in battle. He said that he was not the owner of the SUV, but he had seen a young man who was still in the lavatory pull up in the vehicle. When that man exited the lavatory, he denied being the driver of the SUV, but the police found the keys in his knapsack. It is now believed that the keys had been planted there by Bagwell.

Bagwell had left the gas station on foot when Jerry Curtin, another patron of the gas station picked him up after being impressed with Bagwell's story of serving in the marines. Curtin, and his fourteen-year-old daughter, Danielle, agreed to help Bagwell get to Utah.

Citing a history of back problems, Curtin stopped late in the afternoon so they could rest for the night in a hotel en route to Utah. The Good Samaritan even paid for Bagwell's room. While Curtin relaxed, Bagwell sat out by the pool with Danielle. Their friendly conversation turned uncomfortable for the girl, and she ran to her father for help when Bagwell got a little too close. Her father told her to wait outside while he dealt with the matter. Bagwell, noted for his history of violence, turned the tables and beat the man badly. Bagwell then stole the their car and escaped, heading west on I-80.

Excerpt from Danielle Curtin interview:

FBI INVESTIGATOR: Danielle, I just want to make sure we've got some of our facts right, okay?

DANIELLE CURTIN: Okay.

FBI: Your father picked up Mr. Bagwell hitchhiking along the road?

DANIELLE: Yeah. We had seen him at the gas station. He was talking to some cops about when he was in the war. My dad always helps people from the war.

FBI: I see. And how did Mr. Bagwell and your father end up in a fight?

DANIELLE: Well, Daddy had decided to stop for the night. He was tired and his back needed rest. I was reading my magazine by the pool of the motel we were stayin' at, and Mr. Bagwell sat next to me. At first he was just talking to me, but then he put his arm around me, and I really didn't like it. So I ran and told my dad.

FBI: And then what happened?

DANIELLE: Mr. Bagwell followed me into our motel room saying he didn't touch me. He was lying, but my dad didn't believe him anyway.

FBI: What happened next?

DANIELLE: My dad told me to leave so he could talk to Mr. Bagwell.

FBI: And you went outside?

DANIELLE: Yeah. I waited outside for my dad to come. But he never did. As I was sitting there, I saw Bagwell drive away in our car.

FBI: What did you do?

DANIELLE: I ran back inside. And that's where I found my dad. He was lying on the carpet and bleeding.

City

Informant key in prosecutor's case against Abruzzi

The Press Association

In the end, it was one of mob boss John Abruzzi's best friends that proved to be his undoing. The informant, who agreed to assist the state in its prosecution against Abruzzi in exchange for immunity, provided crucial information into the workings of the mob boss' empire of organized crime. What emerged was a clear picture of Abruzzi's involvement in almost a decade's worth of extortion and other crimes against competing teamster unions, more than two dozen Chicago-area businessmen, as well as the mob boss' complicity in a nationwide internet fraud scheme as well as money laundering activities in offshore banks as widespread in location as Bermuda and Belize.

Brut in this case is the court-protected witness said to be part of Abruzzi's 'extreme inner circle' that proved to be the crucial piece in the government's case in the mob boss' extortion and racketeering trial. The witness, granted immunity in exchange for his testimony and whose identity is currently shielded by the Witness Protection Program provided what prosecutors said was the 'not just the smoking gun, but rather the smoking armory': a veritable treasure trove of information linking the Newark business man to a series ofintimidation crimes that have spanned the last decade.

Location: Globe Motel, Washington, D.C.
Fugitive Sighted: John Abruzzi

Among the initial information pulled off Scofield's hard drive was an article on John Abruzzi and his ties to mob informant Otto Fibonacci. Mahone extrapolated that Scofield used Fibonacci as a bargaining chip with Abruzzi and thought the FBI could now do the same. Assuming that Abruzzi would want revenge on the man whose testimony had led to his arrest, Mahone had it leaked that Fibonacci was in D.C. waiting to testify before a congressional hearing. The leak went through a New Jersey mob boss being held on a RICO charge.

Abruzzi took the bait, driving to D.C. with one of his lieutenants to exact his vengeance. Instead, he was heading for a trap laid by the FBI. Abruzzi's man called ahead and arranged for the motel manager to unlock the door to the room that was supposed to belong to Fibonacci. Once there, Abruzzi entered the room with his

gun drawn, but found it empty. FBI agents then converged on the parking lot outside the room, instructing Abruzzi to come out unarmed. He did come out, but with his gun in hand. Mahone asked him a second time to drop the weapon. As Abruzzi raised his gun, agents fired multiple shots, killing him.

Questions were immediately raised by Mahone's superiors as to why Mahone did not corner Abruzzi before he entered the motel room. The way Mahone played the collar, Abruzzi's death was the only way the scenario could have played out. Mahone continues to defend his actions.

Location: Lotus Motel. Utah

Fugitive Sighted: David Apolskis

Apolskis reportedly picked up a ride in St. Louis from a Debra Jean Belle. The college student was heading home to Utah and had been looking for someone to share the trip with her. While the pair was stopped in Mack, Colorado, police received several calls from residents claiming they had seen Apolskis in the area. Police went door-to-door in the neighborhood with a photo of the escaped convict. Debra Jean Belle answered the motel room door and when presented with a photo of Apolskis, claimed she had never seen him before. It is now assumed that the pair had developed a relationship during their time together and that Belle was covering for him.

Belle later told authorities that after the police left, she went for a walk. An hour after returning from that walk, she reported her car had been stolen, although she could not explain why it took her so long to report it. The car was later located in Utah with the word ALOHA written in the dust on the window.

Location: Train traveling southwest through Green River,
　　Wyoming to Preston, Idaho

Fugitive Sighted: Benjamin Miles Franklin

Franklin hopped a train heading toward Utah without a valid ticket. He gave the conductor the half ticket that he had, presenting a false story that the other half had ripped away. The conductor accepted the ticket but then proceeded to check out Franklin's story.

On the way to Utah, Franklin asked the woman beside him if he could check his email on her computer, using the train's wireless internet. A later search of the woman's computer revealed that he had accessed the U.S. Army Signal Corps site search, locating the GPS coordinates for the "K K Ranch" in Tooele, Utah (circa 1971).

The conductor then returned to inform Franklin that his story had not checked out and that he had alerted local police, who would be waiting at the next stop. As train security moved in to secure Franklin, the fugitive took off in the opposite direction. Realizing he had nowhere to run, he jumped from the train as it went over a bridge. Franklin dropped into the river below, disappeared, and was not sighted again until Tooele, Utah.

Location: Las Vegas, Nevada

Fugitive Sighted: Fernando Sucre

A call came in from Hector Avila reporting that Fernando Sucre had shown up at Avila's Las Vegas wedding to Maricruz Delgado. Theresa Delgado, Maricruz's sister, had been the first to speak with Sucre. The fugitive had arrived to stop the marriage, but failing that, he at least wanted to speak with his former fiancée. But before Theresa could alert her sister, Avila immediately called the police and attempted to delay Sucre himself.

When Sucre heard the police sirens, he punched Avila and took off on a motorcycle before authorities arrived at the church. Following the incident, Maricruz reportedly cancelled her wedding. She was kept under surveillance as she returned home to New York. Shortly after her return home, Maricruz and her sister left the country, taking the honeymoon trip to Belize that Maricruz had originally intended to take with Avila.

An hour after being sighted in Las Vegas, a gas station attendant in Mesquite, Nevada, reported a man matching Sucre's description heading north to the Nevada/Utah border.

Location: Cedar Grove, Wisconsin

Fugitive Sighted: Charles Patoshik

Employees at a local Dairy Gnome found a man matching Patoshik's description on the premises when they opened for work. The kitchen had been rifled through as the escaped convict went on a binge that suggested he had not eaten in some time. This was the first confirmed sighting of Patoshik since he stole a child's bicycle on the night of the escape. Mahone turned the case over to local police, as he wanted his office to focus on a Utah location where the other fugitives seemed to be gathering.

Police later received a call from the home of Eugenia Campbell. The blind woman reported that an intruder had been in her home, posing as her grandson, Billy. While there, he showered and ate, then took some clothes and an oil painting valued at ten dollars. He left the woman unharmed. Police found Patoshik's prison uniform discarded on the premises.

Location: Tooele, Utah

Fugitives Sited: Scofield, Burrows, Bagwell, Apolskis, Sucre, and Franklin

FBI technicians working on Scofield's hard drive were able to restore sixty percent of the contents. The information seemed random at first, but Mahone was able to piece together clues that suggested the inmates were heading to retrieve the ransom money stolen by famed hijacker D.B. Cooper. This seemed to concur with the fact that fugitive sightings indicated most of the surviving members of the group were indeed converging on a spot in Utah.

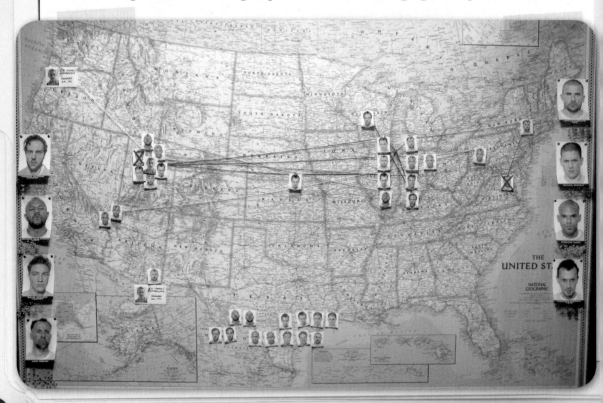

Scofield and Burrows were believed to have been in the tax assessor's office in the municipal building in Tooele, Utah. The assessor thought he recognized the fugitives and went to get a nearby officer to confirm the sighting. When the assessor returned, Scofield was gone. Without corroboration, the assessor doubted the identification and did not report the incident further. A later examination of the book Scofield had been looking at revealed the map on page 1213 had been torn out. But Scofield wasn't the only one interested in that map. Though it wasn't reconciled at the time, only minutes earlier, a man matching Theodore Bagwell's description had been looking at the same book.

The map they had been interested in was for a local property formerly owned by Karl Kokosing. The ranch had been sold several years ago to Briarcliff Land Developers, and a new housing subdivision had been built over it. A section of that page was later found in a car driven by David Apolskis. In a follow-up investigation, agents located a copy of the map in the files of Briarcliff Land Developers.

On that same day Apolskis entered Wood's Garden Center looking for shovels. The proprietor, known as "Woody," recognized the fugitive from police reports. He pulled out a bat and attacked Apolskis, knocking the young man to the floor. Once the escaped convict was incapacitated, Woody began to tie him up. At that point, Scofield and Burrows entered, pulling a gun on Woody. They bound and gagged him and locked him in the back of the store.

When the fugitives went to find the ranch from the map, it is assumed that they were surprised to find a recently constructed housing subdivision in its place. At this point it is clear they thought that, even though the ranch was gone, the money could still be buried under one of the houses in the development. It was simply a matter of determining which one.

Meanwhile, Agent Mahone flew to Utah, where he reviewed the D.B. Cooper files in the Salt Lake City field headquarters. The file indicated that a gas station employee named Harold Jenkins is the person listed as having the only "D.B. Cooper money" ever in circulation. Cooper had bought gas from Jenkins using a hundred-dollar bill. The serial numbers matched up with the numbers listed in the ransom money. Mahone tracked down Jenkins to question him

about his run-in with Cooper. Jenkins was able to clarify what was initially believed to be a discrepancy in the witness's original statement. According to the file, Cooper had been reported as having filled up his car's gas tank at the station in American Fork City, Utah, either at 7:00 A.M. or 7:00 P.M. Jenkins clarified that Cooper had actually filled the tank twice, at both times.

At the time of the hijacking, D.B. Cooper did not have a car registered in his name, but Charles Westmoreland owned a 1965 Chevy Nova. Taking into consideration that the car had a sixteen-gallon gas tank, Mahone extrapolated that a car that size, at the average of eight miles to the gallon, could have covered about 128 miles on that tank of gas. Taking the return trip into consideration meant that there was a sixty-four-mile radius from American Fork in which authorities could focus their search for Cooper's money, and the fugitives.

While the fugitives convened at the dig site in Tooele, Apolskis went alone into town to gather supplies, returning to Wood's Garden Center. While Apolskis was in the shop, Woody's friend Chet Bingham came looking for him. Chet entered the seemingly empty store, and saw a baseball bat lying on the floor. He immediately placed a call to Sheriff Williams, but Apolskis hit him with a shovel, knocking him out before the call could connect. Apolskis tied up the second victim and hid Chet in the back with Woody. Apolskis then returned to the dig site with the supplies.

Once they had what they needed, the fugitives approached the home of Jeanette Owens, at 1131 Monterey Lane, claiming to be electrical workers from a private electronics and diagnostic company. Scofield explained to

Owens that they needed to perform a systems diagnostic because her electrical line had been corrupted. This would require them to dig up the electrical line in the garage, but he promised they would fill the hole before they left. The homeowner was initially suspicious, but she did allow them the access they needed. The fugitives entered the garage and began digging to find the foundation of the K K Ranch's silo.

Jeanette Owens later entered her garage to find the original group had added Franklin and Sucre as well. She found this suspicious, but Bagwell escorted her out of the garage, claiming that he was a supervisor, and then kept her occupied with flirtatious conversation while the others tore up the garage floor. They quickly found the foundation of what used to be the ranch's silo and began excavating in search of the money. At that point, Apolskis realized that he had forgotten to gas up their escape car's tank and was sent back into town.

At the same time, Mahone was in Tooele, meeting with Sheriff Williams. Mahone was drawn to the town after seeing a report that listed two of the town residents—Woody and Chet—as missing. The sheriff explained that he didn't suspect foul play since these men often took off in the middle of the day without explanation. Mahone insisted they search Wood's Garden Center. They found the door locked, but Mahone saw signs of a struggle inside. He smashed through the window to unlock the door and entered the premises. Inside they found the two missing men tied up in a back room. Woody told Mahone that the escaped convicts were in Tooele. Picks, shovels, and other digging materials were also missing from the store, confirming Agent Mahone's suspicions that the fugitives were in the area attempting to dig up D.B. Cooper's money.

Soon after, a local gas station attendant recognized Apolskis and reported him to police. Apolskis grew suspicious and bolted from the station, but was apprehended by Mahone. He initially refused to talk, but after Mahone spoke with the young man privately, Apolskis agreed to take investigators to the house where the other fugitives were digging for the money. Apolskis said that there was a hostage in the house and suggested that he should go to the door himself to ensure no one was hurt. Mahone agreed with this tactic.

Meanwhile, at the Owens Residence, Michael Scofield accidentally barged in on Jeanette in her second floor bedroom while she was changing. Most likely Scofield was checking on Bagwell and panicked when he saw broken glass on the floor of the dining room. Jeanette immediately ordered the crew out of her house. At that time, Jeanette's daughter, Anne, a police officer, came home to check on her mother. She too was suspicious of the broken glass in the dining room. While searching the house, she heard her mother's muffled shout on the second floor and found Scofield and Bagwell holding her mother against her will in her bedroom. Bagwell had a claw-ended hammer against Jeanette's throat. Officer Owens raised her gun and ordered them to put their hands up, unaware that the other fugitives were in the house. Hearing footsteps behind her, the officer turned and aimed her gun at Sucre, but Burrows subdued her and took her weapon.

Though reportedly most of the fugitives were wary about taking hostages, the Owens women were nonetheless tied to chairs in the dining room. Sucre was charged with watching the women while the other fugitives returned to the garage to continue digging for the money. Officer Owens attempted to engage Sucre in conversation, trying to bond with the man in hopes that she and her mother could find a way out of their predicament.

The men had the TV on in the garage, and Burrows reportedly split from the group at around the same time it was announced in the media that his son, L.J., was being released from prison. He stole Jeanette's car, although he promised to repay her twice what the vehicle was worth. Scofield was clearly reluctant to let Burrows leave, but he soon had other concerns to worry about. A call came in on Anne's radio that Apolskis was in custody.

Apolskis directed investigators to what was thought to be the Owens's house, and he approached the front door alone. He rang the bell, and agents watched as a college-aged woman opened the door. Upon hearing the conversation that ensued, Mahone immediately realized they were at the wrong house. The woman at the door was Debra Jean Belle, the student Apolskis had hitched a ride with in St. Louis. As agents converged on the prisoner, Apolskis was heard telling Belle that he intended to write to her from prison, and asking her if she would write back.

In a move that was clearly against protocol, Mahone drove back to headquarters alone with Apolskis. During transport, Mahone reports that Apolskis managed to get a hold of the agent's primary weapon and forced Mahone to pull over. The men got out of the car, but Mahone pulled his secondary weapon and shot and killed the prisoner, in an act of self-defense.

At the Owens house, a neighbor had arrived to pick up Jeanette for an afternoon appointment. Scofield turned away the suspicious neighbor, telling him that Jeanette had already left. Scofield returned to the garage, and soon after, the hostages heard a gunshot, although none of the men appeared to have been injured. Sucre then left the house alone, carrying a large backpack. This seemed to upset the other fugitives. The other three men then left also, but Scofield first handed Jeanette a knife so she could work on severing the ropes that bound her. Before she could get free, Bagwell returned and took a second backpack from the premises. He slipped a hundred-dollar bill into Jeanette's brassiere and said it was to cover the damages. Around the time the fugitives were departing, a call came in from neighbors reporting the gunshot. Police were dispatched to the house, where they found Officer Owens and her mother still bound.

Dogs picked up multiple scents at the scene, and the police split up to follow the different fugitives' trails. Later, two of the trails merged, leading police to a motorcycle that had been abandoned in the woods by the river. The bike was attached to a rope that had been thrown over a branch and tied to a log mired in the river. It is possible that one of the prisoners had been trapped under the log and someone used the bike to pull it off him. Although the fugitives were suspected of being only minutes ahead of their pursuers, they managed to elude capture.

Location: Algoma, Wisconsin

Fugitive Sighted: Charles Patoshik

A camping goods storeowner reported Charles Patoshik stealing numerous items from his store, including camping equipment and foodstuffs. When the proprietor attempted to question the fugitive, Patoshik fled with everything he could carry. The owner let his dog loose to give chase, but the dog did not return. Patoshik was last seen by a passing camper on the beach along Lake Michigan with the dog. According to the camper it appeared that Patoshik was trying to build a raft out of driftwood.

Location: Kingman, Arizona

Fugitive Sighted: Lincoln Burrows

Police report that, upon L.J. Burrows's release from the Klipton Detention Center, a local vagrant attacked the boy without provocation. An anonymous call came into 911 reporting the incident. A subsequent review of the 911 tape revealed that the caller had been Lincoln Burrows.

Transcript of Burrows's 911 call:

911 OPERATOR: Kingman 911.
CALLER: I'd like to report an incident. Some guy's attacking a kid near Park and 4th. It looks like the man is on drugs or something. Send the cops. Fast.
911 OPERATOR: Can you give me a description of the attacker?
CALLER DISCONNECTS.

L.J. was taken to a local hospital where the police interviewed both L.J. and his attacker. The vagrant claimed that a man had paid him to attack the boy. At the same time, a pair of federal agents entered the hospital, inquiring about L.J. Upon hearing the vagrant's story, they realized that Burrows had paid the man to attack his son. That way, Burrows could make contact in the hospital without risking being caught by the street surveillance team. They ran to the examination room where the boy had been receiving stitches, but L.J. was already gone, and his father presumably with him.

Location: Blanding Botanical Gardens. Blanding, Utah

Fugitive Sighted: Michael Scofield

FBI agents managed to get ahead of Scofield at one point by searching his tattoo design for more clues. An image of the **Apache Desert Ghost**, a rare tropical flower, led investigators to the Blanding Botanical Gardens in Utah. Wearing a volunteer's vest, Scofield entered the gardens through the personnel area. While in the garden, Scofield saw the agents waiting for him, turned, and fled into a maze of shrubbery. He managed to climb out of the maze and off the property to evade capture, but without achieving his objective.

Agents found 3,200 nitroglycerin ampules buried in the section of the gardens housing the Apache Desert Ghost. All of it was medical grade, which is appropriate in small doses and safely used on patients with heart irregularities all the time. However, the amount Scofield collected as a whole, could have been used to take out an entire building.

Video cameras at a copy store in nearby Moab, Utah, later picked up Scofield using the internet on one of their computers. A review of the computer history showed he was researching sites related to Special Agent Alexander Mahone.

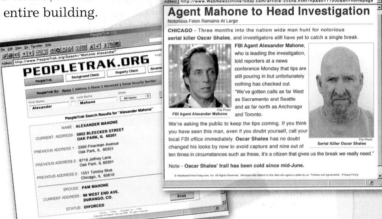

Agent Mahone to Head Investigation

Notorious Felon Remains At Large

CHICAGO — Three months into the nation wide man hunt for notorious serial killer Oscar Shales, and investigators still have yet to catch a single break.

FBI Agent Alexander Mahone, who is leading the investigation, told reporters at a news conference Monday that tips are still pouring in but unfortunately nothing has checked out.

"We've gotten calls as far West as Sacramento and Seattle and as far north as Anchorage and Toronto.

We're asking the public to keep the tips coming. If you think you have seen this man, even if you doubt yourself, call your local FBI office immediately. Oscar Shales has no doubt changed his looks by now to avoid capture and nine out of ten times in circumstances such as these, it's a citizen that gives us the break we really need."

Note - Oscar Shales' trail has been cold since mid-June.

Location: St. David, Arizona

Fugitive Sighted: Lincoln Burrows

L.J. Burrows purchased a meal for himself and his father at a roadside diner, but returned to the car without his change. When the waitress went out to the car to deliver his money, she recognized Burrows in the driver's seat. Realizing he had been spotted, Burrows peeled out of the parking lot while the waitress called the police. Mahone ordered a road team out to the location immediately to confirm the sighting.

Location: Fairgrounds Carnival. Chicago, Illinois

Fugitive Sighted: Benjamin Miles Franklin

On the day that Kacee Franklin was scheduled to meet her husband in the "rainbow room," surveillance revealed that Kacee did not appear to be heading to New York any time soon. It was assumed the rainbow room clue had a different meaning. Agent Lang approached Kacee and reminded the woman that if she was caught helping her husband, not only could she go to jail as an accessory, she could also lose custody of her child. Kacee finally admitted that the "rainbow room" was a reference to her daughter Dede's bedroom because of the rainbow painted on the wall. Her husband had been referring to the location where they had taken a photo that hung on the wall in Dede's room: the Fairgrounds Carnival Arcade. Under duress, Kacee took the agents with her to the arcade to wait for Franklin.

While Kacee waited and surveillance kept watch in a van nearby, an unknown man approached her and said something that agents were unable to hear. Before investigators could respond, Kacee dashed across the park and jumped into a black Jeep with the license plates removed. FBI agents were about to give chase when a delivery truck pulled in their way, blocking their route. Kacee escaped in the vehicle.

Lang contacted agents monitoring Dawson Elementary, ordering them to remove Franklin's daughter, Dede, from school immediately. As agents approached the school, Franklin was seen exiting with the child. He jumped into a waiting car and the driver took off. The family successfully escaped capture.

Location: 90 West End Avenue, Durango, CO

Fugitive Sighted: Michael Scofield

Based on the information he found about Special Agent Alexander Mahone on the internet, Scofield went to the home of the agent's ex-wife posing as FBI Agent Wayne Merrick. He said that he was performing a background check because Agent Mahone was about to be promoted to a higher clearance. During the conversation, it is believed that the fugitive learned personal information on the lead investigator. It is also possible that Scofield may have made contact with Mahone afterward.

Excerpt from Pamela Mahone interview:

FBI INVESTIGATOR: Ms. Mahone, when Michael Scofield knocked on your door, you believed that he was in fact Wayne Merrick, an FBI agent?

PAM MAHONE: I didn't have reason to believe otherwise.

FBI: Were you aware of the Fox River Eight at that time?

PAM: Vaguely. I had heard about it on the news, but obviously I didn't know their faces on sight.

FBI: Right. So you let Scofield into your home, and then what?

PAM: He was pretending to do a background check on Alex. I'd done these sorts of interviews before so I didn't think too much of it. I probably should have jumped on the fact that he hadn't called to make an appointment, but I guess I was taken off guard.

FBI: And while he was in your home, did Michael Scofield do anything out of the ordinary? Were you concerned for your safety?

PAM: No. Well, not at first. He was behaving normally, and just asking me different questions about Alex. He got a little personal, but it wouldn't be the first time that an agent went there, so I just rolled with it.

FBI: When did you begin to suspect that something was off?

PAM: He cut the interview off after a very short amount of time. These things can go on for hours, but he didn't stay longer then twenty or thirty minutes. He hadn't asked anything about Alex's social history, his education, childhood. All that's usually standard procedure. Then he made mention that he was in the Strategic Operations Department. Which as you know, sounds wrong because—

FBI: After the 9/11 realignment, the chief information officer handles them.

PAM: Exactly. He gave me some B.S. story about how S.O. takes over when you get to a high enough level, but—

FBI: That's not true.

PAM: That's what I thought. Anyway, a few minutes after he left, I realized my cell phone was missing, and that's when I really started to freak out.

Location: Willcox, Arizona

Fugitives Sighted: Lincoln and L.J. Burrows

A passenger at the Willcox train station recognized Lincoln Burrows and pointed him out to a station police officer. Lincoln and his son, L.J., attempted to flee the station, but the officer gave chase while reporting the sighting over his walkie-talkie. A patrol car hurried to the scene, cutting off the fugitives' escape. Authorities managed to subdue Burrows and take him and his son into custody.

While en route to headquarters, a black van slammed into the police car, pushing it off the road and into an embankment. The officers were knocked unconscious and did not see how Burrows and his son made their escape. It is still unknown who was driving the black van.

Location: 1605 Midberry Hill. Tribune, Kansas

Fugitive Sighted: Theodore Bagwell

A 911 call was logged, reporting a break-in at 1605 Midberry Hill, the former home of Susan Hollander and her children. Ms. Hollander was the woman who had turned Bagwell in after seeing his image on the TV show *America's Most Wanted*. She reportedly abandoned her home and moved as soon as she heard that Bagwell had escaped. When police arrived at the residence, they found it empty, but a downstairs window was wide open.

In a separate, but related incident, suspected murderer Brad Bellick claimed that he and his victim, Roy Geary, had been on the premises at the time the call was made to police. Bellick wove several tales about his actions on the day of Geary's death, but the one related to this address was most interesting. Bellick claimed that

he and Geary had tracked Bagwell to the address under the belief that the fugitive was carrying five million dollars. The men reportedly forced Bagwell to reveal the location of the money, before tying him up and calling his location in to 911. Bellick said that he and his partner had found the money at a bus station, when Geary turned on him and knocked him unconscious. Geary's body was found in the Fauntleroy Hotel later that evening. (For more on the murder investigation, see the file on Bradley Bellick.)

Location: Sundown Hotel. Gila, New Mexico

Fugitive Sighted: Michael Scofield, Sara Tancredi

Agent Mahone provided a series of phone numbers to cryptographers, informing them that the information was regarding a rendezvous point related to Scofield. It is unclear where the numbers came from, but the code, combined with other information Mahone gathered, indicated the meeting was to take place in Gila, New Mexico, on June 3.

On June 2, Sara Tancredi reportedly checked into the Sundown Hotel in Gila. At the time, the hotel manager, Charlie Jenkins, was unaware of the fact that the woman he put in room nine was Sara Tancredi. Upon check-in, Tancredi presented what Jenkins took to be her driver's license, but which was actually the ID of the deceased Kelli Foster.

Mr. Jenkins reports that a phone call came in early on the morning of June 3. The caller was a male who did not identify himself and asked for the hotel's fax number. About twenty minutes later, a fax was received from an unknown fax number, addressed to Tancredi. It stated, "One Hour. 16781 Butterfield Road." Jenkins delivered the fax to Tancredi's room

From 555-7835   11:33/ST 16: 16/ No. 750000110 P. 1

16781 ONE HOUR. BUTTERFIELD ROAD.

and reports that he knocked several times before she eventually answered and asked Jenkins to slide the fax under the door, which he did. Tancredi promptly left the hotel, but did not check out.

FBI Agent Alexander Mahone arrived at the Sundown Hotel and questioned Jenkins. Mahone showed him a mugshot of Sara Tancredi, and Jenkins immediately recognized her as the woman who identified herself as Kelli Foster. Jenkins told Mahone she was alone and asked Mahone what he should do upon her return, to which Mahone responded, "She's not coming back." Mahone immediately set off in pursuit of the fugitives.

When Scofield saw Mahone's car approaching the rendezvous point, he and Tancredi got into his vehicle and sped away. Agent Mahone chased the pair into an industrial area, where he found the car abandoned. He switched to a foot pursuit, playing a game of cat and mouse with Scofield inside a factory on the premises, while Tancredi used the distraction to disable Mahone's car. Scofield trapped Mahone in a section of the factory and made his escape with Tancredi. Mahone later managed to free himself, but it was not clear in his report how he managed to do so.

Scofield was injured during the confrontation. It is believed he and Dr. Tancredi fled to a motel, where she tended to his wounds. Afterward, Tancredi was seen walking away from the motel property.

Location: GPS Coordinates 32° 0' 09" N by 104° 57' 09" W.
A location in the New Mexico desert.

Fugitives Sighted: Scofield, Burrows, and Sucre

Working on an anonymous tip that Scofield's **Bolshoi Booze** tattoo had some relevance on the day of June 4, Mahone set himself the task of translating the design's significance. After several unsuccessful attempts, he realized that when the words were upside down, the letters became numbers. Those numbers were GPS coordinates for a point in the desert of New Mexico. Once Mahone had the coordinates confirmed, he cut off communication with the FBI command center, instead of calling for backup as dictated by agency protocol. This raised concerns among the agents.

At that location, Scofield met with Pedro Ramos, a drug dealer and illegal immigrant runner wanted along both sides of the U.S./Mexican border, to deliver a container of medicinal nitroglycerin. Since the FBI had intercepted Scofield's intended shipment at the Blanding Botanical Garden, Scofield was forced to fake the "nitro," replacing it with sugar water. The nitro was intended as a payment for passage on a plane ride to which Ramos had access.

Ramos tested the nitroglycerin, but found that it was fake. When he attempted to punish Scofield for trying to double-cross him, Fernando Sucre burst onto the scene, surprising them and taking control of the situation. During the brief shootout that followed, Ramos was shot and critically wounded. Sucre and Scofield then tied up Ramos and his men, Carlos and Ernesto. Seeing that Ramos would clearly die without medical attention, Scofield cut the men free before he and Sucre fled the scene. In gratitude, Ramos disclosed the location where the plane would be landing to Scofield.

Special Agent Mahone was notified by the Command Center in Chicago that Ramos, who was now in a hospital in New Mexico, wanted to talk. At the hospital, Ramos offered up information on the fugitives' location in exchange for a deal. Agent Mahone told him all charges against him would be dropped and his medical bills would be covered until he was healthy enough to be deported back to Mexico, provided the information he gave was accurate. Ramos refused and demanded U.S. citizenship. Mahone, in a break from protocol, unplugged the life-saving equipment Ramos was connected to and locked himself inside the man's hospital room. Ramos then disclosed the location of where he had last seen the fugitives.

Location: Harvey, North Dakota

Fugitive Sighted: Benjamin Miles Franklin

The Franklin family was hiding out in Harvey, North Dakota, when they must have realized that they had left Dede's kidney medicine behind in Chicago. Kacee went to a local drugstore to fill her daughter's prescription. During the transaction, the pharmacist saw a photo of Kacee and her family in a newspaper under the counter, identifying them as fugitives from the law. When Kacee tried to pay for the medicine with hundred-dollar bills, the pharmacist excused herself to the back to make change, but in actuality she called the police. The pharmacist tried to stall to keep Kacee in the store, but the woman grew increasingly nervous and chose not to wait. She fled the store just as police cars reached the parking lot. Kacee was apprehended without

ID and without the medicine. It is believed she purposely dropped the medicine somewhere so that her husband could pick it up.

Location: Desert Highway, New Mexico

Fugitives Sighted: Scofield, Burrows, and Sucre

By placing the witness, Ramos, under extreme duress, Mahone was able to learn the location of the landing strip where Scofield was going to meet the plane to Panama. Mahone traveled to the seven-mile marker on Route 4 as sunset approached and saw a Beechcraft four-seater taking off as he drove up. Sucre had apparently boarded the plane, but Scofield and Burrows were spotted driving away in their car. There was no sign of the previously unidentified man seen with them in the desert. Mahone called the FBI command center, ordering them to contact Border Patrol and the air force. He also told his agents to get clearance from the Mexican government for an international pursuit of the plane. He added that if the air force pilots had to take down the plane, they should have permission to do so. At that point he lost his cell phone signal.

Soon after the Beechcraft took off, air force jets gave chase, crossing the Mexican border with permission from the Mexican government. Knowing the Beechcraft could not outmaneuver the jets, Sucre and the pilot bailed out over the desert. The air force pilots reported the location where the men punched out, and that information was transmitted to local authorities. The pilot was later found dead in the desert, his parachute having malfunctioned. Sucre was not found anywhere in the area.

At the same time, a few miles north of the border, Agent Mahone caught up with Scofield and Burrows as they were driving away from the makeshift landing strip. Mahone turned off his headlights so he did not give away his location. For an unknown reason, the brothers turned their car around and headed back toward Mahone. Seeing no other alternative, Mahone smashed into their car. Once the dust had settled, Mahone got out of his car and held the men at gunpoint as border patrol floodlights illuminated the site.

Mahone identified himself as FBI, but the border patrol agents ordered

him to drop his weapon until they could confirm his identification. The border patrol agents report that Mahone was reluctant to lower his weapon, but eventually acquiesced.

Scofield and Burrows were taken to a border patrol holding facility, captured less than ten days after their escape from Fox River Penitentiary. They were shackled and kept under tight guard while the Illinois DOC sent a large contingent of guards to New Mexico to retrieve the prisoners. Mahone wanted to handle transport, claiming that it was a federal case, but the new warden at Fox River Penitentiary had already made arrangements with the bureau chief. Mahone then attempted to gain access to the transport vehicle so he could ride alone with the brothers. His request was refused, as it was against protocol. Transport was initiated with Mahone in one of the escort vehicles.

Location: Tribune, Kansas

Fugitive Sighted: Theodore Bagwell

Bagwell was seen in a local bar posing as a veteran who had lost his hand during the war in Iraq. Upon seeing a man with a prosthetic hand in the bar, Bagwell questioned him about how to go about getting one from the Veterans Administration. The conversation was terse, and Bagwell left soon afterward. Later that evening, the man was found in an alley beside the bar, beaten badly. His prosthetic hand was missing.

The following day, Bagwell was seen in the company of postal worker Denise Zidlicky. The pair had lunch together, then met again that evening. During their brief time together, post office video cameras recorded Bagwell with Zidlicky as she looked up information for him on her work computer. During this process, Zidlicky seemed to recognize Bagwell from a nearby WANTED poster. Bagwell realized that he had been made and killed Zidlicky on the spot before leaving the post office. Her body was not found until the following day. A computer history search for the records they had accessed revealed that he had looked up the forwarding address of a Ms. Susan Hollander in Ness City, Kansas.

Location: Albuquerque, New Mexico

Fugitives Sighted: Scofield and Burrows

The convoy transporting Burrows and Scofield to Chicago was stopped in traffic in a tunnel, due to a jack-knifed truck in the roadway that was blocking all lanes. Mahone ordered the van to be boxed in while they planned to reroute the convoy. The chase vehicles were placed bumper to bumper in front of and behind the transport van so that it could not move out of position.

The brothers were then left alone in the van, whereupon they must have noticed that due to a negligent oversight, their chains were not attached to the van interior as they should have been. With nothing holding their chains in place, the prisoners were able to reach the guards' keys that had been left unattended in the front seat. After several minutes stuck in traffic, the brothers made their move. They grabbed the keys and unlocked the four-piece shackles, then burst out of the transport van.

Guards started firing as the brothers headed for the tunnel exit. Before they reached the exit, they entered the subsystem access tunnels for a less direct means of escape. As the guards went in the direction they believed the fugitives were heading, Agent Mahone split off from the group and tracked them to a different location. A minute later a gunshot rang out from that section of the structure. Illinois DOC Captain Tuggle followed the sound to an exit above ground, where he found Agent Mahone had been shot. As the agent was rushed to the hospital, all weapons were accounted for. This raises the question: who fired the gun that shot Mahone? The issue has not been satisfactorily resolved.

Location: Cutback Motel, Montana

Fugitive Sighted: Scofield (and possibly Burrows)

A local news station reported receiving a call from a man claiming to be Michael Scofield. The man said that he was in room eleven of the Cutback Motel and that he was turning himself in. Station employees alerted the authorities and police officers were sent to secure the area. As the police arrived, a shot was heard in the motel room.

An unknown man, posing as an FBI agent, exited the building, claiming to have Burrows and Scofield in custody. When police asked to examine the man's identification, the man pulled a gun and grabbed nearby news cameraman, Greg Rydenour, holding him as a hostage. Rydenour was forced to take the keys from the police cars and then accompany the fugitives as they escaped in their vehicle.

The officers on scene reported the incident and waited for backup. When they entered the motel room, they found the body of yet another unidentified man. Later, Scofield and Burrows released a tape to the media, made using Rydenour's camera equipment in a storage facility somewhere between Great Falls and Helena. In the tape the fugitives made several unsubstantiated accusations, one of which was the claim that the body found in the motel room belonged to Terrance Steadman. According to government investigators working with the FBI, the body was actually that of a janitor.

In an interview with the hostage after his release, Rydenour indicated that he had overheard his abductors refer to their need to travel eight hundred miles in twelve hours. Rydenour did not hear their destination. Based on the time-frame, agents determined that it was likely that the fugitives were en route to intercept President Reynolds, who was scheduled to speak in Des Moines at 7:00 that evening. Though Agents Lang and Wheeler wanted to alert the Secret Service so they could change the president's schedule, Agent Mahone ordered that they continue as planned, hoping to smoke out the fugitives. Wheeler disagreed with this decision and informed Internal Affairs, as he had been instructed to keep them in the loop in light of recent accusations against Mahone.

Upon further review of the video, Mahone felt that the section of record-ing in which Scofield addressed Dr. Sara Tancredi seemed particularly heart-felt, leading him to believe additional clues might be found in Scofield's words. Mahone approached Tancredi's former coworkers at Fox River Peni-tentiary for assistance, ultimately speaking with the recently incarcerated Brad Bellick. The inmate recognized key phrases from the dialogue and agreed to share his knowledge if Mahone arranged to have him moved from general population to Ad Seg.

Excerpt from text of Scofield and Burrows recording:

SCOFIELD: Much blame has been placed on another innocent person: Dr. Sara Tancredi. She had nothing to do with our escape. Sara, if you're listening, I know I can't ask you for another chance. I only hope that you have found your safe haven. I took advantage of you—your commit-ment to help others—and put you in a place that's every doctor's nightmare. I've considered many ways to apolo-gize, but I must arrive at one. I am deeply sorry. I wish I could do things differently, but it's too late for that now.

According to Bellick, the phrases "another chance" and "safe haven" come from chapters in *The Big Book*, used in the Alcoholics Anonymous recovery program. Mahone conducted a further comparison between the tape and the book and discovered that the "doctor's nightmare" also referred to a section of the book in which reference is made to St. Joseph's Hospital in Akron, Ohio. From that point, he concluded that Scofield's line "I must arrive at one" referred to a rendezvous time.

Mahone had his agents contact Akron police, instructing them to head for the hospital, but they were too late. Surveillance tapes showed Burrows and Scofield had accepted a phone call in the hospital at 1:00 A.M. The switchboard indicated that the call was for a Michael Crane. The fugitives departed the hospital shortly thereafter, only moments before police arrived.

Location: Algoma, Wisconsin

Fugitive Sighted: Charles Patoshik

A man fitting Charles Patoshik's description was spotted fleeing a murder scene. The victim's stepdaughter, Sasha, reported that her stepfather was killed by a homeless man who spent all his time in Hancock Square. FBI consultant Brad Bellick poked holes in the young woman's story, convinced that she was covering for a man who had killed her abusive stepfather. Sasha claimed to have no part in the murder and finally gave up Patoshik's location on a local beach. When Bellick arrived to take Patoshik into custody, the fugitive fled, climbing up to the top of a silo. Mahone was called in and he climbed up after the fugitive to arrest him. During their private conversation atop the silo, the mentally unstable Patoshik jumped to his death in what appears to have been an act of suicide. It is unclear what he and Mahone said to each other during their brief exchange.

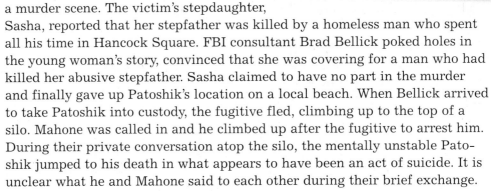

Location: 867 Greenreed Lane. Ness City, Kansas

Fugitive Sighted: Theodore Bagwell

While a realtor was showing a couple the former home of Susan Hollander in Tribune, they discovered a severed hand on the premises. The hand was sent to the coroner, and an officer was dispatched to Hollander's new home in Ness City to inform the woman of the discovery. While the officer was en route, he was informed that fingerprints from that hand matched that of Theodore Bagwell. The officer requested that local authorities be contacted and sent to join him at the residence. When police entered the Hollander home, they found it empty, although an eyewitness confirmed that the family had recently been in residence.

Location: Evansville, Indiana

Fugitives Sighted: Michael Scofield, Lincoln Burrows, and Sara Tancredi

On June 6, Michael Scofield, Lincoln Burrows, Sara Tancredi, and the man who identifies himself as Agent Paul Kellerman boarded a train in Evansville, Indiana, heading to Chicago, Illinois. The ticket taker, Brian Finklestein, reports that "Agent Kellerman" boarded the train with an alleged fugitive who, unbeknownst to him, was Michael Scofield. Finklestein led them to an empty car toward the rear of the train. At this time Lincoln Burrows and Sara Tancredi snuck onto the train as well.

About an hour after the train left Evansville, three college students, Jamie Huang, Sam Salazar, and Benjamin O'Toole, approached Mr. Finklestein to alert him to a disturbance that they witnessed in the rear car. The following is an excerpt from an interview with the three college students conducted by the FBI.

> FBI AGENT: Why don't we begin with you guys telling us what happened that day in your own words.
>
> SALAZAR: It was really weird, man. We were walking through the train looking for the Snack Car, and I guess we went in the wrong direction. Anyways, you know those glass doors that separate the cars?
>
> HUANG: We saw this chick going ape up in there! It was crazy. She was trying to strangle this guy—
>
> O'TOOLE: And the guy was trying to get her off of him, but she was pretty tough. She really had a lock on him. Took a piece of string and just wrapped it around his neck.
>
> HUANG: Then there were these other two dudes who had to rip her off of him, and we got really freaked out so we ran and told the ticket taker about it. We didn't know if anyone was really getting hurt in there.
>
> FBI: And was that the last time that you saw them?
>
> SALAZAR: No. Later on, maybe an hour or two, one of the guys, the big one with the shaved head, he told us we needed to switch our gear with him and his crew—
>
> O'TOOLE: Yeah, and the suit kept a gun on us the whole time. He told us that he would shoot us if we didn't change our jackets and hats and then jump off the train.
>
> FBI: And did you jump off the train?
>
> HUANG: Yeah. Though I'm not gonna lie, it was scary as hell. It's a miracle we didn't break an arm or a leg.

O'TOOLE: He made the ticket taker jump off, too.

HUANG: But the scariest part was when the cops came.

SALAZAR: I think it's more of a miracle we didn't get shot by accident, considering there were cops coming at us, guns pointed. I guess they thought we were the cons on the train since we had all their clothing on.

Location: Ixtapa International Airport, Mexico

Fugitive Sighted: Fernando Sucre

Luis Cadena, an airport security officer, unknowingly picked up Fernando Sucre on his way to the Ixtapa International airport. It was Mr. Cadena's day off, but he had been called in to provide backup on a sting—authorities were planning to ambush an American fugitive at the airport. On his way in, he picked up a hitchhiker, who he was later to realize was Mr. Sucre himself.

Mr. Cadena has stated that Sucre was nonviolent and conversational, but that he grew increasingly nervous as the drive went on. When he arrived at the airport, Cadena pointed Sucre in the direction of the terminal, and Sucre thanked him and ran off.

Moments later, when Cadena greeted his coworkers, he was shown the mugshot of the man they were meant to capture that day. Cadena was floored when he realized it was the very same man he had just given a ride. Cadena immediately notified the guard squad that Sucre was on the premises, and they split up on a search for the fugitive. But by that point, Sucre had already disappeared and was nowhere to be found on the airport premises.

Location: Corona de Oro. Chicago, Illinois

Fugitives Sighted: Sara Tancredi and Michael Scofield

On June 6 at approximately 3:00 P.M., Michael Scofield and Sara Tancredi were spotted at the Corona De Oro Club in Chicago, Illinois. This cigar club is typically frequented by politicians and other public figures of the Chicago metropolitan area. Former Governor Frank Tancredi, now deceased, was a patron of the establishment and had a private humidor at the club.

On this afternoon Tancredi entered the club with a male suspect. As Tancredi was moving toward the back of the club, receptionist Laura Merlotti approached them, questioning Tancredi if she was a member. Tancredi flashed a member's key, and Merlotti nodded for her to proceed. As Tancredi walked down the club's main hallway and out of Merlotti's sight, Merlotti immediately notified the manager on duty, John Friendly, that she recognized Tancredi as the late Governor Tancredi's daughter, who had just skipped bail. Friendly called the Chicago police department, telling them he had an emergency on his hands—and a fugitive on the premises.

Friendly then attempted to stop Tancredi from accessing the area of the club containing the private humidors, but she ignored him and dashed out an emergency exit with the male suspect, who has since been identified as Michael Scofield. This occurred just as members of the CPD were arriving at the club to detain them.

Michael Scofield was also ID'd later that day as the driver of a vehicle that hit grocery store owner Bill Kim. Witness accounts describe Scofield as purposely ramming his car into the pedestrian, who flew onto the hood of the vehicle, and then putting the car into reverse and knocking Kim onto the street. The scenario only grew stranger, as a male, ID'd as Lincoln Burrows, pounced on Kim and began beating him severely. Witnesses say it appeared as if they exchanged words with each other, but no one knew exactly what was said. Upon hearing the sound of ambulance sirens, Burrows stopped his barrage and left Kim injured and bloody on the street while he jumped into the vehicle driven by Scofield. Sara Tancredi was also ID'd as being in this vehicle, and the three of them quickly drove off. Witnesses report that it looked as though another male suspect was attempting to get into the vehicle, but was locked out and left on the side of the road. He quickly fled the scene on foot.

INTERNAL AFFAIRS REVIEW

ALEXANDER MAHONE

AGE: 42   BORN: May 4, 1963, in Davis, California
FATHER: Edward R. Mahone (Assistant Director of Operations—Drushal-Dower Power Plant)
MOTHER: Cynthia L. Mahone (Textiles)   SIBLINGS: One brother (Peter)
MARTIAL STATUS: Divorced from Pamela Mahone
MEDICAL HISTORY: High cholesterol/heart murmur   PSYCH EVALUATIONS: All clean
INTERNAL AFFAIRS REPORTS: One—#B4413958 Re: Oscar F. Shales Investigation

FAMILY HISTORY: Police reports and court documents show a repeated history of physical and mental abuse by Mahone's father toward him and his brother Peter, as well as his mother Cynthia.

In 1993, Alexander married Pamela Austin. The two were married for twelve years and divorced in 2004, citing irreconcilable differences. Alexander kept their primary residence, but forfeited all other assets to his wife. He currently forwards her monthly alimony payments.

MILITARY HISTORY: At eighteen, Alex joined the army. Four years later he re-enlisted and was assigned to the 4th Psychological Operations Group (PSYOP). Used during peacetime, contingencies, and declared war, PSYOP activities are not a form of force. Rather they are force multipliers that use nonviolent means in often violent environments. PSYOP uses persuasion instead of physical force, relying on logic, fear, desire, or other mental factors to promote specific emotions, attitudes, or behaviors. At twenty-seven, under PSYOP, Alexander was part of one of the first American units to touch down in Iraq prior to Operation Desert Storm. He was awarded the Medal of Honor and the Defense Superior Service Medal. After PSYOP, Mahone went to work for the FBI.

WORK HISTORY: Mahone joined the FBI in 1991, working out of Denver, Colorado, doing counter-intelligence. In 2002, he was transferred to the bureau's Chicago office to assist counterterrorism agents there with a Homeland Security intelligence shakeup. In 2003, Alexander was assigned to the infamous Oscar Shales case. Shales, a notorious serial killer based out of Chicago, Illinois, has a violent criminal history. He is wanted for the murder of two Chicago undercover police officers and has been tied to the deaths of several women in the Chicago area, whom he raped and tortured before killing. After years of evading law enforcement officials, Shales was finally apprehended by Evanston, Illinois, authorities in 2004, but later escaped police custody. After Shales absconded, Mahone headed the manhunt to bring him to justice. Despite several close calls, Mahone was never able to catch up with Shales. No one has seen or heard from Oscar Shales since June 2004. He is believed to have fled the United States.

Lang,

Enlcosed is a brief summary of a man who first appeared on our radar during the Cutback Motel standoff in Montana. I have repeatedly tried to discuss his involvement with Mahone, but have consistently been reminded that I am not running the investigation—he is. The gentleman in question is extremely crafty, and has gotten Burrows and Scofield out of several jams. If you think it's wise, I'd like to discuss the matter with Agent Sullins at IA. I feel like Mahone is letting a grudge against me stand in the way of our investigation and this manhunt.

—Wheeler

SECRET SERVICE AGENT KELLERMAN

Little is known about the man who calls himself Secret Service Agent Paul Kellerman. He first appeared at the Cutback Motel in Montana, when he took a hostage, a local news cameraman, before spiriting away Burrows and Scofield from the melee of police cars and media trucks that surrounded them. My contact at the Department of Treasury confirmed that the Secret Service has issued a statement that they have no agent working under that name. It is now believed that Kellerman may be an old friend of Scofield's, who was part of his plan from day one.

Kellerman was next seen at a train station in Evansville, Indiana, where he attempted to use the cover as a federal agent to board a passenger train heading to Chicago. He told a ticket taker there he was transporting a fugitive back to Chicago and wanted to commandeer a train car for the trip. Eyewitness accounts from the scene confirm he was also traveling with Burrows, Scofield, and another unidentified woman, now presumed to be Dr. Sara Tancredi. He was next spotted on Jackson Street outside of the private Corona De Oro cigar club in downtown Chicago. His whereabouts are currently unknown.

Updated on 6/7 by Agent Wheeler.

To: Special Agent Lang
From: Special Agent Wheeler
Re: Fox River Manhunt

Lang,

The following is for <u>your eyes only</u>. As you are aware, the bureau's investigation into the Fox River escape has unearthed some disturbing questions about the actions of certain members of the government. Searching the internet, my assistant and I have come across some interesting websites referencing the Fox River Eight. Of these sites, we've included what has quickly become the most popular: a site dedicated to uncovering an alleged global conspiracy involving the Burrows family. This blog may simply be the ramblings of a paranoid madman, but if even part of what he suggests is true, it's a frightening concept. The blogger has been active for several years now, but he seemed to take an interest in the Burrows case only a week prior to the originally scheduled date of Lincoln's execution. <u>Do not</u> discuss and/or present any of the included files to Mahone. <u>These are for your eyes only</u>. As you review the remainder of the Fox River Eight file, I cannot stress enough the importance of removing this memo before you hand it off to Deputy Agent Malkin for review and publication. There is something seriously amiss behind the Fox River Escape, and while Mahone may not want to get to the bottom of it, I intend to.

POST #598 ·

Sorry I've been gone so long, but I've been collecting evidence on a story that is going to blow all of your minds . . . or not surprise you at all. My spies have been collecting information for weeks now, and I'm telling you that it's time to start paying attention to the case of death row inmate Lincoln Burrows. Seems there are some dark and mysterious figures circling around him. Big Brother is most certainly watching . . . although, I'm beginning to think it might be Big Sister.

Now, we've all talked about corporate interests taking over the government and how they're buying elections and fighting wars so they can make a profit. No news there. We've heard the whispers of this super secret multinational organization known as The Company that's pulling the strings of numerous world governments, including, possibly, our very own Vice President Reynolds. But, fear not, my friends, because I'm also hearing that a group could be out there fighting the good fight for us all. A handful of senators, congressmen, and even former members of this evil organization have banded together to take them on and make the battle public. And I say I'm ready to join up whenever someone contacts me. You've all got my number.

But let's welcome the new players in this game. It all starts with Lincoln Burrows, the man convicted of murdering the vice president's brother, Terrence Steadman. His lawyers, Veronica Donovan and Nick Savrinn, have been our foot soldiers in this latest war. I can't tell you how I know this, but I hear they've been making waves from Chicago to D.C. Then there's Lincoln's brother, Michael Scofield, who just so happens to be in Fox River Penitentiary with his brother. Don't know what he's got to do with it yet, but the vultures seem to be circling. And don't forget Lincoln's son, L.J., who seems more than ready to be taking on the big boys.

Speaking of which, what about this guy? Rumor has it, his name is Secret Service Agent Paul Kellerman. I say rumor, because the Secret Service supposedly has no knowledge of him or his partner, Danny Hale. Yet this Kellerman guy can be seen in the background of photos with Vice President Reynolds going as far back as her second run for the Montgomery, Illinois School Board back in '92. Kellerman has his fingerprints wiped clean from almost all the events I'll be laying out for you over the next couple days. But who is he, really? It promises to be a juicy story.

POST #599 • • • • • • • • •

Okay, okay, I heard you. Some of you are going to need some background on the Burrows case. Guess I was getting ahead of myself. I thought my readers were up on all the news before they came here. Didn't realize I was your #1 source for breaking world developments. I am humbled. Honestly.

This story all starts with the most famous vice-presidential brother in history: Terrence Steadman. The CEO of Ecofield was a pillar in the community. He did a ton of charity work, and his company was making great strides in environmental research and successfully pushing alternative energy. I know. I'm using the word "successfully" here quite loosely. But the company even introduced a prototype electric engine at a technology conference before Steadman's death. It was beginning to look like sixty-dollar barrels of oil would be obsolete if the thing ever made it to the mainstream.

Not that Steadman was a total saint, or anything. Forget the stories you've heard in the mainstream media. Prior to Steadman's death, there were rumors of an indictment coming down. That meant bad things for his business and his investors. CEO of a corporation like Ecofield gets indicted for fraud, and investors could start losing billions of dollars. Considering Ecofield basically crumpled up and folded after his death, I think it's pretty clear that a lot of people were breathing a sigh of relief that the summonses never came.

But the story doesn't really get good until poor, unfortunate Lincoln Burrows stumbles into it. The man had a rough life, highlighted by numerous brushes with the law and brief periods of time served. But how did he become one of the most famous assassins in modern history? Apparently it all began when Burrows was into some lowlife named Crab Simmons for $90,000. Or so Burrows says. To settle his debt, Burrows agreed to go to the parking garage he's now made famous (seriously, it's a stop on Tours of Chicago) to take care of a rival drug dealer. Instead, he says he found Terrence Steadman slumped over in his car. He claims the man was already dead.

Let's start with the official story. These are the facts of the case, according to official police and government sources, who we all know would NEVER lie to us, right? Lincoln Burrows worked in one of the Ecofield warehouses in Chicago, schlepping boxes around all day. It was menial work, but the best someone with his background could get. Witnesses report that one day, for no known reason, Burrows got into a "public altercation" with Terrence Steadman and was fired on the spot. But Burrows claims never to have met the man. Either way, Burrows lost his job two weeks before the big boss was found dead.

On the night of Terrence Steadman's death, Burrows freely admits that he was going to that parking garage because he was up to no good. In order to pay off a debt, Burrows was going there to shoot a nasty drug dealer. Whether or not Burrows would have actually gone through with it is anybody's guess, because he never got the chance. By the time he arrived at the parking garage, his target was already dead. But the target wasn't the guy Burrows thought he had been sent to kill. It was the brother of the then-Vice President, Caroline Reynolds.

When Burrows saw the deceased in the parking garage, he says that he ran (Burrows, not the dead guy), dumping the gun he had on him in a storm drain near Van Buren and Wells. That gun was never recovered. But another one was. We'll get to that in a moment.

A witness called 911, reporting Burrows fleeing from the garage with blood on his pants. The thing about the witness call though, is that a private investigator working for Burrows's lawyers, Veronica Donovan and Nick Savrinn, back traced it to a pay phone at 11th and Constitution . . . in Washington D.C. The "witness" must have had some pretty powerful binoculars to see a murder in Chicago. Turns out, the phone was near an office that is now unoccupied, but was previously the D.C. regional office for Ecofield.

Burrows claims that he then went back to his apartment and splashed some water on his face. I think if I ever saw a dead guy, I'd probably splash some vodka down my throat. Anyway, the official police report claims that he was found standing over the tub, washing the blood of Terrence Steadman off his pants. Both the cops and Burrows admit the pants were in the tub, but Burrows said he had never seen the pants before the cops came bursting in.

But what about that "official police report?" How official is official? Decide for yourselves. Officer Phil Weston was the first to respond to Lincoln's apartment the night of the murder. Here's a copy of his "official" report on the events of that evening.

> *Dispatch called in with a tip that Lincoln Burrows was seen running from the garage where they found the body of Terrence Steadman. The suspect's address was on file from a prior arrest, and our squad car was the nearest to the location. I called our position in and rolled over to the residence with Officer Jacobs. We found the front door open and announced ourselves, but there was no response. We entered the apartment with guns drawn. Officer Jacobs and I spread out to perform a thorough search. I took the bathroom. When I heard water running, I announced myself and kicked in the door to find Burrows standing in the bathroom. I kept my gun on him as I ordered him into the hall.*

And here's his testimony while on the witness stand:

PROSECUTOR: What happened after you and Officer Jacobs entered the premises?
OFFICER WESTON: We split up and performed a room-by-room search.
PROSECUTOR: Where did you start the search?
OFFICER WESTON: The bathroom. I heard water running.
PROSECUTOR: Was the door open?
OFFICER WESTON: No. I announced myself and kicked it in.
PROSECUTOR: What did you find inside?
OFFICER WESTON: The suspect. Lincoln Burrows.
PROSECTOR: What was he doing?
OFFICER WESTON: He was washing something in the tub. Once I had him in cuffs,
    I saw it was a pair of pants with bloodstains still on them.

No one in the courtroom was surprised when forensic experts testified that the blood on the pants matched Terrence Steadman. Weston's testimony factored strongly into Burrows's conviction. But notice how he never said Burrows was washing the pants in his original statement?

Which brings us to the gun that Burrows told his lawyers he dumped. Ballistics matched the slug taken out of Steadman to a gun police did find in Burrows's apartment. Burrows claimed it was planted, but that didn't explain how his fingerprints got on it. Now Burrows thinks it's because of some guy named Bo. This Bo arranged everything with him and Crab Simmons, paying off Burrows's debt in exchange for the hit on the drug dealer. The night before the planned hit, Bo had Burrows try a couple guns to see which one felt good. One of those weapons must have been the murder weapon. When asked how Bo convinced Burrows to kill a man for $90,000, Lincoln admitted the real truth behind his actions: Bo was threatening to kill his son, L.J. Burrows.

More to come . . .

POST #600 ·

Okay, so the story continues. The evidence may have been stacked against Burrows, but he had something almost as valuable: a witness who knew all about what was supposed to go down. Burrows believed that Crab Simmons could have cleared him of the charges, or at least some of the suspicion. All Simmons had to do was admit that this mystery guy, Bo, had paid Burrows's debt in exchange for him agreeing to off some drug dealer. That Terrence Steadman was never supposed to be involved. Whether or not a five-time felon would be a good witness for Burrows is pretty much a moot point. Crab Simmons died only one week after the Steadman assassination.

According to the coroner's report, Simmons died from a heroin overdose. Thing is, his girlfriend, Leticia Barris, claimed that Simmons didn't do drugs because he had a bad heart. 'Course, who's gonna believe the girlfriend of a lowlife? But what if that same girlfriend insisted that she was under surveillance? Said she heard clicks on her phone and saw mysterious cars on her street? Then, what if that girlfriend was found shot dead in the woods shortly after she gave a deposition to Burrows's lawyer, Veronica Donovan?

Kind of makes you think, don't it?

Here's a copy of that deposition obtained directly from Veronica Donovan's assistant. (I know. You're amazed at how I get these things.) Barris never signed the deposition, so it's worthless as a piece of evidence, but it does shine a big ol' light on Burrows's story.

VERONICA DONOVAN: Why don't we start with Lincoln's relationship with your boyfriend.

LETICIA BARRIS: Real simple. He owed my man $90,000, and he wasn't getting it done. Then, all of a sudden . . . it gets done. Crab walks in with ninety K and a big ass smile on his face.

DONOVAN: Who paid him off?

BARRIS: Not Lincoln. They paid his marker.

DONOVAN: Who's "they"?

BARRIS: Crab brought this guy home. I'd never seen him before. Crab did what he always did when he was doing big business. He told me to take a walk. So that's exactly what I did. There was something about this guy, though. He wasn't the kind of guy Crab usually dealth with.

DONOVAN: What do you mean?

BARRIS: Couldn't put my finger on it till he went outside. Then I knew. He had that look.

DONOVAN: What look?

BARRIS: You know, like they own the place. Like they're untouchable. Like they're government.

DONOVAN: So the government paid Lincoln's debt? Did Crab say what they wanted in return?

BARRIS: Uh-uh. (Negative)

Interesting, huh? With Barris gone, the dead bodies sure are starting to pile up. And we haven't even gotten to the actual evidence yet!

POST #601 ▪

So, where's the smoking gun, you ask? Turns out, there was none. It was all special effects. High-end special effects, too. Like the kind they use in Hollywood. But this was a movie the public never saw. The media circus surrounding the case of The State of Illinois vs. Lincoln Burrows forced the judge to make it a closed trial. No one outside that room saw it. And no one ever would, if it weren't for a friend of the blog who shall remain nameless. This friend got a look at the tape with his very own two eyes. And, let me tell you, it was quite a look. But let me back up a minute.

Burrows's lawyers, Veronica Donovan and Nick Savrinn, found out about this tape from Burrows's original lawyer. The tape came from a surveillance camera in the parking garage where Steadman was found dead, and it showed the whole murder. Or so some people would like us to think.

Donovan and Savrinn requested the tape under the Freedom of Information Act and had their own copy made to take home and look over. And they got quite an eyeful. The tape clearly shows Terrence Steadman driving into the parking garage and pulling into an open space. Moments later, Burrows approaches Steadman's car with his gun raised and fires into the driver's side window. Then, Burrows runs to the passenger's side and rifles through the glove compartment to make it look like a theft, before taking off. But does that tell the whole story? Not so much.

First of all, Steadman looks directly into the camera when he pulls into the garage. It's almost like he's saying, "look at me! I'm here!" And when he pulls into the spot, he sits there for almost half a minute, like he's waiting for something to happen. Like he's waiting for Burrows to arrive. And what about when Burrows does arrive? The guy does admit to leading with his gun, but he says he never fired and the tape backs that up. When the gun is fired, there's absolutely no recoil at all. His wrist is totally steady. Now, Burrows isn't exactly a pipsqueak, but for there to be no recoil at all from a 9mm gun? Come on!

After the gunshot, Burrows is seen moving away from the car as he heads off camera. Then he comes around to the passenger side of the car—making sure the camera doesn't see his face—and leans in to rifle through the glove compartment. But he was moving AWAY from the car. Why would Burrows go all the way back just to get Steadman's blood on his pants? But here's where things got real interesting . . .

Our little friend of the blog got to see this tape because he's kind of an expert at these things. Savrinn brought the tape to him to get his opinion, and he had to say that the tape was good. Usually, when someone fakes a tape, if you peel back a few layers all the bogus stuff comes right off. But the changes to this tape were ingrained. It looked like the real deal. But it didn't *sound* that way. Our friend punched up the audio on the tape and something was definitely missing. When Burrows fired his gun on the tape, they heard the sound of a bang, but nothing more. In a concrete parking garage like that, the sound should have echoed. It should have bounced around that room. But this sound didn't. It popped, and then it ended. As if the sound of the gunshot was recorded in a totally different place.

The lawyers wanted our friend to testify to that in court, and he was more than willing, but he couldn't swear to anything because they only had a dupe. If Donovan and Savrinn wanted to get Burrows out, they had to get the real deal. But that's one of those easier said than done situations. First of all, no court clerk is going to let an original piece of evidence out, but that didn't really matter anyway, because the original was gone. The night before Donovan and Savrinn went to request the original tape, a pipe burst in one of the evidence storage rooms, causing a flood. Files from over 100 cases were lost to the damage, including the original tape. But at least they had a dupe, right? Wrong. When Donovan returned to her home, she found the front door ajar. Nothing looked to be stolen . . . except for the duplicate surveillance tape.

So much for the evidence. It looks like this "Company" had successfully framed Lincoln Burrows for the murder of Terrence Steadman. He was found guilty and sentenced to death. Justice was particularly swift in this case. Most death penalty cases take at least a decade to exhaust all appeals. Lincoln seems to have run out of options in only three years. Burrows is scheduled to die at 12:01 on the morning of May 11.

POST #602 · · ▪ · ▪ · ▪ · ▪ · ▪ · ▪ · ▪ · ▪ · ▪ · ▪ · ▪ ·

So . . . Someone's been very busy lately. Busy making sure Lincoln Burrows dies. I'm gonna go out on a limb here and say that Bishop McMorrow was the first in a string of recent murders possibly connected to the Burrows case. The bishop had made it clear that if Burrows appealed to him for his intervention, McMorrow would have gone to the governor. This surely would have put enough political pressure on Governor Tancredi that he would have had to consider the request. But about one month before the execution, the bishop was shot by an intruder while he slept. Police are still searching for the killer, but he's never going to be found, if you ask me. Bishop McMorrow's death was far from the last one related to this case.

But where are Donovan and Savrinn? If you believe what you read in the papers, one or both of them could be dead. I know I've been trying to get in touch with them, but my spies can't find them anywhere. They were last seen unloading some boxes outside Donovan's Gold Coast apartment. The maintenance man in Donovan's building, Lucasz Peshcopi, offered his help getting the boxes into the building for them. A few minutes later, Donovan's apartment exploded in a huge fireball. Initial reports

indicated that only one body was found in the aftermath. Until the body was identified, it was assumed that Donovan had died in the fire. But it really turned out to be her poor maintenance guy. The "official" cause was listed as a gas leak. But that was not the only death that day.

If you've been following this blog, I assume you're starting to catch up with the local mainstream media. You know there's currently a search for the son of Lincoln Burrows. On the same afternoon that Donovan's apartment exploded, L.J. Burrows reportedly killed his mom and stepdad across town in Oak Park. The official line is that L.J. is a troubled youth who took out his aggression on his parental units. His grades had recently suffered a decline, and that combined with his father's arrest and his own recent arrest for drug possession, showed that he was on a path to self-destruction. And just one day prior to the murders, neighbors say that they heard yelling coming from the house. It paints a picture that makes the boy look pretty guilty. Then, of course, there's the evidence: L.J.'s fingerprints were found on the gun and his bloody footprints were leading away from the scene. But I think we all know how easily those things can be faked. But here's where we have some more fun with secrets.

Shortly after L.J. was suspected of the murders, he sent a text message to a friend of his. That girl, who I'm not going to name here, got in touch with yours truly right before she and her brother took it on the lam to protect themselves from the same shadowy figures that seem to be all over the Burrows case. Here's a copy of that message:

i didn't do it. this is the guy. help me. lj

But what's REALLY interesting is the photo that came as an attachment. The file that was forwarded was partially corrupt, but a little techno magic helped fill in the blanks and complete the picture. One heck of a coincidence, wouldn't you say? The time logged on the photo showed that L.J. Burrows took it at 4:34 P.M. on April 24. His mother's time of death was listed as occurring between 4:15 P.M. and 4:45 P.M. on that same day.

Paul Kellerman
Special Agent

Cell: 773.555.0111
Fax: 773.555.0121

But who is this armed villain that was on the premises at the same time L.J. was supposedly committing murder? He seems to keep popping up all over the place, but never sticks around long enough for anyone to nail him down. According to Veronica Donovan, his name is Paul Kellerman, and he's an agent with the Secret Service. We even got a copy of his business card. Of course, we all know anyone can print up a fake government business card or I.D. (I mean, who among us has not done this before?) So, there's no way to know for sure that this guy is government. But since I first posted his picture asking if anyone knew who he was way back in POST 598, I've gotten even more responses linking him to Caroline Reynolds, as far back as the early 90s. The Secret Service still denies any knowledge of this man, or his partner, Daniel Hale, but when have we ever trusted the government to tell us the truth?

POST #603 ·

Okay folks, Veronica Donovan and Nick Savrinn are still missing. I only hope that one of my faithful readers out there is keeping them safe. In the meantime, it's been a little like Christmas in May out here (and I'm not talking about the late-in-the-season cold snap we've been experiencing). I found something on my doorstep this morning that could blow the lid off this whole conspiracy.

Remember how I mentioned that the SEC was about to come down hard on Terrence Steadman? Well, according to Ecofield's SEC findings, Terrence Steadman's company had over a half billion dollars in federal grants for alternative fuel research. But here's the thing: not only did the company never make a profit, it looks to me like they never made ANYTHING. No fuel cells. No patents. Nothing beyond the promise of a revolutionary prototype electric engine that never saw the light of day. So where did this money go?

Anybody hear the report yesterday that Vice President Reynolds has the largest war chest in history as she prepares her run for President? Now, you all know I'm not one to carelessly throw around false accusations but, is it possible that Vice President Reynolds was funneling millions of dollars in research grants to her brother's company? Then, is it further possible that brother dear was filtering that money into millions of small accounts that then made millions of small donations to her campaign? Who can get the SEC on the line? I think somebody needs to look a little closer at the Vice President's campaign finances.

Oh, and here's some more sad news on what is quickly becoming the "Death Watch" portion of our programming . . . Veronica Donovan's former fiancé, Sebastian, was found dead in his apartment this morning. Now, this could certainly just be another one of those random acts of violence, but I don't think so. It looks like we're not the only ones wondering about the whereabouts of Veronica Donovan.

POST #604 ·

Did you see it? Please tell me you saw it! Our girl, Donovan, is back on the case. And boy does she have a tale to tell. Where's she been all this time? I don't know, but I'm noticing Nick Savrinn seems to be looking a little worse for wear. Rumor has it that wherever they were in hiding, more of those Company Men came after them. Nick seems to be nursing a serious

203

wound, but he's up and moving around now. And as for Veronica . . . well, she's gone public in a big way. In case you missed it, here's what she had to say this afternoon, straight from outside the walls of Fox River Penitentiary to the local FOX affiliate WDOZ News 6.

REPORTER: Evening Peter. I'm with Veronica Donovan, the lawyer for Lincoln Burrows. You're petitioning for a stay. Is that right?

DONOVAN: That's right.

REPORTER: On what grounds?

DONOVAN: On the grounds that my client's been framed.

REPORTER: Ms. Donovan, do you have any proof to that effect?

DONOVAN: There's a whole string of proof. Murders. Leticia Barris, a potential exculpatory witness. Lisa Rix, the mother of Lincoln's child. Bishop McMorrow, the man that could've petitioned the governor for clemency . . .

REPORTER: You're saying someone's killing these people off?

DONOVAN: I'm saying somebody's trying to hide what really happened. What the truth about Terrence Steadman really was.

REPORTER: Is this all just speculation, or is there hard evidence that can substantiate your claims?

DONOVAN: I have a source.

REPORTER: Could you elaborate on that?

DONOVAN: Not at this time. But somebody on the inside that claims they can exonerate Lincoln, that Terrence Steadman wasn't even in the car that night . . .

He's alive! Alive!

POST #605 · ▪ ▪ ▪ ▪ ▪ ▪ ▪ ▪ ▪ ▪ ▪ ▪ ▪ ▪ ▪ ▪ ▪ ·

Talk about anticlimactic. Terrence Steadman may be alive, but Veronica Donovan's mole is not. According to Donovan, she went to meet with her informant in an alley behind the Highland Cafe on Kennedy Avenue. She named him as Daniel Hale, a member of the Secret Service and partner to Paul Kellerman (go back and check out my earlier posts). Hale reaffirmed that Steadman is alive and claimed to have a list of names of people in The Company, from top to bottom. He told her that Burrows had been picked to be the assassin long before that night, but he never pulled the trigger. Then their meeting was interrupted when Kellerman arrived. Donovan claims she ducked behind a car and watched as Kellerman shot and killed Hale.

This morning, Donovan and Savrinn presented oral arguments to Judge Randall Kessler, leading with all the circumstantial evidence they had, hoping for a delay of the execution. Their goal? To have the body of Terrence Steadman exhumed to prove once and for all that he's not dead. They fought the good fight, but in the end, they didn't have much to go on. Donovan and Savrinn were the petitioners, while Petter Tucci represented the Respondent, Vice President Reynolds. The following is taken from the court records representing the end of the twenty minutes of petitioning:

SAVRINN: Judge Kessler, Mr. Tucci might not appreciate the weight of what we've just presented but surely you must. As Ms. Donovan stated, a top video forensic analyst has disputed the authenticity of the surveillance tape that was the key piece of evidence in convicting Lincoln Burrows.

TUCCI: That's the tape that no longer exists, right?

DONOVAN: Because your client had it destroyed.

TUCCI: Unless my client is a rusted water pipe in the County Records office, I'm afraid you're mistaken.

SAVRINN: Judge, Ms. Donovan's apartment was blown up in an attempt to silence both her and me.

TUCCI: That was independently corroborated as a gas leak, Your Honor.

DONOVAN: Judge, a month ago a Secret Service Agent named Paul Kellerman visited my office. I saw Kellerman last night, when he shot and killed another agent—Daniel Hale—right after Hale told me that Terrence Steadman was alive and well.

TUCCI: Your Honor, I'm presenting the clerk with an affidavit from the Director of the Secret Service Agency. It states that at no time has there ever been an agent of that organization by the name of Paul Kellerman or Daniel Hale. In addition, there were no other witnesses to this shooting. No bullets found, no blood, no shell casings. The only witness to this alleged murder is Veronica Donovan. Lincoln Burrows's ex-girlfriend. Now, Your Honor, I feel for Ms. Donovan—

DONOVAN: Save it.

TUCCI: I do. But desperation causes desperate acts. And that's what we're seeing here today, Your Honor. My client, the Vice President of the United States—

SAVRINN: Judge Kessler—

JUDGE KESSLER: Do either of you have any evidence that is admissible? Even just tangible? Your claims, if true, are terrifying. But anything, or anyone, that could verify your story is either gone, missing, or dead. I know time is of the essence. I'll reserve judgment for now. I'll take your arguments into consideration, and I'll have a decision within a few hours.

So now, all we can do is wait. Things don't look good for Lincoln Burrows. The conspiracy is staring Judge Kessler right in the eye, but we all know there's no legal ground to stand on here. This Company has been so good at covering its tracks . . . well, maybe not at "covering" its tracks, but certainly they've been good at destroying the evidence once someone *found* the tracks. My guess is Judge Kessler won't grant the exhumation request, and Lincoln Burrows will meet his maker tonight at one minute past midnight.

May God have mercy on his soul.

POST #606 ·

I CAN'T BELIEVE IT!! It isn't often that I'm wrong, but who could have seen this one coming? Oh, sure, I was right about Judge Kessler. He didn't grant the stay, based on what

Donovan and Savrinn had presented. Governor Tancredi proved fairly useless, too. I have it on pretty good authority that his daughter, Sara Tancredi—a doctor at Fox River Penitentiary—gave the governor all the collected files on the Burrows's case. You ask me, there was more than enough circumstantial evidence there for the governor to grant a pardon, but we are in an election year, you know. Mere minutes before midnight, Frontier Justice Frank made the call informing the warden that he was not going to grant clemency.

The Burrows execution continued as scheduled. The condemned was strapped into the electric chair and prepared for death. But, with only seconds before the switch was to be flipped, Judge Kessler called to halt the execution based on NEW evidence. He was working

OPERATION SURGICAL ADMISSION REPORT

ROS:	POS	NEG	EXPLAIN RELEVANT POSITIVES:
FEVER	☑	☐	Severe abdominal pain, upon inspection
WEIGHT LOSS	☑	☐	the appendix was at the point
LOSS OF APPETITE	☑	☐	of bursting.
PAIN	☑	☐	
HEENT	☐	☑	An appendectomy was performed
CARDIO-RESPIRATORY	☐	☑	the results where here
GI	☐	☑	and the surgery
GU	☐	☑	was successful
OB/GYN	☐	☑	
EXTREMITIES	☐	☑	
NEURO	☐	☑	
LAST MAMMOGRAM	☐	☑	Date: 8/8/65
LAST PAP SMEAR	☐	☑	Date:
OTHER			

BP: 90/20   Pulse: 48   Resp: Temp: 101°   Ht: 5'5   Wt: 135.

GENERAL APPEARANCE: Explain Positive/Abnormal Findings: _There to be more for now the surgeon._

SKIN & LYMPH NODES:	☑ Normal	
HEAD & NECK:	☑ Normal	
CHEST:	☑ Normal	
LUNGS:	☑ Normal	
HEART:	☑ Normal	
BREASTS:	☑ Normal	
ABDOMEN:	☐ Normal	Scar from an abdomen
RECTAL:	☑ Normal	
PELVIC:	☑ Normal	

EXTREMITIES:
NEUROLOGICAL: _every thing seemed fine_
PULSES: _Pulses fine_

OTHER PERTINENT FINDINGS: _We found no other ailments. Patient was healthy in print for this operation, we can soon will see the time when we will be out –_

CORONERS REPORT

CERTIFIED COPY

Date: _14/15_   County: _Cook_

Certified By: _Dr S/Manlyon_   Reference Number: _GS120_

County Medical Examiner's Office _Wm Mach_

DECEDENT _Andre Collin_   RACE: _W_   SEX: _M_   AGE: _56_

HOME ADDRESS: _2610 S Westborn Downs Chi Il_   M W S D   OCCUPATION: _Not releaved Con_

TYPE OF DEATH: ☒ Violent   ☐ Casualty   ☐ Suicide   ☐ Suddenly when in apparent health   ☐ Found Dead

DESCRIPTION OF BODY:

Eyes: _Blue_   Hair: _grey_   Mustache: —   Beard: —

Weight: _175lbs_   Legs: _35 in_   Body temp: _40°_   Date and Time: _Feb 334_   Body Color: _White_

Marks and Wounds: _Gun shot wound to head. Entered through right temple lobe and exited out of back bleeding from mouth and ear_

The time if death was instant

The victim felt no pain and was dead at the arrival

All the victims vital organs are in place the next of ken has been notified and the operation to remove all valyable organs will take place upon the families consent

PROBABLE CAUSE OF DEATH

gun shot wound to head

MANNER OF DEATH

(Check one only)

Accident ☐	Homicide ☒
Suicide ☐	Unknown ☐

I hereby, declare that after receiving notice death described and changes of the body and made inquiries regarding the cause of the death in accordance with Section 38-7-101 Chicago Code that all of the information contained herein regarding such information to ones death, I witness full response and knowledge.

Dr S/Manlyon

late in his office when he found an envelope slipped under his door. There were two pieces of paper inside. One was Terrence Steadman's autopsy report, listing his appendix as present and unremarkable. The other was an operative report from when Steadman was twelve years old, showing that he had had an appendectomy. Since the judge didn't know for certain what the papers were, he delayed the execution for two weeks so the lawyers can exhume the body and hopefully bring some resolution to this case.

The vice president's reaction was immediate and expected:

"My family and I are more than dismayed by Judge Kessler's decision to allow the exhumation of my brother. This stunt by Lincoln Burrows's defense counsel is an affront, and an insult to the memory of my brother, a good man who tried to make positive change in this country. This is being done in the name of trying to release a convicted killer from prison."

As luck would have it (or, more likely, really good planning) Steadman had reportedly asked for a "green burial." That means no embalming and a biodegradable coffin. Now, while it wasn't surprising (to most of the public) that Steadman would be so environmentally aware, it was also a good way to make sure that the body couldn't be identified due to decomposition. The forensic examiner was, however, able to compare the teeth in the body to Steadman's records. It was a match. Obviously, this meant it was Terrence Steadman's body in the coffin . . . or it meant someone switched his dental records. You decide.

But what about this mysterious last-minute evidence? Assuming it wasn't fabricated, who could get a hold of medical records from Steadman's childhood? Well, my friends, it just so happens that one of my spies was able to get a screen grab from the surveillance video outside the judge's chambers, before that videotape mysteriously disappeared. A bit of image reconstruction netted us the following picture. Is it just me or does this guy have some features that seem reminiscent of Lincoln Burrows?

POST #607 ·

In some pretty big national news . . . and this is surprising news . . . the Senate deadlocked for the first time this term. The vote on the new energy bill ended up in a fifty-fifty tie. We haven't gotten to the surprise yet. It was up to Vice President Reynolds to cast the deciding vote. Again, we suspected the status quo. Sources said that Reynolds was prepared to vote down the energy bill, which, by the way, would probably help bring billions of dollars to certain interested parties. But wait! She went against her longstanding history of voting against laws like this and voted IN FAVOR of it. Is she just positioning herself for her presidential run?

As surprising as this news is, the odds are President Mills will just veto the thing when it gets to his desk.

Now, on to something a little more local. I don't know about this whole "apple falls far from the tree" business. I mean, yes, it does look like L.J. Burrows is in some real trouble right now. And things do look bad for him. Getting caught robbing the home of a buffalo jerky salesman, and shooting the poor guy doesn't really help him. Now, this Owen Kravecki has been doing his best to stay out of the news since he's just some poor working stiff who doesn't need the attention. Or is he? My spies say he looks an awful lot like the guy in the picture L.J. sent to his friend on the day he supposedly killed his mother and stepfather. You know, that mysterious Kellerman guy.

But here's a story you're not going to see in the mainstream media. Seems we've got a friend in the Kane County Sheriff's department that tells me Lincoln Burrows may have made an escape attempt this morning. At least, that's what the sheriff and the folks at Fox River are trying to hush up. But this friend—and me too—thinks there was something more than a simple escape attempt. Here's what happened:

Lincoln Burrows—a death row inmate in solitary at the time—was given permission to visit his son, who was up for a hearing on those two counts of murdering his mom and step-dad. Now, I ask you, how often do prisoner requests of that nature get honored by the DOC? Um . . . never. While Burrows was en route to the courthouse, a big ol' truck comes barreling into the van, knocking it off the road and leaving two guards dead and one critical. Then the truck keeps on going.

A witness on the scene, named Roy Hawkins, reports that he tried to render aid when someone knocked him out and took off with Lincoln. Police searched for the better part of the afternoon, and found Burrows in a junkyard, nowhere near the accident. He was quietly taken back into custody, but the mystery man that saved him disappeared. What is it with Burrows and this mystery man? Is it the same mystery man who got his execution delayed? We'll never know, because the witness was kind of vague on his description. But how 'bout a description that's not so vague. Our friend in the sheriff's office tells me that this Roy Hawkins guy looked very much like the same Paul Kellerman and Owen Kravecki that we've heard about before. Makes you wonder just how many names this guy's got.

POST #608 ·

Okay, here's a quick one. A lot going on today. You all know that it's your posts that keep me going. In addition to my network of spies, your tips keep my blog alive. So, I'd like to thank a friend who wants to remain way nameless for the following email I just received:

Hey! Love your blog! Keep fighting the good fight. I think I've got a scoop for you. On the identity of this mystery man that keeps popping up. It's Aldo Burrows. Lincoln Burrows's dad. The guy everyone thought was a deadbeat drunk that abandoned his family. But that's not right at all. Aldo used to work for "The Company" many years ago. But he turned his back on them and went underground. He left his wife and his sons to keep them safe.

Aldo was the one who leaked the Ecofield information to the SEC. That's why The

Company set up Burrows for Steadman's alleged murder. To get back at Aldo and to smoke him out. I mean, what man is going to sit back and do nothing while his son is on death row? I know people think Aldo—this "mystery man"—is behind the accident that temporarily freed Lincoln, but that's not true at all. It was staged by The Company in an attempt to quiet Lincoln and bury this whole situation. But Aldo turned the tables on them and tried to help his son go free. But, that wouldn't have helped his other son still in Fox River, would it?

Keep looking into the Kellerman guy. He's the key to everything.

Interesting, huh? Kind of puts things in a whole new perspective.

In other news, it looks like Governor Tancredi is on the short list for Caroline Reynold's running mate. Anyone surprised by this? Yeah, me neither. Seems to me like a nice way to thank the guy that refused to grant clemency to your brother's alleged murderer. Looks like ol' Frontier Justice Frank is going to be reaching a much wider audience with his views on crime and punishment. Maybe it IS time to move to France.

POST #609 · · · · · · · ·

 Whoa! What a night!! When one of the largest prison breaks in U.S. history is hardly a blip on the news radar, you know the world has turned upside down. But first, let me weigh in on the story everyone's talking about: the death of President Mills. Now, I'll be the first to admit that President Mills was no friend to this blog. Go back to some of my earlier posts to see what I really thought of the man. But you all know I've never endorsed a violent overthrow of the government. We want to get this corruption out in the open where the law can run its course as it was intended to do. Certainly, a presidential assassination is never the answer. Now, I know my loyal readers are not sitting there wondering what I'm talking about. I know you get where I'm going. Who among us really believes the "official" line being reported by mainstream media?

"Doctors at Washington Medical Center have corroborated that President Mills was admitted into emergency care here a little more than forty-five minutes ago. In the chief surgeon's words, 'President Mills suffered massive cardiac arrest' and doctors were unable to revive him . . . The news out of Washington Medical Center is official now. The President of the United States, Richard Mills, is dead. And keeping with protocol, Vice President Reynolds is at an undisclosed location, being sworn in as the 44th president of the United States."

Massive cardiac arrest? Now, we all know President Mills was no spring chicken (may he rest in peace), but isn't the timing of this all a little suspect? Rumor has it he was about to SIGN the energy bill that people were saying he was going to veto. Now, how was The Company going to stop that?

And what about the new president? Everyone knows how much Reynolds has been slipping in the polls recently. This whole Burrows affair has had a major effect on her numbers. I think this says something about a person who can't even drum up sympathy votes when going against her brother's murderer. Maybe my readers aren't the only ones out there who refuse to buy what the new president is selling. Add to that the recent grumblings about how Reynolds was losing favor in the party and losing some of her funding; well, it could have just been faster to assume the president's position following his death rather than wait for those pesky voters to decide for you.

Now, I'm not suggesting that Reynolds killed the president. That would be high treason. Besides, he died of a heart attack. According to the toxicology reports, there was nothing in President Mills's system. The cause seemed natural. But we all know that there are chemicals out there that can do these kinds of things. Glycoside saxitoxin hybrid comes to mind. Why do I mention that particular chemical? Maybe I know even more than I usually let on.

POST #610 · · · · · · · · · · · · · · · · · · ·

I know some of you already know this, but in case you missed it, Nick Savrinn's body was just added to the list of deaths associated to the Burrows case. He and his father were found dead in Savrinn's apartment this afternoon. Veronica Donovan is reported as missing. I did some quick investigating and found her name listed on a flight to Montana last night. Then, there's a record of her picking up a rental car at the airport. It's believed that she was on the trail of Terrence Steadman. Now, both she and the car are missing. Maybe President Reynolds can help in the search. Rumor has it she owns some mondo-pricey property in the town of Blackfoot.

POST #611 · · · · ·

Things have been pretty quiet lately with everyone so focused on the manhunt for the Fox River Eight. I know I haven't posted much in a while, but I've been working a new angle and I'm hearing some very interesting things. But first, I want to know your thoughts.

How do you think the manhunt's being handled? I don't want to call the FBI a rogue agency, but Special Agent Alexander Mahone seems to be leaning a little heavy on the "dead" side of "dead or alive," don't you think? According to my sources, the guy kept going off the grid as the manhunt heated up. And I've heard from more than one source that when Burrows and his brother were finally captured, Mahone was THIS CLOSE to plugging them both.

Speaking of which, is anyone else wondering about the sudden suicide of Governor Tancredi? Rumor has it he hanged himself only hours after President Reynolds withdrew his nomination for vice president. A nomination that was GUARANTEED to sail through Congress? And then a man who had probably never expected to be considered as a candidate in the first place suddenly becomes suicidal because he was taken off the short list? Yeah. I'm not seeing it.

And how about his daughter? She's been missing for a while now. I can't say I blame

her. Only hours after she found her father dead, there were reports that somebody had been trying to kill her, too. In fact, I hear that a poor innocent bystander who looked a little like Dr. Sara Tancredi was shot to death at a pay phone that had recently been used by the governor's daughter. Even more interesting is that right before Dr. Tancredi's disappearance, she'd been seen in the company of a friend from her Narcotics Anonymous group. From what I hear, it's some guy named Lance. And wouldn't you know, he looks a lot like our friend Paul Kellerman.

And what about Mr. Kellerman? Well, I'm hearing some very interesting things about him lately.

POST #612 ·

Just how many times can one man escape custody? Seriously. This Lincoln Burrows has got some angel looking over his shoulder. Burrows and his brother got away again, in what only can be called a complete and total screwup on the part of the Illinois DOC. And things looked a little touch-and-go there for our rogue agent Mahone. Either Burrows or Scofield supposedly shot Mahone during their escape. Interesting, considering that neither of the fugitives had a gun. Don't worry about Mahone, though. He got himself patched up right quick. Coincidentally (or maybe NOT so coincidentally) some blond dude in a specifically nondescript-looking suit was found in a dumpster not far from the hospital. Now, I'm not saying this guy looked like a Company man, but he reeked of more than just garbage . . . um . . . may he rest in peace.

Now, just how did Burrows and Scofield get away? And where did they go? Well, a Sergeant Humphries reported having a run-in with Agent Paul Kellerman. You know, the guy the Secret Service still claims to have never heard of. (Seriously, I can't even find a reference to him anywhere nowadays. And you know I've got the best connections in the business. That guy has been totally wiped from the system.) Well, ol' Kellerman was pretty intense about not letting the officer search his vehicle while he traveled away from the scene of the fugitives' escape. Kellerman's attitude was so intense that Humphries immediately reported this incident to his superiors, fearing repercussions if he didn't.

But wait! Here's where things really start to come together. Just so happens that one of our loyal readers is a pilot based in New Mexico. Now, this friend of the blog reports taking an Owen Kravecki (Yes! THAT Owen Kravecki!) to Montana along with his buddies Ben and Phil. Anyone want to guess who this Ben and Phil looked like? And if you're thinking Montana sounds familiar, you'd be right. That's where our old friend, Veronica Donovan was last seen before she disappeared.

POST #613 ·

Tell me you caught the news! And, seriously, you'd have to catch it real fast before our great mainstream media pushed it back to low-level human-interest story. I guess it was indeed Burrows and Scofield on that plane to Montana (my sources are the BEST), because Michael Scofield called one of those local Montana newsrooms saying that he wanted to turn himself in. Now, why would he go to the press before the police? We'll get to that in a moment. It didn't matter much, because the newsroom called the cops and everyone swarmed in on the Cutback Motel. But, as we've all come to expect by now, Burrows and Scofield escaped, along with a mystery man who sounds an awful lot like everybody's favorite imaginary Secret Service Agent Paul Kellerman. Oh, and they took a cameraman, too. They didn't hurt the guy, but they DID use him to record a message, which is probably all they wanted to do in the first place. Even though it's gone from the mainstream media airwaves, it's still all over the internet. You can either link to it HERE or just read the transcripts below.

BURROWS: My name is Lincoln Burrows and I'm innocent. I escaped from Fox River Penitentiary because I was sentenced to die for a murder I did not commit. I didn't murder Terrence Steadman. He committed suicide last night in the Cutback Motel thirty miles outside of his home in Blackfoot, Montana.

SCOFIELD: He killed himself out of fear. Fear of the people who have been hiding him for the past three years—the same people who want my brother dead. They don't want you to know who they are. But know this: they are working with the highest levels of government, including the president of the United States. All told, they've stolen billions of dollars and murdered dozens of innocent people. Yet they plaster our faces on the news and tell you to be afraid. They are the ones to fear, and they operate with impunity, under the cover of the Secret Service. The very people meant to protect and serve.

BURROWS: They are a group of multi-nationals, corporate interests. Together, they are known as the Company. Twenty years ago our father worked for them. He went into hiding when he realized their real agenda. That's why they staged Steadman's death—to pin the murder on me and draw my dad out. It worked. Now our father is dead. And so's the mother of my son. An innocent woman who had nothing to do with this.

SCOFIELD: Much blame has been placed on another innocent person: Dr. Sara Tancredi. She had nothing to do with our escape. Sara, if you're listening, I know I can't ask you for another chance. I only hope that you have found your safe haven. I took advantage of you, your commitment to help others, and put you in a place that's every doctor's nightmare. I've considered many ways to apologize, but I must arrive at one. I am deeply sorry. I wish I could do things differently, but it's too late for that now. For you, and for others. People murdered by government operatives. One man, Special Agent Alexander Mahone, has been responsible for several deaths. He murdered not only John Abruzzi and David Apolskis, but also the last fugitive he was assigned to chase. A man named Oscar Shales, who escaped from prison two years ago, who remains one of this country's most wanted, despite the fact he will never be found.

BURROWS: They'll do whatever it takes to make these deaths look official, like they happened in the line of duty. Or to look like disappearances. Accidents. But these people were murdered. Them and anyone else who tried to help us.

SCOFIELD: Like our father, Aldo Burrows, who also died at the hands of Agent Mahone.

SCOFIELD: And our attorney, Veronica Donovan. I was on the phone with her when she was shot like an animal after discovering Steadman in Montana, alive and well three years after the date of his death.

SCOFIELD: The most recent victims include the governor of Illinois. Frank Tancredi

214

Prison Break
THE CLASSIFIED FBI FILES

did not commit suicide. He was killed because he reviewed Lincoln's file and decided to take action on his behalf.

BURROWS: We made this tape to let the world know what these people are capable of doing. This needs to stop.

SCOFIELD: By bringing these matters out in the open, under the harsh light of public scrutiny, it will be more difficult for the Company to continue this cover-up. We hope this testimony will save the lives of countless future victims and bring control of the government back to the American people.

First of all, isn't it pretty amazing how fast the Justice Department dismissed these accusations as totally baseless? Nice to know that our government doesn't even bother to take the time to look at the facts before they close the door on an investigation. And do we really have to question the timing on the government suddenly raising the terror alert to orange? Are we going to do this every time a person of Middle Eastern descent rents a storage facility? Or only when they rent a storage facility on the same day someone accuses the president of taking part in a global conspiracy? Once again, the mainstream media has ignored what's right in front of their faces and bumped Scofield and Burrows to the funny pages. Somehow, I don't think they're going to be there for long.

EXCERPTS FROM
CONSPIRACYSTEW.NET

AGENT BILL KIM · · · · · · · ·

Not a lot is known about this guy, but I'm putting out there what I do know, or rather what my trusty DC source has passed on to me. He comes from a family of wealthy Korean merchants, who were well established in the DC area. However, when he was in his teens, his family emigrated back to South Korea, but Bill Kim decided to remain here to complete his schooling. It is believed that he majored in political science at Bergamont University in Maryland and did the ROTC program to fund his education. After that, things get a little murky. It is not clear what happened first: Kim being inducted into the Secret Service or Kim joining ranks with the Company. Whatever the case, he climbed the ladder quickly, and became a senior level agent in a very short amount of time.

Bill Kim is thought to be in his mid-thirties. To be honest, no one is even sure if Bill Kim is his real name. He's unmarried, no kids, and doesn't seem to have any contact with his family in Korea. He lives in a lavishly furnished apartment within walking distance of the Capitol. A couple of my sources have said that they've seen him at Facchini's, an Italian restaurant on Fifth Street many times. He usually eats alone, though a couple times he's been seen with other Company folk.

Bill Kim works under the mysterious Pad Man. Sorry I don't know more, guys. When I do, I'll post it.

THE PAD MAN ·

This guy really takes the cake. I don't even have a lead on his name if you can believe it. His alias is merely "The Pad Man." He's way, way up there in the Company, though to be honest, I don't even know if he IS Company. I've gotten anonymous tips ranging from rumors that he's old-school Russian mafia, to whispers that he is the leader of the Freemasons. I can't corroborate either of these claims, but what I can confirm is that even if he isn't officially "Company" he's certainly a power broker in the group.

Why is he called the Pad Man, you might ask? Because the man doesn't speak. Ever. He communicates by writing down his thoughts on little white cards. Apparently he only uses Mont Blanc's Limited Edition Starwalker model (which usually retails for about a grand, can you believe this guy?).

It's unclear as to why the Pad Man goes through the rigmarole of writing down all his orders to his little underlings, but one of the theories out there is that he refuses to actually ever

Lang, here's another website that I found while sorting through this stuff. I found the bios on these two guys particularly interesting. . . . Again, this is all confidential and shouldn't be included in any formally filed reports. Thanks—Wheeler speak, for fear that his phone or any room he is in might be bugged. By his paranoid logic, if his voice is never recorded then he can never be brought to trial for criminal activity.

Hopefully, there'll be some more to come on this guy soon. I feel like he could be the key to a lot of things, Company-wise. . . .

OWEN KRAVECKI VS. AGENT KELLERMAN? · · · · · · · ·

For those of you who don't mind gross speculation on this sort of thing, there are some folks out there who actually believe that Owen Kravecki, the buffalo jerky salesman who LJ Burrows was accused of trying to kill, is actually a Secret Service agent known as none other than—Agent Kellerman. Kellerman has very close ties with President Reynolds, or at least he did. Sources that I've been in contact with in the White House have implied that he's been a little scarce in that neck of the woods as of late. Kravecki's neighbors have leaked that he is never in the house, and some have postulated that he keeps it as a front—it's all part of his buffalo jerky identity bit. It's not uncommon for some of these black ops agents to have two identities, but the real question is why Kellerman has disappeared off the president's radar. Sources say he may run with Bill Kim and that crowd, but all the recent information indicates that he has been put out into the cold, and that he's now in the ranks with Michael Scofield and Lincoln Burrows. The real question is, what does he hope to get out of working with those guys?

The story continues at www.fox.com/prisonbreak!

217

PRISON BREAK
EPISODE LIST

SEASON ONE

01 PILOT—Written by: Paul T. Scheuring
Directed by: Brett Ratner

02 ALLEN—Written by: Paul T. Scheuring
Directed by: Michael Watkins

03 CELL TEST—Written by: Mike Pavone
Directed by: Brad Turner

04 CUTE POISON—Written by: Matt Olmstead
Directed by: Matt Earl Beesley

05 ENGLISH, FITZ, OR PERCY—Written by: Zack Estrin
Directed by: Randy Zisk

06 RIOTS, DRILLS, AND THE DEVIL, PART 1—
Written by: Nick Santora Directed by: Robert Mandel

07 RIOTS, DRILLS, AND THE DEVIL, PART 2—
Written by: Karyn Usher Directed by: Vern Gillum

08 THE OLD HEAD—Written by: Monica Macer
Directed by: Jace Alexander

09 TWEENER—Written by: Paul T. Scheuring
Directed by: Matt Earl Beesley

10 SLEIGHT OF HAND—Written by: Nick Santora
Directed by: Dwight Little

11 AND THEN THERE WERE 7—Written by: Zack Estrin
Directed by: Jesus Salvador Trevino

12 ODD MAN OUT—Written by: Karyn Usher
Directed by: Bobby Roth

13 END OF THE TUNNEL—Written by: Paul T. Scheuring
Directed by: Sanford Bookstaver

14 THE RAT—Written by: Matt Olmstead
Directed by: Kevin Hooks

15 BY THE SKIN AND THE TEETH—Written by: Nick Santora
Directed by: Fred Gerber

16 BROTHER'S KEEPER—Written by: Zack Estrin
Directed by: Greg Yaitanes

17 J-CAT—Written by: Karyn Usher Directed by: Guy Ferland

18 BLUFF—Written by: Nick Santora & Karyn Usher
Directed by: Jace Alexander

19 THE KEY—Teleplay by: Zack Estrin & Matt Olmstead
Story by: Paul T. Scheuring
Directed by: Sergio Mimica-Gezzan

20 TONIGHT—Written by: Zack Estrin Directed by: Bobby Roth

21 GO—Written by: Matt Olmstead Directed by: Dean White

22 FLIGHT—Written by: Paul T. Scheuring
Directed by: Kevin Hooks

SEASON TWO

01 MANHUNT—Written by: Paul T. Scheuring
Directed by: Kevin Hooks

02 OTIS—Written by: Matt Olmstead
Directed by: Bobby Roth

03 SCAN—Written by: Zack Estrin
Directed by: Bryan Spicer

04 FIRST DOWN—Written by: Nick Santora
Directed by: Bobby Roth

05 MAP 1213—Written by: Karyn Usher
Directed by: Peter O'Fallon

06 SUBDIVISION—Written by: Monica Macer
Directed by: Eric Laneuville

07 BURIED—Written by: Seth Hoffman
Directed by: Sergio Mimica-Gezzan

08 DEAD FALL—Written by: Zack Estrin
Directed by: Vincent Misiano

09 UNEARTHED—Written by: Nick Santora
Directed by: Kevin Hooks

10 RENDEZVOUS—Written by: Karyn Usher
Directed by: Dwight Little

11 BOLSHOI BOOZE—Written by: Monica Macer & Seth Hoffman
Directed by: Greg Yaitanes

12 DISCONNECT—Written by: Nick Santora & Karyn Usher
Directed by: Karen Gaviola

13 THE KILLING BOX—Written by: Zack Estrin
Directed by: Bobby Roth

14 JOHN DOE—Written by: Matt Olmstead & Nick Santora
Directed by: Kevin Hooks

15 THE MESSAGE—Written by: Zack Estrin & Karyn Usher
Directed by: Bobby Roth

16 CHICAGO—Written by: Nick Santora
Directed by: Jesse Bochco

17 BAD BLOOD—Written by: Paul Scheuring & Karyn Usher
Directed by: Nelson McCormick

18 WASH—Written by: Nick Santora Directed by: Bobby Roth.

19 SWEET CAROLINE—Written by: Karyn Usher
Directed by: Dwight Little

20 PANAMA—Written by: Zack Estrin
Directed by: Vincent Misiano

21 FIN DEL CAMINO—Written by: Seth Hoffman & Matt Olmstead
Directed by: Bobby Roth

22 SONA—Written by: Paul T. Scheuring Directed by: Kevin Hooks

HOW FAR WOULD YOU GO TO SAVE YOUR BROTHER?

"It's pulse-poundingly intense, combining the suspenseful action of 24, and the rawness of OZ with the emotional center of The Shawshank Redemption."

— *In Touch Magazine*

SEASON ONE: NOW AVAILABLE ON DVD
SEASON TWO: CATCH IT THIS FALL